TOEFL
iBT WRITING

不是權威不出書！練托福，
當然就讓最專業的托福總監帶你練！

捷徑文化
Royal Road Publishing Group

托福總監說在前頭

▶托福總監告訴你！
百分百真正的托福考點攻略在這裡！

　　在閱讀本書時，你可能會發現許多特別的語言學習方式，這些都是托福總監秦蘇珊老師精心研發的「有機英語學習法」！透過此學習法讓大家能在時間內有效學習托福必考的考點全攻略。

考點攻略 1. ─ 透過「詞彙語塊」的形式記憶，自然形成大腦資料庫。

　　什麼是「語塊」？語塊是指經常在一起使用的一組詞，類似片語或搭配詞。語塊既有可能是習慣搭配，如：sedimentary rock（沉積岩），也有可能是片語動詞，如follow up on an issue（追蹤一個問題）。

　　語言學家和神經學家發現，比起孤立地記單字，人們對語塊的記憶會更加準確牢固。且當學習者從其大腦的「資料庫」裡「調出」語塊時，因為不是用母語詞對詞地做翻譯，所以語言使用者的犯錯機率減少，反應速度也同時提高了。因此，本書每一章都收錄了精心挑選的、涉及重要情境的學習語塊。

> **例** Franz Schubert 弗朗茨・舒伯特
> in B Minor B 小調
> instrumental work 樂器作品
> three-fourths time 3/4 拍
> three-eighths time 3/8 拍
> Classical heritage 古典主義的傳承

考點攻略 2. ─ 不只要會做題目，更要練習寫作時的文法。

　　很多華人考生寫文法選擇題時沒有什麼困難，但在說話或寫作中情況就大不相同了。ETS 的評分準則指出：「對文法的有效運用」是得到滿分的要求之一。考生能夠寫出結構較複雜的語法，並清楚地表達自己的觀點，將是寫作高分的重要關鍵。因此，書中也設計了「托福總監的寫作句型庫」專欄，精選了重要的句型，考生寫作時可以多多運用。

> **例** 寫社會科學方面話題的作文時，下面的句型都可以用上。
> There has been much discussion about... 關於……有許多種討論。
> There are several reasons for this... 關於……有很多原因？
> First, because we know..., 首先，因為我們知道……

考點攻略3. 會聽／說出道地的英文發音，對托福寫作也能有大大的幫助。

口語發音與寫作看起來八竿子打不著？但其實在托福考試裡兩者卻是息息相關，因為托福寫作試題其中一大題，是在聽完老師的敘述後，以寫作方式寫下自己的看法觀點，所以，**就算你有再無懈可擊的寫作技巧，若是聽不懂題目，則一切都是白搭！**英語的中聽說讀寫本來就是環環相扣，想要馬虎矇混過去的人，在托福這關絕對會重重踢到鐵板。

考點攻略4. 無論聽說讀寫，都要會換句話說。

換句話說的能力是通往考高分最重要的技能！原因有：

➊ **因為 100% 會考**！沒錯，新托福考試的閱讀部分會直接考你會不會換句話說，而聽力、口語和寫作部分也會間接考查這一能力。閱讀和聽力題中很多選擇題的選項都是對原文語句的改述；而在閱讀部分，有一類難度較高的題型：句子簡化題，其實就是在考你怎麼換句話說。

➋ **因為在訓練換句話說的能力時，考生將被迫用英語思考**，這會使考生在考試中更加有自信，並提高做題速度。

➌ 考托福的你，想必是想出國唸書的，要是什麼句子都只會一種說法，在國外會很辛苦，所以除了為了考試做練習，更要**為了你的未來生活做練習**，換句話說的能力是不可或缺的！

把學術性語言換句話說，對於詞彙量不足或對相關主題缺少瞭解的考生會非常難，因此本書從第 1 章開始，就會引導考生熟悉各種類型的情境，幫助考生擴大詞彙量，累積實用句型，提高閱讀速度、聽力能力和用英語思考的能力。

考點攻略 5. 訓練用關鍵字記筆記。

　　有些考試是不允許記筆記的，因此在準備時，大家常會忽略這一項。但**托福可以記筆記，所以考生應儘早開始訓練，嘗試用各種不同方式記筆記**。本書會提供大量有針對性的記筆記策略，例如：

> **例** 1. 以抓核心概念、論點和分論點為目的去閱讀短文。
> 2. 做表格形式的筆記。閱讀部分，可以用縮寫形式簡單記錄三個分論點。而講座部分，盡量捕捉三個分論點的細節，為了節省時間，同樣可以使用縮寫形式。
> 3. 聽講座時，注意聽關於分論點的指示性詞語。例如，當聽到「It's doubtful that...」時，要意識到教授將提出一個反駁閱讀短文中分論點的論點。
> 4. 本書列舉了閱讀短文和講座中常用的實用句型。記住這些句型，進入考場後要充分利用這些指示性詞語，提醒自己什麼時候該做筆記。

考點攻略 6. 掌握篇章中的大特點（如：開頭語、主題擴展、例證、結論等）。

　　預測下文的能力對於任何希望取得新托福考試高分的考生都非常重要。在聽學術類講座時，**如果能預知下文將要呈現的資訊，那作答速度就會快上許多。而且還能更快地抓住要點、更準確地記下關鍵資訊**。在聽講座或對話時，考生如果能預測到教授接下來很可能會講什麼，那麼即使沒聽出一兩個單字，也不必過於擔心。

> **例** 正確預測講座內容，可運用以下策略：
> 1. 充分利用講座結構的可預測性。認真聽第一段核心概念的定義和論點，然後逐一聽三個分論點。
> 2. 運用表格記錄核心概念、論點以及分論點。這有助於理解閱讀和講座的結構，並準確預測教授的觀點。
> 3. 注意聽指示性詞語和其他關鍵詞。例如，注意聽表達教授說話邏輯的指示性詞語，像 although 和 despite what many people say, 通常後面會緊跟一個對比句，如 there is good reason to believe that...。這些暗示教授將比較講座與閱讀中的觀點。

考點攻略 7. 加強略讀與掃讀的能力。

　　寫作部分的閱讀短文只有約 300 字左右，因此在掃讀、略讀方面應該不會有太大的問題，但來是需要多加注意，畢竟考場上分秒必爭，讀得快有好處沒壞處。

考點攻略 8. 掌握篇章中的大特點（如：開頭語、主題擴展、例證、結論等）。

　　篇章中的「大」特點有很多，例如文章的組織結構，或例如作者開始談論某個歷史事件的方式。另外，理解教授在講座中提供範例的能力也是一種重要的技巧。**當考生抓住了篇章的整體，就能進行更細的資訊處理。這樣即使不認識文章裡的某些單字，也能基本理解文章的主要意思**！這種技巧對於獲得寫作高分極為關鍵！本書用了五章的篇幅對其作了介紹。

 1. 表達偏愛的四大規則
在新托福考試的口語和寫作部分，考生必須會表達自己的偏愛。那麼表達個人偏愛有沒有規則可循呢？我為大家總結了四條規則。
規則一：以相對正式的方式去表述自己的偏愛。如果只是簡單地寫 I prefer to study alone. 評分人不會被打動。考生需要把這些句子嵌入複雜的長句中，例如：There is a lot of pressure at my school, and so in general, I prefer to study alone.

考點攻略 9. 掌握篇章中的小特點（如：詞性、單字、修辭等）。

　　這種技能一般是指對一篇閱讀文章或聽力文本的語言特徵的掌握能力。**這些特徵既包括單字的發音方式，也包括在學術類閱讀文章、講座和對話中使用的字彙、片語。**考生一定都希望記住經常出現在新托福考試中的單字和片語，因此本書列出了大量這類單字和片語。

例 有很多方式可以使作文前後更連貫。本章主要透過連接詞這一手法，而第 14 章會具體介紹如何使用指示詞使上下文衛接自然。連接詞的用法很多，既可以連接句內的片語和分句，也可以連接兩個獨立的句子。

▶托福總監告訴你！這本書的結構與重點

★本書內容

- ·新托福寫作題目分析
- ·各題型的解題策略
- ·命題總監的寫作句型庫
- ·命題總監的高分詞彙表
- ·大量練習與寫作預測題
- ·道地的高分範例以及命題總監萬用寫作模板

★本書結構

本書包含兩種新托福寫作題型分析、解題策略、寫作句型庫、詞彙表、練習和寫作模擬試題。除了以上內容外，還提供道地的高分範文和萬用寫作範本。右頁的「內容一覽表」清楚地標示出了寫作題型（關鍵技能）、情境與領域、和各章會學到的技巧與策略。

第一部分整體介紹新托福考試，詳細地描述寫作考試的結構以及題型。

第二部分介紹兩道寫作題型：

前半部分介紹綜合寫作。這部分共有 8 章，每兩章圍繞一個學術領域展開（共四大學術領域）。每一章都有一道寫作題範例、解讀常考題、高分範文、萬用寫作範本、詞彙和寫作句型庫。每一章會集中訓練一個技能或技巧，例如綜合寫作題如何構思、怎樣記筆記等。

後半部分介紹獨立寫作題。這部分也是 8 章，每章有 6 道寫作題（其中有 5 道是寫作模擬試題）、高分範文、萬用寫作範本和寫作句型庫。根據獨立寫作題題目的措辭和邏輯，獨立寫作題分為 8 種類型。每一章介紹一種寫作類型，並提供寫作方法。

由於科學研究指出，在同一題材下學習類似情境的內容會記得比較熟，所以我們將同一情境或題型的高模擬寫作例題和萬用寫作範本都集中在一起，因此考生的學習效率會很高。

考生會發現自己不會忘記從本書學會的詞彙，因為他們是跟隨著本書的結構在情境中學習詞彙的。通過本書的學習，自學者和教師會發現，就複雜性和抽象性而言，本書的寫作題型和技能是按由易至難的順序來編排的。這就減輕了考生的負擔，提高其寫作能力，同時還能縮短準備考試的時間。

本書的編排非常靈活。考生可以按順序學習第 1—8 章，先專注對付綜合寫作題，然後再看第 9—16 章的獨立寫作題。或者，考生可以先看第 1 章，即第一個介紹綜合寫作題的章節，然後再看第 9 章，即第一個介紹獨立寫作題的章節。每個人都可以根據自己的興趣和需要來選擇學習方案。

特別收錄部分介紹新托福寫作考試的評分標準，相信對大家會大有幫助。

以下為本書的內容一覽表，想知道在哪一章可以找到怎樣的內容、技巧與策略，可以先快速看過這個表喔！

【內容一覽表】

章節	寫作題目	情境內容	高分技巧或策略
1	第一題 綜合寫作題	Physical Sciences — Paleontology 物理科學常考主題 1：古生物學	綜合寫作題的快速解題方法和篇章結構
2	第一題 綜合寫作題	Humanities and the Arts— Music History 人文藝術常考主題 1：音樂史	綜合寫作題如何記筆記
3	第一題 綜合寫作題	Life Sciences — Zoology 生命科學常考主題 1：動物學	預測下文：預測講座內容和觀點
4	第一題 綜合寫作題	Social Sciences — Archaeology 社會科學常考主題 1：考古學	連接詞的銜接
5	第一題 綜合寫作題	Physical Sciences — Energy 物理科學常考主題 2：能源	個性化的寫作
6	第一題 綜合寫作題	Humanities and the Arts — Literature 人文藝術常考主題 2：文學	轉述他人觀點
7	第一題 綜合寫作題	Life Sciences — Ecology 生命科學常考主題 2：生態環境	通過重複關鍵字做到前後連貫
8	第一題 綜合寫作題	Social Sciences — Advertising 社會科學常考主題 2：廣告	應對行話與職業術語
9	第二題 獨立寫作題	Choose one from two 1 如何應對二選一題型 1	獨立寫作題的構思和篇章結構
10	第二題 獨立寫作題	Choose one from two 2 如何應對二選一題型 2	表達偏愛

章節	寫作題目	情境內容	高分技巧或策略
11	第二題 獨立寫作題	Explicit compare and contrast Advantages and disadvantages 如何應對「比較與對比」和「利弊」 題型	有條理地進行比較
12	第二題 獨立寫作題	"What": What changes What skills 如何應對 What 題型	如何寫出漂亮的第一段
13	第二題 獨立寫作題	"Why": Why do you think Why is x important 如何應對 Why 題型	解釋原因
14	第二題 獨立寫作題	"How": How does x influence y How is x different from y 如何應對 How 題型	利用指示詞來銜接
15	第二題 獨立寫作題	"Hypothetical if": If you could change one thing If you could x 如何應對假設性題型	描述假設性情形
16	第二題 獨立寫作題	Open-ended describe and discuss: Discuss the causes Describe a custom 如何應對開放型題型	邏輯上做到前後連貫

▶托福總監告訴你！這本書適合誰用？該怎麼用？

★本書適用對象

　　本書專為希望提高寫作能力的新托福考生編寫。通過運用「有機英語學習法」，指導考生進行有重點、有系統的學習，從而在短時間內提高英語技能並順利通過新托福考試。英語自學者以及新托福考試輔導教師均可從本書中獲益。

★自學的我，該怎麼運用這本書？

　　使用本書的自學者將看到立竿見影的效果。首先，自學者應制訂一個自學計畫，列出時間表和學習安排。如果自學者認為自己的文法比較弱，那麼就多花時間在文法結構上；如果自學者在詞彙方面最弱，就應該花更多的時間背詞彙，尤其是不熟悉領域的術語；如果聽力問題最大，考生就應該在聽力上多花時間。我建議考生重視發音，尤其是單字節奏和重音，因為這可以幫助應對聽力。

　　自學者每天都應該背一背詞彙語塊和寫作句型庫裡的實用句型，最好還要記換句話說的方式。例如，自學者可以把 theoretical perspective 記作一個語塊，把 theoretical point of view 記為它的同義改述。或者自學者也可以把 There has been much discussion about... 和 There has been considerable debate about... 放在一起記。兩個放在一起記能達到最好的學習效果！

　　但請記住一點：如果考官認為你是在背別人寫的範文，可能會給你打低分。所以，要把本書的高分範文或範本進行「個性化」處理，即作文中出現你個人經歷過的事情。

★我是老師，該怎麼運用這本書？

　　建議使用本書的教師可以在課堂上使用「有機英語學習方法」。例如，教師可以幫助學生理解什麼是題材、場景。要想瞭解可以利用的資源和更多關於「有機英語學習方法」的建議，可以登錄 http://blog.sina.com.cn/susanchyn，留言給我。你的任何問題我都會悉心回答喔！

Preface 作者序

　　從很久以前開始，我的朋友和學生們就都常跑來求我寫一套新托福考試的備考輔導書。這都是因為我曾在美國教育考試服務中心（ETS）工作過很多年，在那裡取得了終身職位，所以對托福的考試方式、出題方式都非常熟悉。我曾在 ETS 的多個崗位任職過，從最初的單個項目作者，一直到負責多種英語考試研發工作的主管，其中也包括了托福和多益考試的研發工作。因此，我對研發考試方式和英語考試標準化的專業方法都十分熟悉。

　　在 ETS 時，我很幸運有機會向專家們學習，而且隨著職位的上升，還有幸參與制定並調整新的考試評估體系。大家現在所看到的托福 iBT，就是我與團隊成員努力的成果！

　　在本系列書中，我依自己從 ETS 獲得的多年經驗，制定出一套全新的準備考試大綱，以期幫助考生順利通過新托福考試，並為他們以後的語言學習奠定基礎。本系列圖書是專門為以中文為母語的你們量身編寫的。與很多其他西方教育者不同，我因為個人生活和工作的緣故，對華人文化和你們的學習方式都比較瞭解，非常清楚你們在學習英語過程中的優勢和劣勢。所以在本系列圖書的編寫過程中，我結合你們的優勢，幫助你們在最短的時間內取得最顯著的進步；同時也指出你們常見的不足之處，以便於你們有重點地去彌補和提高學習效率。我把這種學習方法稱為「有機英語學習方法」，也就是把大家熟悉的學習方式（如背誦和模擬考）與科學的學習策略（如語言學）結合在一起，可以說是中西合璧的一種學習方法吧！

　　對於考生來說，時間很緊迫，而且壓力很大，高分似乎永遠遙不可及。不過現在你們可以放下心來，因為在本系列圖書中，我所選取的學習材料和提供的學習策略都能確保你快速提升學習能力，並在新托福考試中考取高分。如果認真讀完了本系列圖書，我保證你們的時間不會白費。當你們坐在考場中時，就會知道自己已經做了最充足的準備！

　　祝大家好運！

托福考試命題總監

Susan Chyn 秦蘇珊

Contents 目錄

第1部分

An Overview of the TOEFL ® iBT
新托福考試怎麼命題

第2部分

Integrated Writing and Independent Writing
綜合寫作和獨立寫作

Task 1 Integrated Writing 第一題 綜合寫作題全解

Task 2 Independent Writing 第二題 獨立寫作全解

特別收錄

"Section ①"

An Overview of the TOEFL ® iBT

第①部分
新托福考試怎麼命題

What the TOEFL ® iBT Measures
新托福考試考什麼？

　　進考場前，多少要知道一下新托福考試的實際情況。新托福考試的時間長度大約為四小時，分為四個部分。閱讀與聽力部分在前面，之後有一次短暫的休息，才進入之後的口語與寫作部分。

新托福考試測驗題目與時間表
（上色的字為不計分的實驗性題目）

	題目類別	題數	時間長度
閱讀	3 篇閱讀文章 +2 篇實驗性閱讀文章	每篇 12 ～ 14 道題目	60 分 + 40 分鐘
聽力	2 段對話、4 段講座 或 +1 段考前講座和 1 段考前對話	對話：每篇 5 道題目 講座：每篇 6 道題目	60 分鐘 + 30 分鐘
中間休息			10 分鐘
口語	2 小段閱讀文章、 2 小段對話、 2 小段講座	6 道題目	20 分鐘
寫作	1 小段閱讀文章、 1 小段講座	2 道題目	50 分鐘

★口語和寫作部分沒有不計分的實驗性試題。

★新托福考試的四類考題都允許考生記筆記。考試結束後，所有筆記會被統一收集起來並銷毀。

A Comprehensive Look at the Writing Section
新托福考試怎麼命題：寫作命題全解

　　本章將逐一介紹新托福考試的兩道寫作題，並提供一些概括性的寫作策略。接下來的 16 章會具體介紹備考和應試技巧。

　　似乎大多數考生對新托福寫作考試都懷著複雜的感情。從積極的一面來看，寫作考試不像口語考試那樣讓人膽戰心驚，因為考生作答之後可以修改；而且，很多考生對寫作第二題（即獨立寫作題）的形式已經很熟悉了，因為獨立寫作題的考試形式和舊托福寫作題一致，和很多學校裡的寫作考試形式或者其他考試形式都類似。另外一方面，考生不太喜歡第一道綜合寫作題，因為這篇綜合作文要根據閱讀文章和學術講座進行寫作。請大家不要灰心！本書會教你怎樣攻克所有的這些障礙。

▶寫作考試怎麼進行？

　　和新托福考試的其他部分一樣，寫作考試也在電腦上進行，這也就意味著考生需要用打字的打出自己的文章。寫作考試是最後一部分，考生完成口語最後一道題後，就要根據指示直接進入寫作部分的考試。

　　寫作考試時，電腦螢幕的角落上也會有時鐘。寫作時需要注意時間，因為必須為每道題留出合理的時間：第一題 20 分鐘，第二題 30 分鐘。考生開始做題時，時鐘就會開始倒數計時。考試時間快結束時，電腦上會出現提示資訊。

　　考生可以記筆記，利用筆記資訊來組織文章結構。筆記可以記在紙上，也可以直接記在電腦上。考試結束後，所有的草稿紙都會被收回並銷毀。兩篇作文的電子版會發送到 ETS 的評分網路。

▶新托福寫作題考什麼？

　　下面請看新托福考試寫作題的考試要求：

題目	情境內容	綜合材料	作文字數	寫作時間
第一題：綜合寫作	學術	學術閱讀文章和學術講座	150～225 個單字	20 分鐘
第二題：獨立寫作	個人知識和經驗	無	300～400 個單字	30 分鐘

從上表可知，新托福寫作考試有兩類題型：綜合寫作和獨立寫作。第一題綜合寫作有好幾個步驟：考生先要讀一篇小短文，再聽一個小講座，然後根據小短文和小講座的內容來寫作。

第二題獨立寫作要求考生運用自己的個人知識和經驗來寫作。因此，寫作部分考查的是考生在學術話題和一般話題方面的寫作能力。然而，它也間接考查考生的閱讀和聽力技能、學術詞彙、分析性思維能力和組織觀點的能力。

▶寫作評分準則

寫作評分準則考慮到了兩篇作文的意圖和目的，所以綜合寫作題和獨立寫作題分別有兩套評分準則。評分者能給的最高分是 5 分，最低分是 0 分。一般 0 分很少見，但是如果考生什麼都沒寫、離題，或者完全照抄題目或閱讀文章裡的句子，那麼只能得 0 分。

本書提供了很多如何獲得高分的指導資訊，此外附錄還專門講述評分方式和分數報告。

▶兩種寫作題型的比較

新托福考試寫作部分的兩道寫作題分別考查不同的技能。考生要想得高分，就必須清楚每道題的考試目的、特徵和評分標準。

第一題：綜合寫作

第一道題是關於一個學術話題的綜合寫作題。該話題肯定逃不出 ETS 選材的四大學術領域：物理科學、人文藝術、生命科學和社會科學。考生先要閱讀一篇大約 300 個單字的短文，然後聽一個相同話題的講座錄音。大多數情況下，講座的人是教授，他會針對閱讀短文中的觀點進行辯駁。

聽小講座時，考生應該記筆記，尤其是在教授講述三個不同論點時。聽完講座後，考生會聽到題目，題目也會出現在電腦螢幕上。在這個過程中，考生可以參考閱讀過的短文。

綜合寫作題想拿高分，考生必須完整再現講座中的重要資訊，即必須準確抓住教授提到的三個不同論點。此外，考生的作文還必須前後連貫、易於理解。一些小錯誤不會影響得分。

考生得高分的關鍵就是從閱讀短文和聽力講座中捕捉重要資訊，即輸入內容（INPUT），並通過描述主要話題及解釋三個不同論點把講座中的資訊轉化成自己的語言，即輸出內容（OUTPUT）。

第二題：獨立寫作

　　大部分獨立寫作題給考生提供一些意見性的陳述，要求考生回答「同意或不同意」，並展開論述，說明理由；另一些題目則要求考生比較某個特定現象的優點。事實上，這只是其中的一類題目。總體而言，有八種不同類型的題目。本書會一一解析，並向考生講述評分者期待看到什麼樣的作文！

　　第二題想得高分，考生的作文必須達到以下要求：組織結構有條理、清晰，論證充分展開（考生要有大量的細節和例子來支撐自己的觀點）。觀點之間的邏輯必須通順、易懂。一些小錯誤不影響得分。

▶新托福考試寫作的總體搶分策略

考試前的準備

1. 瞭解兩道作文題的要求。例如，綜合寫作題是否要概括閱讀文章的全文？獨立寫作題到底應該寫多少？

2. 瞭解兩道作文題的評分準則，注意不同之處。例如第一題要求全面討論該話題，指出教授提出的三個反駁閱讀文章的觀點。

3. 按照每一題的考試時間來練習寫作。

4. 儘量多背本書「建立自己的寫作句型庫」中的實用句型，使你的「寫作工具箱」更完善。

5. 平時練習寫作時多把片語和句子換句話說。評分者希望看到考生的換句話說能力。

考試時要注意

綜合寫作題：

1. 快速閱讀文章，找出主要論點。不要擔心細節，因為講座中會出現。

2. 聽力錄音開始播放時，開始思考整個話題。如果有不清楚的地方，利用細節和自己的知識去猜測。

3. 仔細聽錄音，記下閱讀短文和講座的結構性筆記。記下論點，並用英語記下關鍵字和例證。

4. 如果覺得自己第一篇作文寫得不好，不要驚慌。保持良好的心態，集中注意力完成獨立寫作題。

5. 不要逐字使用本書中的萬用寫作範本，儘量使其內容和用詞個性化。

獨立寫作題：

1. 合理分配時間，確保每一步都能夠完成。例如，要有足夠的時間進行構思，以確保論點的連貫性。

2. 不要以「I agree with the statement」開頭。首段的前兩句最好是介紹性的文字，為沒看過題目的讀者解釋情境。

3. 用有效的連接詞把論點串聯起來。

4. 不要用不常用的奇特詞彙。用低頻詞彙並不一定能得高分，但用詞錯誤一定會被扣分。

5. 不要一字不漏地用本書中的萬用寫作範本，儘量使其內容和用詞個性化。

6. 不要以為作文寫得越長就越能得高分。評分者不是外行，作文字數要和作文的品質相平衡。

7. 不要以以下形式結尾：「That's it!」或「That's all!」或「OK, I'm finished.」

Section ❷

Integrated Writing and Independent Writing

第❷部分
綜合寫作和獨立寫作

Task 1 Integrated Writing

第一題 綜合寫作題全解

　　首先，考生要閱讀一篇主題選自四個學術領域的學術短文。接下來會聽到一段講座：一位教授就閱讀短文話題的某一點發表自己的見解。講座結束後，考生需要寫出講座的要點，闡明講座中教授的論點與閱讀短文中的論點是否一致，這是題目明確要求的。考生需寫出論點的相似之處或不同之處。要想得高分，考生需要準確且盡可能多地捕捉並傳達講座的要點。

▶短文

　　閱讀短文的長度大約 230 ～ 300 個單字，考生需要在 3 分鐘內閱讀完。這表示考生平時做練習時至少要達到每分鐘 100 個單字的閱讀速度。閱讀短文涉及的主題選自四大學術領域：物理科學、人文藝術、生命科學和社會科學。閱讀短文通常有四個段落。第一段概述概念、事物或事件，接下來的三段內容針對話題的三個要點進行闡述。如果文章介紹一項新技術，例如太陽能，第一段會給出太陽能的定義並作簡要描述。之後的三段可能會談論太陽能技術的益處。

　　閱讀短文時不一定要記筆記，因為寫作文的過程中考生還可以回頭去看。不過，閱讀時可以記下一兩個詞，以助於集中注意力。

▶講座

　　閱讀時間結束後，閱讀短文將會從電腦螢幕上消失，接著電腦螢幕上出現一張教授的照片。講座主題與閱讀短文的主題一致，但可能會從不同的角度展開討論。也就是說，大多數情況下，教授會質疑閱讀短文的論點，不過偶爾也有贊同閱讀短文論點的時候。錄音材料大約 230 ～ 300 個詞，大約播放 2 分鐘。

　　聽錄音時，考生應該要記筆記。對於綜合寫作題的講座來說，記好筆記非常重要！結構性的筆記能夠抓住閱讀短文論點和講座論點的一致和分歧，有助於拿高分。一般情況下，教授會在講座中就閱讀短文的三個分論點發表看法。如果講座的論點與閱讀短文的論點相悖，那麼教授所提的每個分論點都是在反駁閱讀中的某個分論點。這就體現了筆記的重要性！所以一定要好好記下每個論點和論據。

　　大多數情況下，教授會開篇點題，例如：「……表面看來是個可行的方法，但是實際上，閱讀短文提到的方法不正確」。有時候，教授的表述也可能留有餘地，承認閱讀短文中的觀點並非完全錯誤，只有一些地方有誤。例如，教授可能會說：「沒錯，做某事是有一些缺點，但是其實它沒有文章所說的這麼差」。因此，考生從講座的第一句就能大致瞭解教授的態度。第 3 章會講到如何預測教授講座內容的具體策略。

　　講座結束後，考生會聽到題目，該題目也會顯示在電腦螢幕上。此外，螢幕上會再次出現閱讀短文。

綜合寫作題常見的題目形式

1. Summarize the points made in the lecture, being sure to explain how they **challenge** the specific **points** made in the reading passage.
   總結講座中的論點，闡述這些論點如何質疑閱讀短文中的論點。

2. Summarize the points made in the lecture, being sure to explain how the new laws helped to **address** the specific **problems** discussed in the reading passage.
   總結講座中的論點，闡述新法規如何有助於解決閱讀短文中討論的問題。

3. Summarize the points made in the lecture, being sure to explain how they **cast doubt on** the specific **solutions** presented in the reading passage.
   總結講座中的論點，闡述這些論點如何質疑閱讀短文中提到的具體解決方案。

4. Summarize the points made in the lecture, being sure to explain how they **cast doubt on** the specific **points** made in the reading passage.
   總結講座中的論點，闡述這些論點如何質疑閱讀短文中的具體論點。

5. Summarize the points made in the lecture, being sure to explain how they **oppose** specific **points** made in the reading passage.
   總結講座中的論點，闡述這些論點如何反駁閱讀短文中的具體論點。

6. Summarize the points made in the lecture, being sure to explain how they **respond to** the specific **arguments** made in the reading passage.
   總結講座中的論點，闡述這些論點如何回應閱讀短文中的具體論點。

7. Summarize the points made in the lecture, being sure to explain how they **cast doubt on** specific **theories** discussed in the reading passage.
   總結講座中的論點，闡述這些論點如何質疑閱讀短文中討論的具體看法。

8. Summarize the points made in the lecture, being sure to explain how they **answer** the specific **problems** presented in the reading passage.
   總結講座中的論點，闡述這些論點如何回應閱讀短文中提到的具體問題。

9. Summarize the points made in the lecture, being sure to explain how they **strengthen** the **specific points** made in the reading passage.
   總結講座中的論點，闡述這些論點如何使閱讀短文中的具體論點更有說服力。

評分標準

綜合寫作題對作文中是否涵蓋「講座中的要點」有嚴格的要求。如果遺漏了要點，評分者會扣分。

什麼樣的作文才能吸引閱卷老師？

作文最好控制在 150 ～ 225 個單字，超過 225 個單字不會扣分。許多考生認為寫得越多，評分者給的分數會越高，所以就洋洋灑灑地寫得很長。但作文長度不是衡量能否拿高分的標準喔！綜合寫作題，考生要注意以下幾點：

1. 切題（按照題目要求寫出講座中的要點）。
2. 佈局（包括文章前後連貫、結構合理、表達流暢）。
3. 語言要有連貫性（儘量避免文法和用詞錯誤，注意句子與句子之間的銜接及句型的多樣性）。

作文中偶爾出現一些無關緊要的文法錯誤、用詞不當或拼寫錯誤，不會被扣分。但是，如果評分者發現考生將閱讀短文中的內容照搬過來湊字數，就會毫不留情地扣分。

怎麼樣才能拿到高分？

要想拿高分，有以下幾種方法：

1. 考前多練習寫作。考生可以針對各類學術主題進行句子、段落和文章的寫作練習。在練習過程中多寫幾次並反覆修改。
2. 參考本書的寫作範本和寫作句型庫裡的實用句型。
3. 閱讀各個學科各類主題的學術文章，中英文均可。

一些普通的學術概念或定義特別有用，因為諸多定義在綜合寫作題的閱讀短文和講座中都會有所涉及。

綜合寫作題的四個題材

與新托福考試其他題型一致，綜合寫作題涉及以下四個學術題材：

1. 物理科學
2. 人文藝術
3. 生命科學
4. 社會科學

1 Physical Sciences — Paleontology
物理科學常考主題 1：古生物學

在本章，你將學到……

★綜合寫作題的快速解題方法
★綜合寫作題如何設定最理想的篇章結構

解讀常考題

　　新托福綜合寫作題涉及物理科學的題目覆蓋了十分廣泛的話題，包括氣候、海洋、地震、沙漠、天文學、光與聲、環境、觸覺以及化學、地質學、自然地理學方面的原理。話題和原理涉及的概念不會太高深。

▶模擬試題①

　　閱讀以下的短文並聆聽講座，完成以下這道作文題。

Narrator: This section measures writing to communicate in an academic environment. There are two writing tasks.

For Writing Task 1, the integrated writing task, you will read a short passage and listen to a lecture and then answer a question. For Writing Task 2, the independent writing task, you will answer a question based on your own knowledge and experience.

Now listen to the directions for Writing Task 1.

For Writing Task 1, you will have three minutes to read a short academic passage. You may take notes. The passage will be removed and you will listen to a lecture about the same topic. Again, you may take notes.

You will have 20 minutes to write a response about the relationship between the lecture and the reading. Try to answer the question as completely as possible using information from the reading passage and the lecture. Do not give your personal opinion. You will be able to see the reading passage again. You may use your notes.

An effective response will be 150 to 225 words. You will be rated on the quality of your writing and on the completeness and accuracy of the content. If you finish your response before time is up, you may go on to Writing Task 2.

Begin reading now.

The dinosaurs known as sauropods were the largest animals ever to walk the Earth. One sauropod, the Brachiosaurus or "arm lizard," weighed over 50 tons and was very tall, the equivalent of a three-story building. Brachiosaurus adults measured over 80 feet. Brachiosaurus' necks took up a third of this length, extending 30 feet. Its tail was also very long, serving as a counterbalance for the neck. Because the animal was limited by its huge size and shape, scientists believe it was probably confined to a water habitat.

For one thing, on land the short legs of Brachiosaurus would have been unable to support such a large mass. Its frame would have collapsed, the bones being crushed by the weight. In water, however, buoyancy would help support the bodies of these large animals, allowing them to stand and even move about, just as large crocodiles are supported by water in rivers and swamps.

Second, it is unlikely that Brachiosaurus could have lifted its neck to reach tree leaves on land due to the weight of its head and long neck. Because this giant dinosaur ate 400 pounds of food a day, it would have needed a ready food supply. Thus, Brachiosaurus could only have survived by dipping its long neck under the water and feeding on aquatic plants in the many lakes and swamps that existed in the warm Jurassic Period.

Finally, because its nostrils are located at the top of its head, the Brachiosaurus could have spent much of the time mostly submerged in deep lake waters. In such habitats, the dinosaurs would have used their nostrils to breathe, like swimmers use snorkels.

Narrator: Now listen to part of a lecture on the same topic.

 Track 001 在這裡請播放 Track 001。錄音內容全文可在本章結尾找到。

> **Summarize the points made in the lecture you just heard, explaining how they cast doubt on the specific theories discussed in the reading passage.**

Narrator: You have 20 minutes to write Task 1.

綜合寫作題的快速解題方法和篇章結構

1. 快速解題的三個簡單步驟

1）閱讀短文的過程中，搞清楚作者的立場，找到三個分論點。
2）聽講座的過程中，抓住反駁閱讀短文的論點（少數情況下論點和閱讀短文一致）並做筆記。
3）寫作文時，概括講座教授的立場，列出三個分論點。在時間允許的情況下，寫得越詳細越好。

2. 綜合寫作題最理想的篇章結構

　　第一段總結講座教授的觀點，要充分結合具體的內容，讓並非專家的讀者能夠理解。考生要儘量用自己的話改述。

　　接下來分三段具體闡述講座中的三個分論點。也就是説，綜合寫作題的作文要分為四個段落。記住，在寫綜合寫作題的作文時，不能融入自己的觀點。如果加入自己的觀點，分數會很低。只有寫獨立寫作題作文時才能夠涉及自己的個人觀點。

綜合寫作題的高分策略

1. 仔細閱讀短文，弄清作者的論點或觀點以及三個分論點。例如，上面那篇關於恐龍的閱讀短文，論點是「科學家們認為腕龍有可能生活在水中」。
2. 可以簡要記錄閱讀短文中的關鍵字。不過，寫作文的時候電腦螢幕上會出現閱讀短文，所以不做筆記也沒有關係。
3. 仔細聽講座，認真、有技巧地做筆記。利用閱讀短文中的資訊來理解教授所講的內容和論點。
4. 通常來講，教授的論點與閱讀短文的論點是對立的。不過也有極少數情況，教授會補充一些資訊來支援閱讀短文的論點。
5. 考生無須詳細記錄閱讀短文中的論點，但是一定要詳細記錄講座中的論點。不過更重要的是，考生必須要真正理解教授的推理思路與閱讀短文的推理思路有何不同。
6. 講座的篇章結構一般與閱讀短文的篇章結構相似：開篇提出論點，接下來的三段詳細闡述。聽講座時要謹記這種篇章結構以便抓住關鍵資訊。
7. 不要照搬閱讀短文裡的詞句，要用自己的話改述論點。
8. 作文的篇章結構儘量與講座的篇章結構一致：開篇總結話題，給出陳述教授立場和論點的主題句，接下來的三段分別闡述三個分論點。
9. 不要浪費時間將閱讀短文裡的論點一一羅列出來，評分者可不會被你的小伎倆矇騙。這麼做只會浪費時間，並影響最終的分數。
10. 寫作文時儘量用自己的話進行改述，不要一字不改地照搬題目。可以照搬學術概念和專業術語中的片語，其他就用自己的話來陳述。
11. 不要試圖超越自己真實的英語水準，將作文寫得很高深。清楚、準確的表述要勝過華而不實、沒有條理的文章。一旦出現嚴重的錯誤就會被扣分，表達含糊也會被扣分，因此還是使用自己習慣的語言來表述清楚就可以了。
12. 即便是總結教授的論點，用詞也要恰當、明確，避免模糊的表達，如：The professor talks about changes in recent years. 完整、明確的表達是：The professor talks about the recent trend of people reacting negatively to commercial advertisements. 儘量做到語言達意，富有條理。如果用了華麗的詞彙，但是意思卻含糊不清或用詞不準確，評分者也會扣分。
13. 控制好考試時間。

高分範文　 Track 002

In the lecture, the professor talked about Brachiosaurus' habitat. Disputing the passage's arguments that this particular dinosaur lived in water, she cited several pieces of evidence showing that it lived near water.

First, she said there was fossil evidence of Brachiosaurus' footprints on land. The evidence shows that some sauropods walked on four feet in groups and youngsters may have to run on their hind legs to keep up with the adults. This evidence contradicts the claim in the passage that Brachiosaurus' legs could not support their massive weight and had to rely on water buoyancy.

Second, the professor said Brachiosaurus could easily feed on land plants and thus did not depend on water plants as the passage argued. Anatomically similar to a giraffe, it had relatively long front legs, which allowed it to extend its neck upward with less effort. Moreover, even if it could only reach out its neck horizontally, there were plenty of plants at its body height. What's more, its long neck allowed it to cover a large surface area so it could easily devour a large quantity of food without having to move much.

Third, the professor dismissed the argument in the passage that Brachiosaurus lay submerged in water and used its nostrils to breathe. She cited the evidence of bone fossils indicating that these dinosaurs had narrow feet which were unfit for life in water. For a large animal to live in the lakes or swamps, the professor believed it needed to have broad feet like those of a hippopotamus to walk on the muddy bottom.

萬用模板

　　許多主題為物理科學的綜合寫作題會涉及討論遠古時期一些現象的學科，如地質學、自然地理學和古生物學。針對這些話題，閱讀短文通常會提出一種觀點解釋某一現象，然後講座提出另一種觀點。兩種觀點都提出各自的「證據」。下面的萬用寫作範本就是針對這類寫作題設計的。

　　針對證據類題目的萬用寫作範本：

In the lecture, the professor talked about _____. Disputing the passage's arguments that _____ , she cited several pieces of evidence showing that _____.

First, she said there was evidence of _____. The evidence shows that _____. This evidence contradicts the claim in the passage that _____.

Second, the professor said _____ and thus did not _____as the passage argued. Moreover,_____. What's more, _____ .

Third, the professor dismissed the argument in the passage that _____. She cited the evidence of _____ indicating that _____.

事實上，不僅是物理科學，其他學術內容的作文也可以套用這個範本。例如，社會科學領域討論古文明、考古學及古人類學相關證據的題目，就可以用這個範本進行寫作。

建立自己的寫作句型庫

考試前要多閱讀、多聽和多說，在閱讀英文文章、聽英文材料和說英文的過程中訓練英語思維能力。這需要花很多時間，但是效果肯定是最好的。

另一種訓練英語思維的方法是：熟記本書中的實用句型和片語。這是短時間內提升英語思維能力的最佳方法。

綜合寫作題中遇到涉及物理科學的題目時，下面的句型都可以用上。現在，讓我們開始熟記這些實用句型吧！

• 閱讀好句型，成為我的作文佳句！

1. Because x was…, scientists believe it was probably…

因為……是……，科學家們相信它可能……

Because the animal was limited by its huge size and shape, scientists believe it was probably confined to a water habitat.

延伸說法 Because the large dinosaur would have been unable to move on land, scientists believe it was probably an aquatic species.

2. For one thing, on land x would have been unable to VERB…

首先，X 在陸地上的話，無法……

For one thing, on land the short legs of Brachiosaurus would have been unable to support such a large mass.

延伸說法 For one thing, on land Brachiosaurus would have been unable to go from lying down to a standing position.

3. Second, it is unlikely that x could have VERBed… due to x

其次，因為……的原因，它不可能……

Second, it is unlikely that Brachiosaurus could have lifted its neck to reach tree leaves on land due to the weight of its head and long neck.

延伸說法 Second, it is unlikely that Brachiosaurus could have got enough to eat from land trees due to its heavy neck.

4. Finally, because…, x could have VERBed

最後，因為……，它可以……

Finally, because its nostrils are located at the top of its head, the Brachiosaurus could have spent much of the time mostly submerged in deep lake waters.

延伸說法 Finally, because Brachiosaurus was often under water, it could have breathed through its nostrils.

• 講座好句型，成為我的作文佳句！

1. But these x were without a doubt able to VERB
但是，毫無疑問，⋯⋯能夠⋯⋯

But these dinosaurs were without a doubt able to walk on dry land.

延伸說法 But these animals were without a doubt able to live on land.

2. When we look at all the evidence, we can see that…
當審視所有證據，我們會發現⋯⋯

When we look at all the evidence, we can see that they were not aquatic dwellers.

延伸說法 When we look at all the evidence, we can see that Brachiosaurus lived near water, not in water.

3. First, let's take the argument that x would be unable to VERB because…
首先，我們分析一下「X 因為⋯⋯而不可能⋯⋯」的論點⋯⋯

First, let's take the argument that Brachiosaurus would be unable to stand on land because its legs would not have supported its weight.

延伸說法 First, let's take the argument that Brachiosaurus would be unable to walk around on land because its legs were too weak.

4. Second, because of x, a Brachiosaurus could have VERBed
其次，由於⋯⋯，腕龍可以⋯⋯

Second, because of its small, light head and long forefeet, a Brachiosaurus could have lifted its neck.

延伸說法 Second, because of its proportionately small head, a Brachiosaurus could have lifted its head up to reach trees.

• 高分範文中，有這些作文佳句！

1. In the lecture, the professor talked about x
教授在講座中談論了⋯⋯

In the lecture, the professor talked about Brachiosaurus' habitat.

延伸說法 In the lecture, the professor talked about where Brachiosaurus probably lived.

2. Disputing the passage's arguments that…, she cited several pieces of evidence showing that…
為反駁文章中的⋯⋯觀點，她舉出若干證據，證明⋯⋯

Disputing the passage's arguments that this particular dinosaur lived in water, she cited several pieces of evidence showing that it lived near water.

延伸說法 Disputing the passage's arguments that Brachiosaurus was aquatic, she cited several pieces of evidence showing that it was terrestrial.

3. First, she said there was x evidence of y

首先，她說有……的證據

First, she said there was fossil evidence of Brachiosaurus' footprints on land.

延伸說法 First, she said there was clear evidence of Brachiosaurus' tracks on land.

4. Second, the professor said x could easily VERB and thus did not VERB as the passage argued.

其次，教授說……能輕易……因而不會如文中所說那樣地……

Second, the professor said Brachiosaurus could easily feed on land plants and thus did not depend on water plants as the passage argued.

延伸說法 Second, the professor said Brachiosaurus could easily reach land plants and thus did not need to eat aquatic plants as the passage argued.

5. Third, the professor dismissed the argument in the passage that…

第三，教授不接受閱讀短文中……的論點

Third, the professor dismissed the argument in the passage that Brachiosaurus lay submerged in water and used its nostrils to breathe.

延伸說法 Third, the professor dismissed the argument in the passage that Brachiosaurus spent a lot of time under water.

關鍵語塊

- **dinosaurs** 恐龍
- **aquatic** 水生的
- **sauropod** 蜥腳龍
- **the Jurassic Period** 侏羅紀
- **Brachiosaurus** 腕龍
- **nostrils** 鼻孔
- **equivalent of** 與……相當
- **be submerged in** 潛入……以下
- **extend (number + measure word)**
  伸展到（數字 + 量詞）
- **snorkels** （潛水者使用的）通氣管
- **counterbalance** 平衡（力）
- **aquatic dwellers** 水棲動植物
- **be limited by** 受限於……
- **Let's take the argument that...**
  讓我們分析一下……的論點
- **be confined to**
  限定在（一定範圍以內）

- **fossil tracks** 化石足跡
- **habitat** （動植物的）棲息地
- **herd** 獸群
- **frame** 身體；體型
- **stance** 站姿
- **collapse** 塌陷
- **parallel to**
  與……相同；與……同時
- **crushed by** 被……壓碎
- **horizontal reach** 水平可達距離
- **buoyancy** 浮力
- **sweep x from side to side**
  將……從一端掃到另一端
- **swamps** 沼澤
- **swallow whole** 整個吞下
- **survive by VERBing**
  通過……而活下來
- **wade about** 在水中四處走

▶再練習一次！

> 學習了以上這些策略、實用句型、關鍵詞語、高分範文和萬用寫作範本之後，再回頭看看例題。再讀一遍閱讀短文，然後再聽一遍講座。如果還是聽不懂講座內容，就反覆多聽幾遍，或者參考錄音原稿。然後修改你之前寫的作文，或者重新寫一篇作文。修改或重寫作文時，試著運用本章學到的寫作技巧。完成之後，比較一下修改或重寫前後的兩篇作文，看看是不是很不一樣呢？

附錄：錄音原稿

 Track 001

Narrator: Now listen to part of a lecture on the same topic.

(woman) Professor: Of course, dinosaurs like the Brachiosaurus would have spent considerable time near water—feeding and drinking near the many swamps and lakes that existed in the Jurassic Period. but these dinosaurs were without a doubt able to walk on dry land. When we look at all the evidence, we can see that they were not aquatic dwellers.

First, let's take the argument that Brachiosaurus would be unable to stand on land because its legs ould not have supported its weight. We know Brachiosaurus walked on land on all four legs because any fossil tracks have been found, indicating groups of Brachiosaurus walking together. In fact, scientists have even found track evidence that some sauropod babies could run on two feet alongside the herd.

Second, because of its small, light head and long forefeet, a Brachiosaurus could have lifted its neck. With long front legs and shorter hind legs, its stance was similar to that of a giraffe, and that posture gave it some advantages. At the very minimum, it could raise its neck up parallel to its body, so that it reached the branches of conifers and other trees at that height. Moreover, because the Brachiosaurus had great horizontal reach on land, it could sweep its head from side to side, swallowing whole great quantities of ferns and other terrestrial plants.

Finally, the Brachiosaurus could not have lived in water. From bone fossils we know that its feet and limbs were too narrow to allow it to stand very long in mud. Animals that spend considerable time in muddy waters have short legs and broad, flat feet, which allow them to wade about in swamps without sinking down too far. Water-dwelling hippopotamus and elephants, for example, have these broad, flat feet—very different from Brachiosaurus.

② Humanities and the Arts ── Music History
人文藝術常考主題1：音樂史

❝ 在本章，你將學到…… ❞

★如何記筆記才能抓住閱讀短文和聽力材料中的要點

解讀常考題

在新托福寫作部分，與人文藝術相關的題目涵蓋很多領域，包括建築和設計、藝術作品、藝術史、紡織和紡織工藝、音樂和音樂史以及舞蹈。人文藝術領域的其他學科還包括攝影、新聞、文學（包括小説、詩歌、戲劇以及藝術中的一些「主義」，如浪漫主義和現代主義）以及美國史和世界史。

▶模擬試題①

閱讀以下的短文並聆聽講座，完成以下這道作文題目。

Narrator: This section measures writing to communicate in an academic environment. There are two writing tasks.

For Writing Task 1, the integrated writing task, you will read a short passage and listen to a lecture and then answer a question. For Writing Task 2, the independent writing task, you will answer a question based on your own knowledge and experience.

Now listen to the directions for Writing Task 1.

For Writing Task 1, you will have three minutes to read a short academic passage. You may take notes. The passage will be removed and you will listen to a lecture about the same topic. Again, you may take notes.

You will have 20 minutes to write a response about the relationship between the lecture and the reading. Try to answer the question as completely as possible using information from the reading passage and the lecture. Do not give your personal opinion. You will be able to see the reading passage again. You may use your notes.

An effective response will be 150 to 225 words. You will be rated on the quality of your writing and on the completeness and accuracy of the content. If you finish your response before time is up, you may go on to Writing Task 2.

Begin reading now.

In 1822, at the age of 25, Austrian composer Franz Schubert began to work on a symphony in B Minor, his 8th Symphony. Because Schubert did not write the full four movements normally required for a Classical symphony, the two movements which he did write are now referred to as his "Unfinished" Symphony. The composition is now the most famous and popular of all his instrumental work. Schubert, though young, was already a brilliant and careful composer. There are good reasons to believe that he did not consider this work "incomplete" and intended it to have only two movements.

For one thing, there was precedent for two-movement works in the 19th century. Schubert's hero, Beethoven, had written four piano sonatas with only two movements. Beethoven had also created new forms of symphonies. Like Beethoven, Schubert was searching for an artistic form that would allow his symphony to transcend the Classical models.

Music historians also maintain that Schubert was content with two movements because both movements are written in the same meter; that is to say, three beats to a measure. The first movement is in three-fourths time and the second movement is in three-eighths time. It would be difficult for Schubert to write a third movement because the third movement in most symphonies was usually written in three-fourths time: Three consecutive movements in the same meter would not likely be acceptable to composers or audiences.

Finally, Schubert most likely intentionally left the composition at two movements because he thought the music was perfect as it was. The themes were fully developed and the orchestration was complete. There was nothing he could add to the piece that would add value. And in fact, the Eighth Symphony, in its two-movement form, is often performed by orchestras over the world and regarded as emotionally and structurally satisfying.

Narrator: Now listen to part of a lecture on the same topic.

 Track 003 在這裡請播放 Track 003。錄音內容全文可在本章結尾找到。

Summarize the points made in the lecture you just heard, being sure to explain how they respond to the specific points made in the reading passage.

Narrator: You have 20 minutes to write Task 1.

綜合寫作題如何記筆記

1. 綜合寫作題記筆記的三個簡單步驟

　　1）閱讀時儘快找到論點。這就表示必須理解文中的核心概念，並找出分論點。

　　2）最好運用表格的形式（見下表）做筆記，因為表格會讓你的思路富有條理。不一定要畫很漂亮的表格，只要在紙上畫出橫線和分隔號，出現八個空格即可。考前練習一段時間，就會畫得很順了。這種方法會讓文章結構很自然。

3）仔細閱讀題目要求後開始寫作文，按照上面的兩個步驟把講座的觀點有條理地列出來。

2. 如何記筆記

由於題目要求考生談論講座要點與短文要點之間的聯繫，因此透過筆記將這些觀點組織起來對寫作是很有幫助的。下面的表格就可以幫你輕鬆記下短文和講座中的兩種論點。

綜合寫作題的記筆記方法

要點　　　材料	閱讀短文	講座
論點（Thesis）		
分論點 1（Point 1）		
分論點 2（Point 2）		
分論點 3（Point 3）		

論點一般出現在閱讀短文的第一段。例如，文章的論點是「這幅古老而難以辨認的繪畫，可能是珍・奧斯汀的畫像」，那麼接下來的三段就會列舉作此推測的原因。考生可以快速做筆記抓住這一點資訊。

在講座中，教授會表達自己對短文論點的看法，通常會對論點提出質疑。考生要認真聽講座的前幾句話，以確定教授的立場。接下來，教授會對閱讀短文中的分論點逐一進行反駁，考生要把這些反駁的分論點記錄在表格上「講座」這一欄。例如在上面的例子中，教授可能會說珍・奧斯汀家族裡有很多人，這幅畫也許是她某個親戚的畫像。

下面是上面關於舒伯特這道例題的筆記：

要點　　　材料	閱讀短文	講座
論點	S thought Symph complete (2 movts)	No, S would have liked 4 movts
分論點 1	Precedent for 2 movts symph	Yes, S was pushing boundary, but 8th Symph was written in Classical times
分論點 2	Both movts wrtten in same meter (3/4)	In fact, they found a 3rd movement in 3/4 time
分論點 3	S thought it perfect as it was	The 3rd and 4th draft movts were mediocre, not at all perfect

當然，講座中的每個分論點記錄得越詳細越好。但是沒必要詳細記錄短文的內容，因為寫作時短文會顯示在螢幕上，可以直接看。寫作文時，考生只須順著「分論點」欄一個接一個地詳述就可以了。如此一來，這張表格就相當於寫作提綱。

綜合寫作題的記筆記策略

1. 以「抓好核心概念、論點和分論點」為目標,來閱讀短文。
2. 做表格形式的筆記。閱讀部分,可以用縮寫形式簡單記錄三個分論點。而講座部分,儘量捕捉三個分論點的細節,為了節省時間,同樣可以使用縮寫形式。
3. 聽講座時,注意聽關於分論點的指示性詞語。例如,當聽到「It's doubtful that...」時,要意識到教授將提出一個反駁閱讀短文中分論點的論點。
4. 本書列舉了閱讀短文和講座中常用的實用句型。記住這些句型,進入考場後要充分利用這些指示性詞語,提醒自己什麼時候該做筆記。
5. 做筆記時要放鬆。講座的結構和上下文都是可以預測的,所以教授在介紹或說明每一個分論點時,就可以做好準備把每一點都記錄下來。

高分範文 *Track 004*

The professor talks about the controversy surrounding Schubert's masterpiece, the Eighth Symphony. Some people, including the author of the passage, think the two-movement symphony that we have today was exactly what Schubert intended. Other people, like the professor, believe Schubert hoped to write a four-movement piece but was not able to complete it.

First, the professor disputes the reading's point that Schubert created two movements because he was trying to break out of the Classical mold. He points out that the Eighth Symphony was written at the end of the Classical period and thus followed Classical practices in terms of symphony structure. There is no reason to believe he wanted to deviate from the norm of four movements.

The professor also takes exception to the argument regarding consecutive movements in the same meter, suggesting that Schubert would only write two movements in the same meter. The professor rebuts this point by citing that old manuscripts have been found, proving that Schubert attempted to write a third, and even a fourth, movement.

Third, the professor thinks Schubert was simply not comfortable with the work as a whole, for some reason. This view contradicts the reading, which maintains that because the two-movement "Unfinished Symphony" is now a favorite with audiences worldwide, Schubert must have been happy with his work. The professor again refers to the evidence of the rather ordinary third movement that exists and the missing pages, making the case that Schubert was not happy with the symphony. He probably tried to write the remaining movements, but eventually gave up.

萬用模板

　　描述藝術家、音樂家或劇作家的想法時，可以運用下面的萬用寫作範本。

The professor talks about the controversy surrounding _____
_____.

First, the professor disputes the reading's point that _____ because
_____ [he/she] was trying to _____
_____. There is no reason to believe [he / she] _____.

The professor also takes exception to the argument regarding , _____

suggesting that _____. The professor rebuts this point by
citing that _____, proving that _____
_____.

Third, the professor thinks _____.

This view contradicts the reading, which maintains that because _____,

[he / she] must have been _____. The professor again refers
to the evidence _____, making the case that
_____.

建立自己的寫作句型庫

　　寫人文藝術方面話題的作文時，以下句型都可以用。

• 閱讀好句型，成為我的作文佳句！

1. **There are good reasons to believe that x did not consider this work y and intended it to VERB**
   有充分的理由認為 x 不覺得他的作品很 y，本來打算……

   There are good reasons to believe that he did not consider this work "incomplete" and intended it to have only two movements.

   延伸說法 There are good reasons to believe that the artist did not consider this work unfinished and intended it to be destroyed.

2. **X also maintain that y was / were… because…**
   某人也認為 y 是……因為……

   Music historians also maintain that Schubert was content with two movements because both movements are written in the same meter; that is to say, three beats to a measure.

延伸說法 Experts also maintain that works by Picasso are popular targets for art thieves because of their immense monetary value.

3. Finally, x most likely intentionally VERBed because…
最後，某人極有可能故意……因為……

Finally, Schubert most likely intentionally left the composition at two movements because he thought the music was perfect as it was.

延伸說法 Finally, Plato most likely wrote down the thoughts of Socrates because Socrates was no longer alive to record them.

• 講座好句型，成為我的作文佳句！

1. We can assume that x would have VERBed
我們可以假設 x 本來會……

We can assume that Schubert would have liked to complete all four movements.

延伸說法 We can assume that Schubert would have written four movements had he lived longer.

2. It's true that in the x century y VERBed
確實在 x 世紀，y 做了……

It's true that in the early 19th century some musical compositions had only two movements.

延伸說法 It's true that in the 1800s composers began to explore new musical forms.

3. What about x's use of y?
x 使用 y 的方式如何？

What about Schubert's use of the same meter in the first two movements?

延伸說法 What about Schubert's missing manuscript?

4. Third, it's doubtful that…
第三，……很可疑

Third, it's doubtful that Schubert thought the composition was "perfect" as it was.

延伸說法 Third, it's doubtful that Schubert would have published a three-movement symphony at that time.

• 高分範文中，有這些作文佳句！

1. The professor talks about the controversy surrounding x
該教授談論了圍繞……存在的爭議

The professor talks about the controversy surrounding Schubert's masterpiece, the Eighth Symphony.

延伸說法 The professor talks about the controversy surrounding the Unfinished Symphony.

2. First, the professor disputes the reading's point that x VERBed because x was trying to VERB
首先，該教授對閱讀中的「x 因為試著……而……」的論點表示了異議

First, the professor disputes the reading's point that Schubert created two movements because he was trying to break out of the Classical mold.

延伸說法 First, the professor disputes the reading's point that the composer wrote a new kind of symphony because he was trying to revolutionize music.

3. There is no reason to believe…
沒有理由去相信……

There is no reason to believe he wanted to deviate from the norm of four movements.

延伸說法 There is no reason to believe Schubert would use a radically different musical structure.

4. The professor also takes exception to the argument regarding x, suggesting that…
該教授也不同意關於……的論點，認為……

The professor also takes exception to the argument regarding consecutive movements in the same meter, suggesting that Schubert would only write two movements in the same meter.

延伸說法 The professor also takes exception to the argument regarding movements in the same musical meter, suggesting that there were only supposed to be two movements.

5. The professor rebuts this point by citing that…, proving that…
該教授以……來反駁該論點，證實……

The professor rebuts this point by citing that old manuscripts have been found, proving that Schubert attempted to write a third, and even a fourth, movement.

延伸說法 The professor rebuts this point by citing that pages of old music have been found, proving that Schubert actually tried to write more than two movements.

6. This view contradicts the reading, which maintains that because…, x must have…
該觀點與閱讀短文的觀點相矛盾，閱讀短文的觀點認為因為……，x 一定有……

This view contradicts the reading, which maintains that because the two-movement "Unfinished Symphony" is now a favorite with audiences worldwide, Schubert must have been happy with his work.

延伸說法 This view contradicts the reading, which maintains that because the two-movement work is very popular, Schubert must have considered it a great symphony.

7. The professor again refers to the evidence of x, making the case that...

該教授又引用了……的證據，提出理由證明……

The professor again refers to the evidence of the rather ordinary third movement that exists and the missing pages, making the case that Schubert was not happy with the symphony.

延伸說法 The professor again refers to the evidence of the piano version of the third movement and torn manuscript pages, making the case that Schubert had wanted to finish the symphony.

關鍵語塊

- **composer** 作曲家
- **measure** 小節
- **Franz Schubert** 弗朗茨‧舒伯特
- **three-fourths time** 3/4 拍
- **symphony** 交響樂
- **three-eighths time** 3/8 拍
- **in B Minor B** 小調
- **consecutive** 連貫的；不間斷的
- **movements** 樂章
- **as it was** 按原狀
- **Unfinished Symphony** 《未完成的交響曲》（特指舒伯特《第八交響曲》）
- **themes** 主旋律
- **composition** 音樂作品
- **orchestration** 管弦樂編曲
- **instrumental work** 器樂作品
- **masterful** 精湛的
- **precedent** 前例，先例

- **it's no coincidence that...** ……並非偶然
- **Beethoven** 貝多芬
- **pushing the boundaries of...** 對……進行突破；促進……的進步
- **sonatas** 奏鳴曲
- **Classical heritage** 古典主義的傳承
- **transcend** 超越
- **in a row** 連續
- **be content with...** 對……滿意
- **torn out of...** 從……扯出
- **meter** 韻律
- **it's doubtful that...** ……是值得懷疑的
- **beats** 節拍
- **mediocre** 平庸的，普通的

▼再練習一次！

學習了以上這些策略、實用句型、語塊、高分範文和萬用寫作範本之後，再回頭去看看例題吧！再讀一遍閱讀短文，然後再聽一遍講座。如果還是聽不懂講座內容，就反覆多聽幾遍，或者參考錄音原稿。接下來，再修改你之前寫的作文，或者重新寫一篇作文。修改或重寫作文時，試著運用本章學到的寫作技巧。完成之後，比較一下修改或重寫前後的兩篇作文，注意不同之處。

附錄：錄音原稿

 Track 003

Narrator: Now listen to part of a lecture on the same topic.

(man) **Professor:** As masterful as Schubert's Eighth Symphony is, the fact remains that instead of the four movements required of Classical symphonies, it has only two. And it's no coincidence that this work is called the "Unfinished" Symphony. We can assume that Schubert would have liked to complete all four movements. Let's look at the points mentioned in the reading, one by one.

First, the issue of two-movement works. It's true that in the early 19th century some musical compositions had only two movements. It is also true that Schubert was pushing the boundaries of symphonies, especially by writing musical themes with great emotional power. But remember that the Eighth Symphony was written at the end of the Classical period. The structure of Schubert's symphonies reflects this Classical heritage. This means that, for Schubert, a symphony would always have four movements.

What about Schubert's use of the same meter in the first two movements? Yes, symphonies are not supposed to have three movements in a row with the same meter. What is interesting is that Schubert did in fact try to write a third movement to his Eighth Symphony, in the same meter. Music historians discovered an early version, most of which contained only piano music. At the end, pages appear to have been torn out of the music. These missing pages may have been the fourth movement of his symphony.

Third, it's doubtful that Schubert thought the composition was "perfect" as it was. As I mentioned, it's clear that he was having trouble with his third movement. The version that does exist is considered rather mediocre by music historians. Schubert probably never revised the third and fourth movements; he disliked making small changes to his scores. He sent the unfinished Eighth Symphony to a friend, who kept it secretly for forty years.

3 Life Sciences — Zoology
生命科學常考主題 1：動物學

在本章，你將學到……

★提高預測講座中教授觀點的能力

解讀常考題

綜合寫作題中涉及動植物話題的題占很大的比例。除了動植物話題之外，還會涉及生態學、微觀生物學和公共健康。在典型的生命科學寫作題裡，如果閱讀短文討論的是有袋類動物向低級進化，那麼講座就會反駁此說法，認為有袋類動物向高級進化。

由於動植物的生命形式多樣，名稱和行為各異，所以有些考生覺得生命科學主題的講座很難，詞彙量非常大。儘管原理和定義不會太專業（如果內容的語言是自己的母語就根本沒有絲毫難度），但是英語為非母語的人聽生命科學的術語確實有很大的難度。不過不要擔心，許多詞彙會出現在閱讀短文中，其他詞彙則可根據上下文來猜測。

▶模擬試題①

閱讀以下的短文並聆聽講座，完成以下這道作文題。

Narrator: This section measures writing to communicate in an academic environment. There are two writing tasks.

For Writing Task 1, the integrated writing task, you will read a short passage and listen to a lecture and then answer a question. For Writing Task 2, the independent writing task, you will answer a question based on your own knowledge and experience.

Now listen to the directions for Writing Task 1.

For Writing Task 1, you will have three minutes to read a short academic passage. You may take notes. The passage will be removed and you will listen to a lecture about the same topic. Again, you may take notes.

You will have 20 minutes to write a response about the relationship between the lecture and the reading. Try to answer the question as completely as possible using information from the reading passage and the lecture. Do not give your personal opinion. You will be able to see the reading passage again. You may use your notes.

An effective response will be 150 to 225 words. You will be rated on the quality of your writing and on the completeness and accuracy of the content. If you finish your response before time is up, you may go on to Writing Task 2.

Begin reading now.

One of the more serious threats facing wildlife in North America is the future of bobwhite quails. Native to Mexico, the Caribbean and the US, these "New World" quails have declined dramatically in number. In fact, in the past 40 years, the population of wild bobwhite quail has fallen 82 percent. Recreational hunters and conservationists claim that actions need to be taken to reverse this trend.

First, because so much land is taken up by crops and agriculture, it is necessary for each farmer to create a small area of native plants dedicated to quail. Successful quail habitat management requires meeting all the quail's needs in these small areas.

Next, hunters must stop "over-hunting." The bobwhite's popularity as a game bird has led to excessive hunting, causing a decline in quail populations. By shortening the hunting season to two months in some areas, and by completely banning hunting in areas where quail have disappeared, quail will have the opportunity to reproduce and build in number.

Finally, we need to encourage individuals to breed large numbers of bobwhite quail and release them into the wild. For example, growers can buy quail eggs and raise them. Alternatively, growers can buy a breeding pair of adult quail. Young quail grow quickly and are ready for release at 16 weeks. By artificially restocking quail populations through the release of penraised birds, hunting and conservation interests will benefit.

Narrator: Now listen to part of a lecture on the same topic.

 Track 005 在這裡請播放 Track 005。錄音內容全文可在本章結尾找到。

Summarize the points made in the lecture you just heard, explaining how they cast doubt on the specific solutions presented in the reading.

Narrator: You have 20 minutes to write Task 1.

預測下文：預測講座內容和觀點

綜合寫作題的難點在於理解教授的講座內容和其觀點。對於英語為非母語的學習者而言，教授的語速非常快。不管講座內容是否熟悉，英語術語一閃即逝。聽力語速很快，考生應如何應對？

如果考生能訓練自己預測下文的能力，那麼捕捉講座的要點就會容易得多。

那麼如何預測講座內容和教授的觀點呢？

預測講座內容時，利用以下幾點：

1. 結構和邏輯順序
2. 指示性詞語
3. 主題之外的知識

1. 結構和邏輯順序

綜合寫作題的講座結構大多可以預測。講座第一段通常是介紹性的段落，觀點鮮明，對概念、現象或要描述的事件作簡單的介紹。接下來的段落包含三個分論點。考生可以明顯感覺到講座中的分論點是對閱讀短文分論點的具體回應。通常情況下，講座會反駁閱讀中的觀點。如果考生漏聽了一兩個詞，要充分利用這種「可預測性」來預測甚至猜測下文內容。此外，正如上章所說，透過製作筆記表格也可以很快抓住講座的結構。

2. 指示性詞語

講座第一段經常會有一個表示部分贊同閱讀短文論點的陳述，但是接下來會反駁其論證的某些方面。邏輯上的指示性詞語包括下面句子中的底線詞語：

Solar energy <u>may appear</u>（看起來可能） to be easy to implement, but <u>actually</u>（事實上） it is quite problematic.

再舉一個例子：

The reading is correct in pointing out that there are some benefits associated with micro credit. <u>However</u>（然而）, the reading neglects to mention the serious problems that occur.

考生從這些指示性詞語便可知道，接下來要開始反駁閱讀短文的觀點了。

指示性詞語最明顯的用法是表示順序，即教授將 first、second、third 或 lastly 置於每段最前面，引出三個分論點。然而並不是所有教授都透過這種形式來陳述自己的觀點。有時候，教授可能用 To begin with... 來開始陳述第一個分論點。而對於第二個和第三個分論點，教授可能會用 And regarding the issue of x,... 或者 X is also a problem with...。因此考生需要了解各種表示順序的詞彙及片語，以提醒自己接下來就是一個反駁性分論點。

還有一些講座中經常用到的指示性詞語是和短文中概念的性質相關的實義詞，諸如 benefits、advantages、drawbacks、likelihood of success（或 failure），以及用 increases、decreases 等表示未來趨勢的詞。如果你已掌握這些實義詞，那麼就能更理解上下文。例如，如果在講座中聽到：The steps proposed by the reading are likely to be unsuccessful and may even cause environmental damage. 你就可以做好準備去聽下面說這些步驟無效且有害的原因。

3. 主題之外的知識

對於學術話題，哪怕僅有一點背景知識，理解該話題也會相對容易一些。因此，考生應該充分利用自己的知識，結合閱讀中的資訊來預測教授即將說什麼。用自己已有的經驗和對世界的認知來推斷和預測講座內容，這叫做「自上而下」的聽力策略。運用這一策略可以更成功地預測教授的觀點（並猜測一些模糊性詞語的意思）。這樣一來記筆記就會容易很多，也有助於得高分。

現在你們已經瞭解了上面談的這些方法，以後練習寫作的時候就可以用這些方法了。認真研讀本書中的錄音原稿，熟悉其結構和片語的用法。掌握好這些，相信你一定能提高綜合寫作題的分數！

正確預測講座內容，可運用以下策略

1. 充分利用講座結構的可預測性。認真聽第一段核心概念的定義和論點，然後逐一聽三個分論點。

2. 運用表格記錄核心概念、論點以及分論點。這有助於理解閱讀和講座的結構，並準確預測教授的觀點。

3. 注意聽指示性詞語和其他關鍵字。例如，注意聽表達教授說話邏輯的指示性詞語，像 although 和 despite what many people say，通常後面會緊跟一個對比子句，如 there is good reason to believe that...。這些暗示教授將比較講座與閱讀中的觀點。

4. 注意聽表示順序的指示性詞語，如 first、second 和 lastly。一旦聽到這些詞，就要集中注意力抓住每一個分論點的內容。

5. 注意聽可預測下文內容的實義詞，如 benefits 和 problems。這些詞在閱讀和講座中都可能出現。但在講座中聽到的這些詞會更有價值，因為它們暗示教授即將講述的觀點的性質。

6. 用閱讀短文中的事實和實義詞在心裡形成一個框架或綱要，這些事實和詞彙會幫助你預測講座中教授要說的內容。

7. 運用自己的知識大膽猜測教授的講話內容。事實上，你懂的遠比自己想像的要多！如果講座是關於農藥，而這一話題可能你正好瞭解一些，那就儘量多想想用以描述農藥的基本概念，包括其好處和潛在的危害等。

8. 預測教授的講話內容時，如果有一兩個單字沒聽清楚，不要驚慌。只要好好運用上述策略，就一定會理解所聽的話題；一些不熟悉的詞彙不影響對全文的把握。

高分範文　 *Track 006*

The bobwhite quail has been under tremendous ecological pressure. In the past few decades, over four-fifths of the population has been killed. Suggestions for how to restore the quail numbers have been proposed, but there are differences in opinion. For example, in the lecture, the professor disagrees with the views expressed in the reading passage.

First, the professor disputes the effectiveness of the suggestion to set aside many small patches of land for the quails to live on. He believes isolated islands of land cannot duplicate the quail's natural environment. Instead, he thinks tracts of land connecting many regions need to be allotted for this purpose. Moreover, he believes these plots should be integrated with agricultural land.

Second, the professor contradicts the reading regarding the issue of hunting. In his mind, overhunting is not the main factor leading to the dwindling of the quail's population. Not even a complete ban on hunting will solve the problem. He argues that bobwhite quail is a prolific species. As long as there are suitable habitats that meet quails' complex ecological requirements, they can quickly regain their numbers.

Third, he is against the idea of using farm-raised bobwhites to replenish the quail stock. He believes farm breeding will produce quail genes that weaken their abilities to adapt to the natural environment. Consequently, the farm-born quails will not survive in the wild. He thinks "trap and transfer" is a much better approach. By trapping bobwhites in areas with dense populations and moving them to a low density but suitable areas, we can increase their numbers while preserving the strong genes of the wild bobwhite.

萬用模板

綜合寫作題有很多會提出一個需要解決的問題，而短文中會提出一系列的解決方法。講座中教授會反駁這些解決方法，指出其缺陷。下面的萬用寫作範本適用於所有「解決問題」的文章。

針對解決問題類題目的萬用寫作範本：

[開頭第一句可以簡單地陳述一下問題]. Suggestions for how to _____ have been proposed, but there are differences in opinion. For example, in the lecture, the professor disagrees with the views expressed in the reading passage.

First, the professor disputes the effectiveness of the suggestion to _____ _____.

Second, the professor contradicts the reading regarding the issue of _____.

Not even _____ will solve the problem. He argues that _____ _____.

Third, he is against the idea of _____ _____.

建立自己的寫作句型庫

下面的實用句型適用於綜合寫作題中關於生命科學的題目。

• 閱讀好句型，成為我的作文佳句！

1. x claim that actions need to be taken to reverse this trend.
某人主張需要採取一些行動來扭轉這一趨勢。

Recreational hunters and conservationists claim that actions need to be taken to reverse this trend.

延伸說法 Policy makers claim that actions need to be taken to reverse this trend.

2. First, because…, it is necessary for y to VERB

首先，因為……，所以 y 有必要……

First, because so much land is taken up by crops and agriculture, it is necessary for each farmer to create a small area of native plants dedicated to quail.

延伸說法 First, because there are very few bushes on farms nowadays, it is necessary for people to plant areas of wild plants especially for quail.

3. x has led to y, causing z

……導致……，從而引發……

The bobwhite's popularity as a game bird has led to excessive hunting, causing a decline in quail populations.

延伸說法 Modern farming has led to fewer patches of wild grass, causing the number of quail to shrink.

• 講座好句型，成為我的作文佳句！

1. Yet the steps proposed in the reading passage will not be effective in VERBing

但是，閱讀短文中提議的措施在……方面不會有成效

Yet the steps proposed in the reading passage will not be effective in increasing quail populations.

延伸說法 Yet the steps proposed in the reading passage will not be effective in restoring quail populations.

2. First, people need to recognize that we…

首先，人們需要認識到我們……

First, people need to recognize that we can't increase the quail population with little plots of land here and there.

延伸說法 First, people need to recognize that we need to take action to save the bobwhite quail.

3. Second, x is not a major factor contributing to y

其次，……不是促成……的主要因素

Second, over-hunting is not a major factor contributing to the decline of quail populations.

延伸說法 Second, pollution is not a major factor contributing to the decrease in quail.

4. **Finally, the proposal to VERB is a bad idea.**
最後，……的提議不是一個好主意。

Finally, the proposal to release pen-raised bobwhite quail into the wild is a bad idea.

延伸說法 Finally, the proposal to raise quail domestically is a bad idea.

• **高分範文中，有這些作文佳句！**

1. **Suggestions for how to VERB have been proposed, but there are differences in opinion.**
有人已經提出……的建議，但是人們對此有不同看法。

Suggestions for how to restore the quail numbers have been proposed, but there are differences in opinion.

延伸說法 Suggestions for how to provide new habitat for quail have been proposed, but there are differences in opinion.

2. **For example, in the lecture, the professor disagrees with x in the reading passage.**
例如，在講座中，教授不贊同閱讀短文中的……

For example, in the lecture, the professor disagrees with the views expressed in the reading passage.

延伸說法 For example, in the lecture, the professor disagrees with the opinions presented in the reading passage.

3. **First, the professor disputes the effectiveness of the suggestion to VERB**
首先，教授質疑……建議的有效性

First, the professor disputes the effectiveness of the suggestion to set aside many small patches of land for the quails to live on.

延伸說法 First, the professor disputes the effectiveness of the suggestion to reserve small plots of farm land.

4. **Second, the professor contradicts the reading regarding the issue of VERBing**
其次，教授在關於……的問題上與短文中的觀點不一致

Second, the professor contradicts the reading regarding the issue of hunting.

延伸說法 Second, the professor contradicts the reading regarding the issue of quail reproduction.

5. Third, he is against the idea of VERBing

第三，他反對……的想法

Third, he is against the idea of using farm-raised bobwhites to replenish the quail stock.

延伸說法 Third, he is against the idea of releasing domestic quail into the wild.

關鍵語塊

- **bobwhite quail** 美洲鶉
- **restocking (quail) populations** 補充（鵪鶉的）數量
- **threats facing...** 對……的威脅
- **pen-raised birds** 圈養的鳥
- **decline dramatically** 急劇下降
- **hunting enthusiasts** 狩獵愛好者
- **recreational hunters** 把打獵作為娛樂的狩獵者
- **boost (bobwhite quail populations)** （美洲鶉數量）激增
- **conservationists** （動植物）保護工作者
- **plots of land** 土地
- **reverse (this) trend** 扭轉（這一）趨勢
- **It hasn't worked.** 這沒有效果。
- **be taken up by...** 被……佔據
- **isolated islands of land** 隔離的幾塊土地
- **native plants** 土生土長的植物，本地生植物
- **hunting season** 狩獵季
- **dedicated to...** 專門為……

- **prolific breeders** 繁殖力很高的動物
- **habitat management** 生態環境管理
- **timely access to...** 及時進入……
- **over-hunting** 過度捕獵
- **nesting habitats** 築巢之地
- **popularity as a(n)...** 作為……廣受歡迎
- **genetic DNA** 遺傳基因
- **game bird** 獵鳥；供捕獵的鳥
- **tends to be (inferior)** 往往是（低等的）
- **banning hunting** 禁獵
- **inter-breeding** 純種雜交
- **build in number** 數量增加
- **docile** 馴服的；溫順的
- **breed** 飼養；培育
- **have trouble (surviving)** 很難（倖存）
- **release** 釋放
- **trap and transfer** 陷阱捕獵和轉移
- **a breeding pair of adult quail** 育種配對的成年鵪鶉
- **genetic integrity** 遺傳完整性

▶再練習一次！

　　學習了以上這些策略、實用句型、語塊、高分範文和萬用寫作範本之後，返回去看例題。再讀一遍閱讀短文，然後再聽一遍講座。如果還是聽不懂講座內容，就反覆多聽幾遍，或者參考錄音原稿。然後修改你之前寫的作文，或者重新寫一篇作文。修改或重寫作文時，試著運用本章學到的寫作技巧。完成之後，比較一下修改或重寫前後的兩篇作文，注意不同之處。

附錄：錄音原稿

 Track 005

Narrator: Now listen to part of a lecture on the same topic.

(woman) Professor: Both hunting enthusiasts and biologists are searching for ways to boost bobwhite quail populations. It's not an easy task because bobwhite quail have complex habitat requirements, much more complex than most other animals. Yet the steps proposed in the reading passage will not be effective in increasing quail populations.

First, people need to recognize that we can't increase the quail population with little plots of land here and there. Rather, what is needed is a cooperative strategy that involves wildlife management across multiple regions. Professionals have been saying that creating small-scale plots on a farm will be enough, but it hasn't worked. The reason is that these isolated islands of land are not connected to one another. Biologists now realize we must have pieces of land that are connected to one another. The habitat areas must be managed across regional borders, integrated with pre-existing pieces of agricultural land.

Second, over-hunting is not a major factor contributing to the decline of quail populations. Even where the hunting season has been eliminated entirely, quail numbers have decreased. Quail are extremely prolific breeders — a single hen may lay a dozen eggs. But their life cycles are short — which makes it important for quail to have timely access to proper nesting habitats, where they can reproduce.

Finally, the proposal to release pen-raised bobwhite quail into the wild is a bad idea. Captive-bred bobwhites will seriously harm wild quail populations because their genetic DNA tends to be inferior, due to years of inter-breeding. Moreover, pen-raised quail often are docile and have trouble surviving in the wild. A better plan is to trap wild bobwhite quail in areas where they are abundant and then transfer them to areas of good habitat where quail are few. This "trap and transfer" approach maintains the genetic integrity of the breeding population of the wild quails.

4 Social Sciences ─ Archaeology
社會科學常考主題 1：考古學

在本章，你將學到……

★如何運用連接詞使作文銜接自然
★學習「讓步與反駁」的作文結構，讓作文更有說服力

解讀常考題

綜合寫作題中有很多關於社會科學的情境（在新托福考試的四個部分中，心理學和社會學是出現頻率很高的主題）。社會科學的話題涉及人類學、考古學、商業和管理、通訊、教育和經濟等。社會科學的話題主要關注人類的行為，例如，工人就業問題。因此，經濟學領域的作文題可能會談論私營企業的投資有沒有可能創造新的就業機會等等。

▶模擬試題①

閱讀以下的短文並聆聽講座，完成以下這道作文題。

Narrator: This section measures writing to communicate in an academic environment. There are two writing tasks.

For Writing Task 1, the integrated writing task, you will read a short passage and listen to a lecture and then answer a question. For Writing Task 2, the independent writing task, you will answer a question based on your own knowledge and experience.

Now listen to the directions for Writing Task 1.

For Writing Task 1, you will have three minutes to read a short academic passage. You may take notes. The passage will be removed and you will listen to a lecture about the same topic. Again, you may take notes.

You will have 20 minutes to write a response about the relationship between the lecture and the reading. Try to answer the question as completely as possible using information from the reading passage and the lecture. Do not give your personal opinion. You will be able to see the reading passage again. You may use your notes.

An effective response will be 150 to 225 words. You will be rated on the quality of your writing and on the completeness and accuracy of the content. If you finish your response before time is up, you may go on to Writing Task 2.

Begin reading now.

There has been much discussion about when our early human ancestors were first able to control fire on a regular basis. Many archaeologists believe that some 1.6 million years ago, the early human ancestors referred to as Hominins had control over fire when they emerged from Africa. These predecessors of modern human beings could walk on two feet and were always on the move. They were hunters and gatherers who could use simple stone tools. We can logically assume that the Homo erectus species — the name we often give the first upright Hominins — had control of fire when they arrived in Europe. There are several reasons for this thinking.

First, because we know the Homo erectus species colonizing Europe had rapidly evolving bodies and relatively large brains, they would have required a steady source of energy. Heat greatly increases the nutritional quality of food. Cooked foods are more efficiently digested and boost metabolic energy. In cold climates, the consumption of raw foods would have been an insufficient source of energy to fuel the growth and evolution of Homo erectus that took place.

Also, archaeologists have discovered traces of fireplaces and burned materials in many excavations in Europe. Although the nomadic Homo erectus did not take time to build formal hearths, the clusters of burnt materials that have been found indicate that heating took place. For example, there are reddened sediments (showing iron oxidation), charred bone fragments and small pieces of charcoal.

Moreover, we know that during this time the temperatures in Europe routinely dropped below freezing. It would have been impossible for Homo erectus to survive in the northern latitudes of Europe during the Ice Age without relying on fire to stay warm, especially during the coldest periods of winter.

Narrator: Now listen to part of a lecture on the same topic.

 Track 007 在這裡請播放 Track 007。錄音內容全文可在本章結尾找到。

Summarize the points made in the lecture you just heard, being sure to explain how they respond to the specific arguments made in the reading passage.

Narrator: You have 20 minutes to write Task 1.

連接詞的銜接

　　僅僅熟練掌握詞彙和文法還遠遠不夠，考生還需要具備一種能夠準確地組詞成句和組句成段的能力。這正是我的「有機英語學習法」中，如此強調「銜接能力」的原因。很多情況下銜接就像膠水一樣，將單字和片語連接在一起。銜接自然的作文能夠讓評分者輕鬆讀懂文章的邏輯。一旦考生在新托福考試的作文中能夠做到銜接自然，評分者就會注意到這一點，並順理成章打出高分。文章觀點統一也是一種連貫，做到這一點，文章的分數就能從 3 分上升到 4 分。

　　根據 ETS 評分準則，綜合作文題若想得到 4 分，作文必須連貫而準確地傳達講座的要點。若只拿到 3 分，這種作文一般是模糊、籠統且不太準確地表達了講座觀點與閱讀觀點的聯繫。由此可見，銜接自然的作文拿 4 分的可能性就會增大。因此，下面就教給大家怎樣做到銜接自然和前後連貫。

　　有很多方法可以使作文前後更連貫。本章主要透過連接詞這一手法，第 14 章會具體介紹如何使用指示詞，使上下文銜接自然。

　　連接詞的用法很多。連接詞既可以連接句內的片語和分句，也可以連接兩個獨立的句子。連接詞種類繁多，下面的表格列舉了一些寫作中常用的連接詞和連接副詞。

並列連接詞	從屬連接詞	連接副詞
and	although	as a result
but	because	consequently
for	even though	however
nor	if	moreover
or	unless	nevertheless
so	until	rather
yet	in order that	yet

　　用連接詞使上下文連貫需要注意以下兩點：

1）複習連接詞位置的文法知識。學習不同連接詞的位置，判斷它們是放在句中的不同地方還是放在獨立分句之前。如：

Micro credit loans are in some ways inefficient; <u>on the other hand</u>, they can help entrepreneurs in remote villages.

<u>Although</u> micro credit loans are in some ways inefficient, they can help entrepreneurs in remote villages.

It's true that micro credit loans are in some ways inefficient. They can help entrepreneurs in remote villages, <u>however</u>.

2）選擇連接詞時，除了文法外，還要考慮邏輯。例如，moreover 表示要在原義的基礎上增加一些資訊；however 表示要陳述與之前的觀點相矛盾或相反的觀點。如：

The passage says celebrity endorsements can grab the attention of consumers. Moreover, celebrity advertisements can be used to promote a wide variety of products and services.

The passage says celebrity endorsements can grab the attention of consumers. However, the professor asserts that consumers aren't really persuaded by this tactic.

運用連接詞做到上下文銜接自然的策略

1. 學習基本的幾個連接詞的功能和用法，考試前練習寫作時要學著運用。這對掌握銜接和連貫的技巧非常重要，且會直接影響你的分數。

2. 寫作時不要在句子開頭使用 and 作為連接詞。在一個句子開頭用 and 會讓評分者覺得考生的連接詞運用能力欠佳，如：The professor said that consumer resistance to advertising had never been greater. And she also said that the consumers are aware that they are being manipulated.

3. 不要忘記邏輯！銜接自然的文章，邏輯一定是連貫的。寫作時要注意觀點間的邏輯。（關於邏輯連貫性的策略將在第 16 章詳述。）

4. 考試時不要只用連接詞這一單一手法來銜接。銜接和連貫都需要各種語言表達策略，包括使用指示性代名詞（如 this project）、限定詞（the team model），或者重複關鍵字。簡而言之，寫作需要連接詞，但不能只用連接詞這一種手段。

高分範文   *Track 008*

Early humans knew how to use fire. But the question of just when they learned to control the use of fire is far from being settled. Examining the evidence left by the Homo erectus living in Europe, the writer of the reading passage believes it was 1.6 million years ago, while the professor thinks it was much later — about 400,000 years ago.

The professor concurs that cooking enhances the nutritional value of food, but he thinks early Hominins got enough nutrition through raw food. The professor cites fossil records of teeth which are well-suited for tearing and chewing. He implies they would not have had this kind of teeth unless they had to consume raw food.

Second, the professor disputes the dating of the charcoal and burnt bones. Referring to the fireplace evidence cited in the reading, the professor says the burnt materials were from a much later time. He says there is no archeological evidence of the control use of fire in Europe that goes back a million years. Homo erectus in Africa may have taken advantage of natural fires, but that does not mean they were able to create fire.

On the third point, about how the Homo erectus kept warm in the frigid temperatures of the time, the professor does not believe fire played a role. Homo erectus were persistent and adaptable. Their hunting lifestyle kept them moving with herds of animals and they could use furs for clothing. He also says they could stay in natural shelters to keep warm.

萬用模板

綜合寫作題的閱讀短文有一個論點和幾個分論點，然後講座會反駁這些論點和分論點。有些教授反駁時，會先同意閱讀短文中的一個觀點，然後再反駁整體論斷。這種「讓步與反駁」的文章複雜但具有說服力，右頁的範本可以用於這類文章。

針對讓步與反駁類題目的萬用寫作範本：

[用簡短的一句話表示認同閱讀短文的部分觀點]. But the question of _____ is far from being settled. Examining the evidence left by _____, the writer of the reading passage believes _____, while the professor thinks _____.

The professor concurs that _____, but he thinks _____.

Second, the professor disputes the _____ of _____. _____ may have _____, but that does not mean they were able to _____.

On the third point, about how _____, the professor does not believe _____ played a role.

建立自己的寫作句型庫

寫社會科學方面話題的作文時，下面的句型都可以用上。

• 閱讀好句型，成為我的作文佳句！

1　There has been much discussion about when…
關於……當時的事，有許多種討論

There has been much discussion about when our early human ancestors were first able to control fire on a regular basis.

延伸說法 There has been much discussion about when humans first used fire.

2. There are several reasons for this x
關於這個……有很多原因

There are several reasons for this thinking.

延伸說法 There are several reasons for this opinion.

3. First, because we know x…, they would have required y
首先，因為我們知道……，所以他們可能需要……

First, because we know the Homo erectus species colonizing Europe had rapidly evolving bodies and relatively large brains, they would have required a steady source of energy.

延伸說法 First, because we know the Hominids of that time were involving increasingly large brains, they would have required good nutrition.

4. Although x did not VERB, y indicate(s) that...

雖然…… 沒有…… ，但是……暗示……

Although the nomadic Homo erectus did not take time to build formal hearths, the clusters of burnt materials that have been found indicate that heating took place.

延伸說法 Although the European Hominins of that time did not settle in one place, pieces of charcoal indicate that heating took place.

5. Moreover, we know that during this time x VERBed

此外，我們知道在此期間 x 做了……

Moreover, we know that during this time the temperatures in Europe routinely dropped below freezing.

延伸說法 Moreover, we know that during this time the European climate was colder than it is today.

• **講座好句型，成為我的作文佳句！**

1. Research findings suggest that humans did not VERB until…

研究結果顯示人們直到……才

Research findings suggest that humans did not control fire until much later, about 400,000 years ago.

延伸說法 Research findings suggest that humans did not learn to use fire until approximately 400,000 years ago.

2. What about the claim that x must have VERBed…?

關於 x 一定有……的說法怎麼樣呢？

What about the claim that Homo erectus must have eaten cooked food to have enough energy to evolve?

延伸說法 What about the claim that early humans must have absorbed nutrients from cooked food?

3. And third, whereas it's true that…, x proved able to VERB

第三，雖然……確實是事實，但……證明能夠……

And third, whereas it's true that a million years ago temperatures in Europe dipped below freezing as glaciers advanced and retreated, the Homo erectus who colonized these parts proved able to survive without fire.

延伸說法 And third, whereas it's true that it was extremely cold in Europe during the Ice Age, our early ancestors proved able to endure this cold without fire.

• **高分範文中，有這些作文佳句！**

1. **But the question of x is far from being settled.**

   但是關於……的問題遠沒有解決。

   But the question of just when they learned to control the use of fire is far from being settled.

   延伸說法 But the question of when our human ancestors actually gained control over fire is far from being settled.

2. **Examining the evidence [left] by x, the writer of the reading passage believes…, while the professor thinks…**

   仔細研究……留下的證據，短文作者認為……，而教授認為……

   Examining the evidence left by the Homo erectus living in Europe, the writer of the reading passage believes it was 1.6 million years ago, while the professor thinks it was much later — about 400,000 years ago.

   延伸說法 Examining the evidence left by the European Hominins, the writer of the reading passage believes fire was controlled almost 1.6 million years ago, while the professor thinks the actual date was closer to 400,000 years ago.

3. **The professor concurs that…, but he thinks…**

   教授認同……，但他認為……

   The professor concurs that cooking enhances the nutritional value of food, but he thinks early Hominins got enough nutrition through raw food.

4. **Second, the professor disputes the x of y**

   其次，該教授質疑……

   Second, the professor disputes the dating of the charcoal and burnt bones.

   延伸說法 Second, the professor disputes the passage's interpretations of the evidence.

5. **x may have VERBed, but that does not mean they were able to VERB**

   也許 x 有……，但是那不表示他們能夠……（may have done 結構表示對過去發生的行為的推測）

   Homo erectus in Africa may have taken advantage of natural fires, but that does not mean they were able to create fire.

   延伸說法 Early humans may have taken advantage of forest fires started by lightning, but that does not mean they were able to build fires by themselves.

6. On the third point, about how x..., the professor does not believe y played a role.

第三，關於……，該教授不相信……有影響。

On the third point, about how the Homo erectus kept warm in the frigid temperatures of the time, the professor does not believe fire played a role.

延伸說法 On the third point, about how early humans in Europe kept warm, the professor does not believe fire played a role.

關鍵語塊

- **archaeologists** 考古學家
- **bone fragments** 骨片
- **Hominin** 人類，古人類
- **charcoal** 木炭
- **predecessors of...** ……的祖先
- **northern latitudes** 北緯
- **Homo erectus** 直立人
- **Ice Age** 冰川期
- **metabolic energy** 維持新陳代謝的能量
- **energy efficient** 節能的
- **consumption of...** 吃，喝
- **crunchy** 酥脆的
- **fuel (growth and evolution)** 刺激（生長和進化）
- **geologic time** 地質時期
- **traces of...** ……的痕跡
- **domestic use** 家用
- **fireplaces** 生火之地
- **(lightning) struck** （雷）擊
- **excavations** 挖掘現場
- **(volcanoes) erupted** （火山）爆發
- **nomadic** 遊牧的
- **on a habitual basis** 按照常規
- **hearths** 生火之地
- **glaciers** 冰川
- **clusters of...** 一叢一叢的……
- **tenacious** 頑強的
- **sediments** 沉積物
- **resilient** 適應性強的
- **iron oxidation** 鐵的氧化
- **natural shelters** 自然庇護所
- **charred** 燒焦的
- **adapting to...** 適應……

▶再練習一次！

　　學習了以上這些策略、實用句型、語塊、高分範文和萬用寫作範本之後，再回頭去看例題。再讀一遍閱讀短文，然後再聽一遍講座。如果還是聽不懂講座內容，就反覆多聽幾遍，或者參考錄音原稿。然後修改你之前寫的作文，或者重新寫一篇作文。修改或重寫作文時，試著運用本章學到的寫作技巧。完成之後，比較一下修改或重寫前後的兩篇作文，注意不同之處。

Track 007

Narrator: Now listen to part of a lecture on the same topic.

(man) Professor: Of course, our early human ancestors made use of natural fires in Africa, but they were not able to control the technology. There is simply no evidence in Europe that the early Hominins had regular control of fire almost two million years ago. Research findings suggest that humans did not control fire until much later, about 400,000 years ago.

What about the claim that Homo erectus must have eaten cooked food to have enough energy to evolve? To be sure, cooked food is more energy efficient for human bodies. However, even in cold climates, Homo erectus would have had an excellent source of meat and fish. And archaeologists who have analyzed fossils of teeth have found that Homo erectus munched on crunchy and tough foods, such as raw meat and root vegetables. The size and shape of their teeth were well suited for tearing and chewing meat, a source of protein that supports brain development.

As for fireplaces, no charcoal or charred bones have been found in European archaeological sites dating a million years back that can be linked to the controlled use of fire. The charcoal particles and burnt bones that have been found seem to be products of fires which occurred much later in geologic time. Furthermore, while our ancestors in Africa certainly made good domestic use of fire when lightning struck or when volcanoes erupted, they were unable to create fire on a habitual basis.

And third, whereas it's true that a million years ago temperatures in Europe dipped below freezing as glaciers advanced and retreated, the Homo erectus who colonized these parts proved able to survive without fire. How? They were tenacious and resilient. They followed herds of game and took advantage of natural shelters such as caves. Adapting to the cold, they used primitive tools to create warm clothing out of animal skins.

5 Physical Sciences — Energy
物理科學常考主題 2：能源

❝ 在本章，你將學到…… ❞

★如何運用本書的萬用寫作範本和高分範文寫出個性化的作文
★如何清晰地陳述兩方的觀點

解讀常考題

能源利用是新托福寫作的熱門話題。

▶模擬試題①

閱讀以下的短文並聆聽講座，完成以下這道作文題目。

Narrator: This section measures writing to communicate in an academic environment. There are two writing tasks.

For Writing Task 1, the integrated writing task, you will read a short passage and listen to a lecture and then answer a question. For Writing Task 2, the independent writing task, you will answer a question based on your own knowledge and experience.

Now listen to the directions for Writing Task 1.

For Writing Task 1, you will have three minutes to read a short academic passage. You may take notes. The passage will be removed and you will listen to a lecture about the same topic. Again, you may take notes.

You will have 20 minutes to write a response about the relationship between the lecture and the reading. Try to answer the question as completely as possible using information from the reading passage and the lecture. Do not give your personal opinion. You will be able to see the reading passage again. You may use your notes.

An effective response will be 150 to 225 words. You will be rated on the quality of your writing and on the completeness and accuracy of the content. If you finish your response before time is up, you may go on to Writing Task 2.

Begin reading now.

Wind is a clean, renewable source of energy which holds much promise, and so private companies and governments have been actively exploring ways to commercially exploit wind power. Wind generators are currently operating in over 70 countries in the world, producing electrical power for small-scale applications and large utility companies. Yet there are several problems with using wind power that may prove obstacles to widespread implementation of this resource in the future.

One of the main challenges that the energy developers face is the large amount of land that is required to support wind generators. A safety zone of 5 acres is necessary for each wind turbine. Moreover, because the wind must be free from dust and debris, trees within 30 feet of the turbines should be cleared away. In order to generate the electrical output equivalent to a conventional power plant, a wind power system requires hundreds of acres of land.

Another challenge for the new technology is that wind energy turbines destroy vast numbers of birds and bats every year. In one wind farm in California, for example, it is estimated that 10,000 birds — all protected by the migratory bird act — are killed every year. In addition, bat fatalities have been documented at high rates near wind projects. Endangered species of both birds and bats are at great risk from wind turbines, including the golden eagle.

Third, wind farms destroy the natural beauty of the land. The wind turbines and the many wires and poles that must be constructed to transmit electricity are not aesthetically pleasing. They cannot "blend" into the landscape. No homeowner wants to look at and listen to 200-meter towers, and homeowners should not have to worry about the value of their property. Furthermore, public property with open space and scenic views adds value to communities.

Narrator: Now listen to part of a lecture on the same topic.

 Track 009 在這裡請播放 Track 009。錄音內容全文可在本章結尾找到。

> **Summarize the points made in the lecture, being sure to explain how they oppose the specific points made in the reading passage.**

Narrator: You have 20 minutes to write Task 1.

個性化的寫作

　　評分者看過成千上萬篇的作文，對於常用範本一眼就能看出來，而且 ETS 有專門的軟體檢測異常的語言雷同現象。如果評分者或 ETS 工作人員發現某篇作文可能是抄襲的，不能反映考生的真實能力，那麼這篇文章很可能會被打低分，嚴重的甚至會被判零分。相反，如果能讀到一篇描述情景和論據都與眾不同的文章，評分者會非常開心。因為這讓他們的工作變得不那麼枯燥，而且他們喜歡瞭解新事物。不管是個人經歷還是獨特的論點，個性化的文字會讓評分者確信自己評估的是考生的真實能力。所以說，考生應儘量把作文寫得個性化一點。

考生多背些高分範文以增強自信心的做法固然可取，但是怎樣才能使自己的文章更有個人特徵，讓評分者覺得有趣、真實並給高分呢？

文章個性化的三個步驟

1）根據題目判斷情境或上下文，以確定使用哪些模板句型，包括模板的結構和邏輯。

2）在合適的模板中選擇你已經熟記的實用句型。例如，對於綜合寫作題，The professor disputes the claim that... 用於聲稱找到解決方案的作文是很好的方法。

3）然後用自己的情況填充空白處。可以加一些自己的生活細節來支持自己的觀點。例如：The family meals my mother prepared were not fancy, but we sat down together every evening to eat.（摘自第 14 章的高分範文）

現在請認真閱讀本章後面關於風力發電的高分範文，研究它是怎麼運用模板句型的。

第一句提到有一場關於風力發電的爭論。考生透過陳述一個大家公認的事實做出總結，例如：Wind power is a renewable energy source with great potential. 然後告訴讀者有一場爭論。換句話說，大家對於風力發電是好是壞持有不同的見解。

第二句解釋各種意見是如何產生分歧的：風力發電的反對者（opponents）關注技術方面帶來的問題，而支持者（proponents）對這些問題比較樂觀。在這篇高分範文中，考生表示是科技帶來了這些問題。另一個較好的陳述是：Opponents focus on the problems that plague the technology...（這些句子在「建立自己的寫作句型庫」裡可以找到）。

第一段的最後一句指出短文如何表達反對者的觀點，而教授如何表達相反觀點來支持風力發電。

考生可以記住這些實用句型，在綜合寫作題任何一篇作文的第一段都可以用它們來描述爭論。然後，接下來三個段落的每段開頭都可以用本章提供的實用句型來表達教授對閱讀短文分論點的看法。寫作時，可以在每個論點之後另加一兩個句子。例如，在第二段，考生可以為該論點多提供一些細節。正如本章的高分範文，考生說教授同意風力發電需要大片土地這一觀點，還提出問題的解決辦法。

只要考生能正確理解講座、記好筆記，寫詳細的句子就不是太難。對考生而言，最重要的是抓住三個分論點並在最後三段中對它們進行陳述。

現在請研究一下本章後面的高分範文，看看如何在模板中填入正確的句子。由於這種寫法會得到高分，所以你要記住「萬用寫作範本」和「建立自己的寫作句型庫」裡的實用句型，讓它們成為你的寫作工具箱，用在你的個性化寫作中。

個性化寫作的策略

1. 對於綜合寫作題，記住本書前八章的「萬用寫作範本」和「建立自己的寫作句型庫」裡的實用句型。這些實用句型很重要，一定要熟練掌握！

2. 研究並記住前八章閱讀和講座裡的實用句型，寫作文時可以借用這些句型。請記住，在真正的新托福考試中，你要將閱讀和講座中的語言進行換句話說。如果直接從短文甚至講座中照搬太多詞彙，評分者給你的分數會比較低。

3. 獨立寫作題基本上可以用同樣的方法：研究本書的高分範文和「萬用寫作範本」，並記住「建立自己的寫作句型庫」裡的實用句型。但是，要寫出一篇具有個性化的作文，你還必須瀏覽所有的練習題並用英語列出自己的個性化內容。例如，題目問你喜歡什麼，你要寫下自己喜歡的東西並列出原因。如果你業餘時間喜歡呆在戶外，那就要用英語寫下你喜歡去的地方，並寫出原因。不要逐字逐句照搬別人的文字，嘗試原創。用這樣的方式寫下你喜歡的東西就像一場腦力激盪練習，幫你拿到最高分 5 分。

4. 準備寫作文時，有很多方法可以用上你準備的句型。可以從「建立自己的寫作句型庫」中選擇幾個句型，添加個性化內容，寫出自己的句子；也可以把本書高分範文中的所有句子當實用句型使用，然後加入個性化的內容。當然你也可以根據本章介紹的原則和策略寫出一篇全新的作文。

5. 不管使用哪種方法，練習寫作時最好用英語記下你自己的個性化內容，然後高聲朗讀，盡量記住。

高分範文　 *Track 010*

Wind power is a renewable energy source with great potential, but it is surrounded by controversy. Opponents focus on the problems that plague the technology, while proponents are optimistic about resolving the problems. The reading sides with the views of the opponents, and the professor is obviously a proponent.

First, the professor thinks the issue of land usage can be resolved. The reading talks about the large amount of land required by a wind power system. The professor does not dispute this fact, but she offers a way to solve the problem. She suggests placing wind power systems offshore or on top of mountains where they do not compete with other uses for land.

Second, the professor thinks bird and bat fatalities can be ameliorated. She reminds us of the fact that any structure can potentially kill a flying animal. She then attributes the problem discussed in the reading to the old design of the fast-spinning turbine blade and the fact that some power systems are placed in the animals' fly zones or near their nesting grounds. She says the new design of slow-moving blades will not kill as many birds and bats.

Finally, on the issue of aesthetics, the professor argues that this problem can be avoided by placing power systems out of sight of most people. She says current technologies allow power systems to be located more than 12 miles offshore, implying people living on land will not be able to see them. Then she repeats the same suggestion she made for the solution to the land usage problem, i.e., that wind turbines should be placed on mountaintops where few people live.

萬用模板

以下範本可以用於任何描述爭議並明確提出支持者與反對者的意見的作文。爭論型作文可能是關於諸如天文學等物理科學，例如，支持者與反對者對月球是否由大爆炸形式的假設持不同觀點。也可能關於其他學科，如社會科學的人類學，例如，有人稱某種古文明消失於乾旱，而有人則反對此說法。

_____ is [正面陳述] _____, but it is surrounded by controversy. Opponents focus on the problems that _____, while proponents are optimistic about resolving the problems. The reading sides with the views of the _____, and the professor is obviously a _____.

First, the professor thinks the issue of _____ can be resolved. [用兩三個句子來陳述] _____.

Second, the professor thinks [反面例子] _____ can be ameliorated. [用兩三個句子來陳述] _____.

Finally, on the issue of _____, the professor argues that this problem can be avoided by _____.

建立自己的寫作句型庫

寫物理科學方面話題的作文時，下面的句型都可以用上。

• 閱讀好句型，成為我的作文佳句！

1. Yet there are several problems with VERBing that may prove obstacles to x in the future.
但是關於……有許多問題可能會是……的障礙。

Yet there are several problems with using wind power that may prove obstacles to widespread implementation of this resource in the future.

延伸說法 Yet there are several problems with designing wind turbines that may prove obstacles to successful operations in the future.

2. Another challenge for the new technology is that...
這種新科技的另一個難題是……

Another challenge for the new technology is that wind energy turbines destroy vast numbers of birds and bats every year.

延伸說法 Another challenge for the new technology is that it is not yet economically practical.

3. Third, x destroy the natural beauty of y
第三，……毀了……的自然美

Third, wind farms destroy the natural beauty of the land.

延伸說法 Third, oil spills destroy the natural beauty of the coastline.

4. Furthermore, x adds value to y
而且，……提升了……的價值

Furthermore, public property with open space and scenic views adds value to communities.

延伸說法 Furthermore, clean energy adds value to the environment.

• 講座好句型，成為我的作文佳句！

1. The reading is correct in saying that x is…
談到……時，短文的觀點是正確的

The reading is correct in saying that wind power is being aggressively pursued as an alternative energy form with much potential.

延伸說法 The reading is correct in saying that wind power is an alternative energy source that should be explored further.

2. Let's take a look at x and the challenge that brings.
我們來看看……和它帶來的難題。

Let's take a look at land usage and the challenge that brings.

延伸說法 Let's take a look at the loud noise produced by wind turbines and the challenge that brings.

3. For one thing, people should keep in mind that any x — including y and even z — can VERB
首先，人們必須記住任何 x（包括 y，甚至 z）都能……

For one thing, people should keep in mind that any structure — including skyscrapers and even two-story homes — can kill birds when they fly into them.

延伸說法 For one thing, people should keep in mind that any generator — including those powered by gas and even oil — can harm wildlife.

4. As I mentioned earlier, in the future, x will be VERBed
正如我之前提到的，在未來，x 會被……

As I mentioned earlier, in the future, many wind generators will be placed out in the ocean.

延伸說法 As I mentioned earlier, in the future, many traditional sources of energy will be depleted.

• 高分範文中，有這些作文佳句！

1. x is…, but it is surrounded by controversy.

x 是……，但是圍繞這一問題還存在爭議。

Wind power is a renewable energy source with great potential, but it is surrounded by controversy.

延伸說法 Wind power is considered a clean energy, but it is surrounded by controversy.

2. Opponents focus on the problems that VERB, while proponents are optimistic about resolving the problems.

反對者關注……的問題，而支持者對這些問題的解決抱樂觀態度。

Opponents focus on the problems that plague the technology, while proponents are optimistic about resolving the problems.

延伸說法 Opponents focus on the problems that make this technology inefficient, while proponents are optimistic about resolving the problems.

3. The reading sides with the views of the x, and the professor is obviously a y

短文支持……的觀點，而教授顯然是……

The reading sides with the views of the opponents, and the professor is obviously a proponent.

延伸說法 The reading sides with the views of the critics, and the professor is obviously a supporter.

4. First, the professor thinks the issue of x can be resolved.

首先，該教授認為……的問題能夠解決。

First, the professor thinks the issue of land usage can be resolved.

延伸說法 First, the professor thinks the issue of how land is used can be resolved.

5. Second, the professor thinks x [a problem] can be ameliorated.

第二，該教授認為……（問題）可以改善。

Second, the professor thinks bird and bat fatalities can be ameliorated.

延伸說法 Second, the professor thinks accidental bird deaths can be ameliorated.

6. Finally, on the issue of x, the professor argues that this problem can be avoided by VERBing

最後，關於……問題，該教授認為這個問題能夠透過……避免

Finally, on the issue of aesthetics, the professor argues that this problem can be avoided by placing power systems out of sight of most people.

延伸說法 Finally, on the issue of wind turbine noise, the professor argues that this problem can be avoided by placing the turbines in remote areas.

關鍵語塊

- **renewable (source of energy)**
  （能源）可再生的
- **blend into...** 融入……
- **holds much promise** 具有很大的
  前途
- **scenic views** 風景
- **commercially exploit ...**
  商業開發……
- **adds value to...** 使……增值
- **wind generators** 風力發電機
- **aggressively pursued as ...**
  把……作為目標積極追求
- **small-scale** 小規模的
- **alternative energy** 替代能源
- **utility companies** 公用事業公司
- **problematic issues** 棘手問題
- **may prove obstacles to...** 對……
  來說可能是個障礙
- **policy makers** 政策制定者
- **safety zone** 安全區域
- **cost effective** 成本划算的，節省
  成本的

- **wind turbine** 風力渦輪機
- **offshore** 離岸，向海
- **free from...** 沒有……的
- **fly zones** 飛行區域
- **debris** 碎片
- **nesting areas** 築巢區
- **cleared away** 清除
- **aesthetics** 美學
- **migratory bird act** 候鳥法案
- **drill** 在……上鑽孔
- **fatalities** 死亡
- **electric cables** 電纜
- **endangered species**
  瀕臨絕種物種
- **atop** 在……頂上
- **golden eagle** 金雕
- **population centers** 人口聚居中心
- **aesthetically pleasing**
  有美感的，美觀的
- **out of sight** 看不見，在視野之外

▶再練習一次！

　　學習了以上這些策略、實用句型、語塊、高分範文和萬用寫作範本之後，再回頭去看例題。再讀一遍閱讀短文，然後再聽一遍講座。如果還是聽不懂講座內容，就反覆多聽幾遍，或者參考錄音原稿。然後修改你之前寫的作文，或者重新寫一篇作文。修改或重寫作文時，試著運用本章學到的寫作技巧。完成之後，比較一下修改或重寫前後的兩篇作文，注意不同之處。

附錄：錄音原稿

 Track 009

Narrator: Now listen to part of a lecture on the same topic.

(woman) Professor: The reading is correct in saying that wind power is being aggressively pursued as an alternative energy form with much potential. And yes, there are still problematic issues. But engineers and policy makers are in the process of improving the technology underlying wind turbines. What's more, as this alternative form of energy becomes increasingly cost effective, more time and money will be devoted to overcoming each of the obstacles.

Let's take a look at land usage and the challenge that brings. A large percentage of our energy needs can be supplied by wind generators offshore and on top of mountains. That will reduce the need for wind projects to use large amounts of land.

Second, the issue related to the fatalities of birds and bats. For one thing, people should keep in mind that any structure — including skyscrapers and even two-story homes — can kill birds when they fly into them. The California wind project mentioned in the reading uses a relatively old turbine design. Old turbines kill more wildlife because they move quickly. Moreover, they are often placed near the fly zones and nesting areas of bird populations. The blades of new turbine models move slowly. Birds are able to avoid these slow-moving blades more easily.

Third, the issue of aesthetics. As I mentioned earlier, in the future, many wind generators will be placed out in the ocean. Developers can drill more than 12 miles offshore and put electric cables underground, so that they are not visible from the land. Additional wind generators will be placed atop mountains, far from major population centers. That means that the unattractive high towers of the turbines will be out of sight of most people.

Humanities and the Arts — Literature
人文藝術常考主題 2：文學

❝ 在本章，你將學到…… ❞

★如何轉述合作廠商觀點
★轉述合作廠商觀點時應該用什麼時態

解讀常考題

文學也是人文藝術的常考主題，一般討論如何更好地學習某個人文科目。

▶模擬試題①

閱讀以下的短文並聆聽講座，完成以下這道作文題目。

Narrator: This section measures writing to communicate in an academic environment. There are two writing tasks.

For Writing Task 1, the integrated writing task, you will read a short passage and listen to a lecture and then answer a question. For Writing Task 2, the independent writing task, you will answer a question based on your own knowledge and experience.

Now listen to the directions for Writing Task 1.

For Writing Task 1, you will have three minutes to read a short academic passage. You may take notes. The passage will be removed and you will listen to a lecture about the same topic. Again, you may take notes.

You will have 20 minutes to write a response about the relationship between the lecture and the reading. Try to answer the question as completely as possible using information from the reading passage and the lecture. Do not give your personal opinion. You will be able to see the reading passage again. You may use your notes.

An effective response will be 150 to 225 words. You will be rated on the quality of your writing and on the completeness and accuracy of the content. If you finish your response before time is up, you may go on to Writing Task 2.

Begin reading now.

Poetry has a lot to teach us. Through an analysis of a poem, we can become familiar with its form, content and history. Yet in Literature classes, young people become unhappy when they are asked to rigorously analyze poetry. They fail to realize that only through the benefits of this investigative approach can one gain a deeper appreciation of the poem's meaning, along with useful critical skills.

First, when the poetry analysis method is not used in the classroom, students miss out on the core meaning of the poem. Because poems tend to be short, young people tend to rush through the text. They might skim a poem once or twice, notice one or two things and then jump to a conclusion — which is often wrong. However, by picking apart each stanza, line and word, the Literature teacher can serve as a catalyst for learning, allowing students to understand precisely what meaning the poet intended to communicate.

Also, by carefully analyzing the structure of a poem, students become aware of the craft that went into making the poem. Young people need to learn about the rules for various poetic forms, such as sonnets and odes. There is also a benefit to learning about a poem's rhyme scheme (that is to say, which lines rhyme with each other) and the use of language, as in the line "Life is a barren field."

Third and last, poetry analysis trains young people to develop disciplined critical skills that can be applied not only to poetry, but to other forms of literature, and even to personal and work settings. By learning how to extract meaning from different types of poems, students become adept at "reading between the lines," appreciating nuance in all sorts of communication.

Narrator: Now listen to part of a lecture on the same topic.

 Track 011 在這裡請播放 Track 011。錄音內容全文可在本章結尾找到。

Summarize the points made in the lecture, being sure to explain how they challenge the specific points made in the reading passage.

Narrator: You have 20 minutes to write Task 1.

轉述他人觀點

由於綜合寫作題要概括教授的觀點，所以轉述他人觀點（也叫間接引語）的能力對獲得高分至關重要。因此，綜合寫作題的作文中應該要包含很多間接引語。

轉述他人觀點有很多種方式：

The professor **says** that...
The professor **claims** that...

The lecturer **points out** that...
She **argues** that...
The professor **talks about** how...
The lecturer **states** that...
The professor **wonders** if...
He **denies** that...

上面句子中加粗的動詞都可以轉述他人的觀點。顯然，從傳達資訊的可理解程度與文法的準確性兩個方面來判斷，掌握間接引語會幫助你提高綜合寫作題的分數。

現在先複習一下間接引語。用自己的話轉述別人的話時，被轉述的部分稱為間接引語。寫綜合寫作題的作文時，很多地方需要引用或轉述教授的話。不像報紙和小說可以使用引號來直接引用，而新托福綜合寫作題，考生必須抓住教授的觀點或想法然後轉述。

間接引語有一些特定規則：
1）從屬連接詞 that 一般放在間接引語之前。
2）間接引語中，主要動詞（轉述動詞後面的動詞）的時態要變換，例如：

直接引語	間接引語
一般現在式	一般過去式
一般過去式	過去完成式
現在進行式	過去進行式
一般將來式	過去將來式
現在完成式	過去完成式

3）涉及時間和地點的副詞、指示代名詞等一般要作變動。
4）例外：如果轉述的內容涉及真理或事實，那麼就不變換時態。

第四點在新托福考試中很重要，因為閱讀短文和聽力中會有很多「觀點」和「事實」。轉述這樣的內容就不需變換時態，如：

Professor: The meaning of a poem will vary from one reader to another. That's because each person brings his or her own experiences and insights to a poem. Of all the types of literature, poetry is the most subjective, the most personal.

教授在陳述自己的觀點，說的是一種「事實」，所以當用間接引語轉述他的觀點時，用一般現在式：

He thinks that it is impossible to know precisely the meaning intended by the poet and therefore useless to try to achieve an understanding through detailed analysis.

為了對間接引語有個整體的感知，請再看一遍下面的高分範文，並與本章後面的聽力原稿進行比較。注意間接引語中，不同的動詞時態是如何結合的。你會發現，這篇範文基本上用一般現在式，但是在最後，用現在完成式描述正在發生的現象：... have robbed the students of the opportunity to critique poetry from a fresh start. 由此可見，用間接引語之前，應做好判斷。

考生們需注意，在一篇有四個段落的文章中，間接引語一般用在第二段至第四段，因為這三段是引用教授分論點的段落。

運用間接引語的策略

1. 一般情況下，間接引語中的動詞比原句動詞往過去推一個時態。
2. 考試前認真研究本書中的實用句型和高分範文，學習怎樣用間接引語轉述教授的觀點。
3. 總結事實性的觀點時，即轉述短文和聽力講座時，可以在間接引語中使用一般現在式。
4. 注意整篇文章中間接引語時態的統一。如果開始的時候用一般現在式，The professor says that...，那麼接下來都用一般現在式，不要隨便更換時態。
5. 轉述教授說的話或閱讀短文的觀點時儘量換句話說。用自己的話轉述得越精彩，越容易得高分。
6. 綜合寫作題中的間接引語往往綜合了一些觀點，這些觀點組成一個複雜的結構，考生要把握好。如：The professor wonders if students will ever be able to think critically if they simply repeat what famous people have said.

高分範文 Track 012

There is a dichotomy of opinion about the usefulness of poetry analysis for students. One school of thought, as represented by the reading, says it helps students gain a deeper appreciation of the poems. The opposing camp, of which the professor is a member, emphasizes the pitfalls of alienating young people from poems.

First, the professor opposes the reading's view as regards the meaning of poems. He thinks that it is impossible to know precisely the meaning intended by the poet and therefore useless to try to achieve an understanding through detailed analysis. Instead, he argues that poetry is the most subjective form of literature and that each person can have a personal interpretation of the work because of his or her own unique life experiences.

Second, the professor disagrees with the reading on how best to learn the special language usage and forms of poetry. He discounts the importance of the learning of poetry-writing rules and places a high value on fully experiencing the emotional force of poems. By avoiding analyzing a poem ad nauseam, he argues, a student will be able to appreciate its sound and imagery directly.

Finally, while concurring with the importance of critical thinking, the professor takes an issue with how poetry analysis skills are taught in the classroom. He thinks that by presenting the orthodox views of established literary critics, the teachers have robbed the students of the opportunity to critique poetry from a fresh start. He does not believe the students can learn to think critically this way.

萬用模板

本模板句型和第五章的模板句型（關於支持者和反對者的爭論）很相似，都在第一段明確列出兩種不同的觀點。但是，本章範本的獨特之處在於，它專門討論學生該怎樣更好地學習某科目或技能（這是綜合寫作題中常見的話題）。這種範本還可以用於組織正反兩方關於人文藝術教學方法或者其他學科教學方法的辯論。例如，討論學生學習寫小説、詩歌、畫畫或唱歌等的最佳方法；討論學習科學、數學或歷史的最好方法；討論網路線上學習和在傳統教室學習哪種方式更好等。

本範本的語言和邏輯都有些複雜，只要運用得當，就能拿高分。

There is a dichotomy of opinion about _____. One school of thought, as represented by the reading, says _____ helps students gain a deeper appreciation of _____. The opposing camp, of which the professor is a member, emphasizes the pitfalls of _____.

First, the professor opposes the reading's view as regards _____. Instead, he argues that _____ is _____.

Second, the professor disagrees with the reading on how best to _____ _____. He discounts the importance of _____ and places a high value on _____. By _____, he argues, a student will be able to _____.

Finally, while concurring with the importance of _____, the professor takes an issue with how _____ skills are _____.

建立自己的寫作句型庫

寫人文藝術方面話題的作文時，下面的句型都可以用上。

• 閱讀好句型，成為我的作文佳句！

1. x has a lot to teach us.
……能教我們很多東西。

Poetry has a lot to teach us.

延伸説法 Literature has a lot to teach us.

2. They fail to realize that only through the benefits of x can one gain a deeper appreciation of y
他們沒有意識到只有靠著……我們才能更瞭解……

They fail to realize that only through the benefits of this investigative approach can one gain a deeper appreciation of the poem's meaning, along with useful critical skills.

延伸說法 They fail to realize that only through the benefits of detailed research can one gain a deeper appreciation of the poet's feelings.

3. Also, by carefully analyzing x, students become aware of y
此外，透過仔細分析……，學生會知道……

Also, by carefully analyzing the structure of a poem, students become aware of the craft that went into making the poem.

延伸說法 Also, by carefully analyzing the poem's imagery, students become aware of the symbolism used by the poet.

4. Third and last, x trains young people to develop y skills that can be applied not only to x, but to z, and even to personal and work settings.
第三點也就是最後一點，x 可以訓練年輕人發展 y 的能力，不但可用在 x 上，也可用在 z 上，甚至個人與工作場合上。

Third and last, poetry analysis trains young people to develop disciplined critical skills that can be applied not only to poetry, but to other forms of literature, and even to personal and work settings.

延伸說法 Third and last, memorizing poetry trains young people to develop language skills that can be applied not only to literature, but to other types of writing, and even to personal and work settings.

• **講座好句型，成為我的作文佳句！**

1. The reading is correct in saying that x…
短文中說……的說法是正確的

The reading is correct in saying that poetry has much to teach us.

延伸說法 The reading is correct in saying that students should learn about poetry analysis.

2. First off, let's take x
首先，舉個……的例子吧

First off, let's take meaning.

延伸說法 First off, let's take the poet's vision.

3. And what about things like x and y such as z?
那像 x、y 這樣的事物（例如 z），又如何呢？

And what about things like rhyming patterns and figurative language such as metaphors?

延伸說法 And what about things like biographies and personal writings such as a poet's diary?

4. As for the value of x, no doubt y skills are good skills to hone.
關於⋯⋯的價值，毫無疑問⋯⋯是該訓練的良好技巧。

As for the value of critical thinking, no doubt critical skills are good skills to hone.

延伸說法 As for the value of a foreign language, no doubt English language skills are good skills to hone.

5. But how can x learn to VERB by simply VERBing?
但是僅僅透過⋯⋯，x 如何能夠學會⋯⋯？

But how can they learn to think critically for themselves by simply parroting what many famous critics have said?

延伸說法 But how can students learn to analyze a poem by simply memorizing other people's poems?

• 高分範文中，有這些作文佳句！

1. There is a dichotomy of opinion about x
關於⋯⋯，有兩種截然對立的觀點。

There is a dichotomy of opinion about the usefulness of poetry analysis for students.

延伸說法 There is a dichotomy of opinion about the best way to teach poetry to young people.

2. One school of thought, as represented by the reading, says x helps students gain a deeper appreciation of y
一個學派的觀點（正如短文所代表的）認為 x 能幫助學生更深地瞭解⋯⋯

One school of thought, as represented by the reading, says it helps students gain a deeper appreciation of the poems.

延伸說法 One school of thought, as represented by the reading, says analysis helps students gain a more accurate understanding of poetry.

3. The opposing camp, of which the professor is a member, emphasizes the pitfalls of x
反對陣營（教授就是其中之一）強調⋯⋯的問題

The opposing camp, of which the professor is a member, emphasizes the pitfalls of alienating young people from poems.

延伸說法 The opposing camp, of which the professor is a member, emphasizes the pitfalls of a tedious analytical method.

4. First, the professor opposes the reading's view as regards x
首先，該教授反對閱讀短文中有關……的觀點

First, the professor opposes the reading's view as regards the meaning of poems.

延伸說法 First, the professor opposes the reading's view as regards how teachers should approach the meaning of a poem.

5. Instead, he argues that x is…
相反，他認為 x 是……

Instead, he argues that poetry is the most subjective form of literature and that each person can have a personal interpretation of the work because of his or her own unique life experiences.

延伸說法 Instead, he argues that poetry can only be meaningful to someone when it has a personal meaning.

6. Second, the professor disagrees with the reading on how best to VERB
其次，該教授不同意閱讀短文中有關……的論點

Second, the professor disagrees with the reading on how best to learn the special language usage and forms of poetry.

延伸說法 Second, the professor disagrees with the reading on how best to appreciate the structures and word choices in poetry.

7. He discounts the importance of x and places a high value on y
他認為……不重要，而給予……高度的評價

He discounts the importance of the learning of poetry-writing rules and places a high value on fully experiencing the emotional force of poems.

延伸說法 He discounts the importance of memorizing formulae and places a high value on a listener's intuitive reactions to the poem.

8. Finally, while concurring with the importance of x, the professor takes an issue with how y skills are VERBed
最後，雖然同意……的重要性，但教授對……能力如何……提出了異議

Finally, while concurring with the importance of critical thinking, the professor takes an issue with how poetry analysis skills are taught in the classroom.

延伸說法 Finally, while concurring with the importance of critical skills, the professor takes an issue with how these skills are best developed.

關鍵語塊

- **rigorously** 嚴密地，縝密地
- **extract meaning from...**
  從……推測含義
- **investigative approach**
  探究細節的方法
- **be adept at ...**
  對……熟練的，擅長的
- **appreciation** 理解，領會
- **reading between the lines**
  體會言外之意
- **poetry analysis** 詩歌分析
- **nuance** 細微差別
- **miss out on** 錯過；漏掉
- **doing... a disservice**
  對……不利，損害……
- **core meaning**
  核心意義，中心意思
- **tedious** 枯燥的，乏味的
- **rush through** 匆忙完成
- **worth this risk**
  可能的事，能做到的事
- **skim** 瀏覽

- **first off** 首先，一開始
- **jump to a conclusion** 過早下結
  論；貿然下結論
- **subjective** 主觀的
- **stanza** 詩節
- **meaningful** 有意義的
- **catalyst for...** ……的誘導者
- **figurative language** 形象化的語
  言，比喻性語言
- **craft** 藝術手法
- **metaphors** 隱喻
- **sonnets** 十四行詩
- **long-winded analysis**
  冗長的分析
- **ode** 頌詩
- **emotional impact** 情感上的衝擊
- **rhyme scheme** 韻律；韻腳
- **hone** 改進，改善
- **disciplined critical skills**
  訓練有素的批判技能
- **parroting** 機械地模仿

▶再練習一次！

　　學習了以上這些策略、實用句型、語塊、高分範文和萬用寫作範本之後，再回頭去看例題。再讀一遍閱讀短文，然後再聽一遍講座。如果還是聽不懂講座內容，就反覆多聽幾遍，或者參考錄音原稿。然後修改你之前寫的作文，或者重新寫一篇作文。修改或重寫作文時，試著運用本章學到的寫作技巧。完成之後，比較一下修改或重寫前後的兩篇作文，注意不同之處。

Track 011

Narrator: Now listen to part of a lecture on the same topic.

(man) Professor: The reading is correct in saying that poetry has much to teach us. Unfortunately, teachers who insist on making students do a poetry analysis every time they read poems are doing their students a disservice. The only thing that teachers accomplish through tedious poetry analysis is making young people want to stay far away from poetry. None of the benefits mentioned in the reading is worth this risk.

First off, let's take meaning. The meaning of a poem will vary from one reader to another. That's because each person brings his or her own experiences and insights to a poem. Of all the types of literature, poetry is the most subjective, the most personal. The more a teacher lectures about the deep meaning of this or that phrase, the less likely it is that a student will be affected by the poem in a meaningful way.

And what about things like rhyming patterns and figurative language such as metaphors? Don't teachers need to identify each of these for students? No, not really. When young people read or listen to poetry, they should be able to directly experience the pure pleasure of sound and image. Even if they can't understand all the words, they can still enjoy them, in much the same way we enjoy listening to a song and don't catch the meaning of every word. A long-winded analysis of poetry weakens a poem's emotional impact.

As for the value of critical thinking, no doubt critical skills are good skills to hone. The problem is, most teachers doing poetry analyses with their students present all the "accepted" interpretations that have been made by scholars over the years. Teachers expect students to learn from these critiques. But how can they learn to think critically for themselves by simply parroting what many famous critics have said?

Life Sciences — Ecology
生命科學常考主題 2：生態環境

在本章，你將學到……

　　★如何有技巧地重複關鍵字使上下文連貫
　　★如何描述雙方的爭論

解讀常考題

　　本章重新回到生命科學這一學術情境，探討考試中常見的一個主題：生態環境。

▶模擬試題①

　　閱讀以下的短文並聆聽講座，完成以下這道作文題目。

Narrator: This section measures writing to communicate in an academic environment. There are two writing tasks.

For Writing Task 1, the integrated writing task, you will read a short passage and listen to a lecture and then answer a question. For Writing Task 2, the independent writing task, you will answer a question based on your own knowledge and experience.

Now listen to the directions for Writing Task 1.

For Writing Task 1, you will have three minutes to read a short academic passage. You may take notes. The passage will be removed and you will listen to a lecture about the same topic. Again, you may take notes.

You will have 20 minutes to write a response about the relationship between the lecture and the reading. Try to answer the question as completely as possible using information from the reading passage and the lecture. Do not give your personal opinion. You will be able to see the reading passage again. You may use your notes.

An effective response will be 150 to 225 words. You will be rated on the quality of your writing and on the completeness and accuracy of the content. If you finish your response before time is up, you may go on to Writing Task 2.

Begin reading now.

A variety of carp are native to Asia, including the bighead and silver carp. More than forty years ago, several species of Asian carp were imported to the southern US to control algae in fish farms. However, in their new environment they are very aggressive and have been migrating northwards, causing economic and ecological damage to the Mississippi River watershed. Now, five states that adjoin the Great Lakes have filed suit against several government agencies, demanding that the Chicago area shipping locks be temporarily shut to prevent the carp from entering the Great Lakes water system. They base their lawsuit on several arguments.

The first point the States make is that the problem is urgent. Asian carp may soon infiltrate the Great Lakes system through the shipping locks and sewage facilities near Chicago. To support the claim of urgency, the States cite a research study by a professor who found Asian carp DNA in the water of the canals leading to Lake Michigan. This DNA is proof that live Asian carp are already very close to the Great Lakes system.

The States also claim that once Asian carp penetrate the locks, they will multiply and overpower the Great Lakes ecosystems. If Asian carp are present in a water system, they quickly dominate that system. They eat voraciously and reproduce rapidly, disrupting the food chain of native fish species. These giant fish even disturb human activity; when boats pass, they jump in the air, often striking passengers.

Third, the States maintain that if Asian carp enter Lake Michigan, they could have a significant negative impact on the $7 billion Great Lakes fishery industry. Although shutting the locks will cause some loss of revenue to shipping companies and tourist boats, this hardship to the economy would, it is argued, be minor compared to the financial damage caused by Asian carp.

Narrator: Now listen to part of a lecture on the same topic.

 Track 013 在這裡請播放 Track 013。錄音內容全文可在本章結尾找到。

Summarize the points made in the lecture you just heard, explaining how they answer the specific arguments made in the reading.

Narrator: You have 20 minutes to write Task 1.

透過重複關鍵字做到前後連貫

　　銜接自然和前後連貫是一篇優秀作文的必備要素。「銜接自然」指的是句與句或段落與段落之間緊湊、文法正確;而「連貫」則指寫作時思維的順暢,其核心在於語義的銜接。

　　大部分考生認為使作文更連貫的最好方法是在分論點段落中用上 first、second 和 third 這類詞彙。綜合寫作題的作文包含三個分論點,這一特點讓考生自然想到使用這種形式的連接詞。但是,這種方法很難拿到高分,尤其是結構不容易預測的獨立寫作題。

　　綜合寫作題和獨立寫作題做到前後連貫的有效方法是重複關鍵字。重複關鍵字並不是機械、無意義地重複所有的片語和分句，而是必須有技巧。利用重複手法來營造一篇前後連貫的作文，需要做到三個簡單的步驟。

寫出連貫句子的三個簡單步驟

　　1）寫作時，把重點放在語義和內容上。
　　2）根據語義從前一句（或前一段）抓住最重要的話題或觀點，然後選出關鍵字或關鍵片語。
　　3）站在讀者（也就是評分者）的角度，一步步試著用關鍵字連接上下兩個句子，把前後兩個句子結合起來。

　　下面是從綜合寫作題和獨立寫作題中節選的段落，用來說明怎樣有技巧地重複關鍵字（重複的關鍵字為粗體）。

Task 1:

> First, the agencies question the results of **the DNA study** cited by the States. They think the **methodology** of **the DNA study** was flawed and argue that **the study** does not prove there are live carp in the Great Lakes. In fact, no one was able to find **live Asian Carp** in the Great Lakes.

　　這是本章高分範文的第二段。本段反駁閱讀短文中的第一個分論點。本段透過重複關鍵詞 the DNA study，the study 和 methodology 把講座和閱讀短文聯繫了起來。同時，本段的觀點表達順暢，邏輯清晰（閱讀短文提到 the DNA study，而教授則提及 new DNA methodology）。

　　同樣，live Asian carp 也是使文章連貫、通順的關鍵字。Live Asian carp 出現在閱讀短文中，living carp 和 live Asian carp 出現在講座中。透過重複 live Asian carp，考生以連貫且強有力的方式表達了自己的觀點。

Task 2:

> **Borrowing money** from a friend is something that I would never do. In fact, if a friend ever wants to **borrow money** from me, he had better have a compelling reason. I am relieved to say I don't think any of my friends would even attempt to **ask me for money**. **Money borrowing** is one of the most often cited causes for the demise of a friendship.

　　本段是第 9 章第三篇寫作預測題高分範文的開頭段落，第一句就是文章的論點句，考生明確表明了自己的觀點。注意第二句是如何做到連貫性的：考生重複了關鍵字 borrow money。再看第三句，考生透過換句話說再次進行重複，ask me for money 是 borrow money from me 的換句話說。最後一句用了 money borrowing，只改了第一句中 borrowing money 的順序。這種方法很有技巧，因為它不僅使文章前後連貫，也總結了文章的論點，為接下來更詳細的分論點段落做了鋪陳。

透過重複關鍵字使文章連貫的策略

1. 重點關注自己想要表達的意思。
2. 在綜合寫作題中總結教授觀點時，簡要指出講座與閱讀短文的不同之處或相同之處。可以選擇一兩個在閱讀短文和講座中都出現的關鍵字，例如 the DNA study。這會增加作文語言上的連貫性。
3. 對於獨立寫作題中的句子，有選擇地從前面的句子中挑出一兩個關鍵字。但注意不要隨便重複某個詞。
4. 要記得：讀者（也就是評分者）不見得瞭解這個學術領域，所以要儘量使觀點簡單易懂。把每個句子想像成連接上下句的橋樑。

　　看高分範文和萬用寫作範本之前，大家需要瞭解 ETS 出的這類題型與其他題目題型的不同之處。大多數的綜合寫作題，閱讀短文提出一個觀點（有三個分論點），教授在講座中提出反駁性的觀點（也有三個分論點）。但是本題的閱讀短文描述一個問題（北美五大湖中亞洲鯉魚的泛濫）和問題的解決方案。閱讀短文出現了一方的觀點，即提起訴訟的五個州的觀點和論述，外加三個分論點和論證。而在講座中，教授沒有說自己的觀點，而是總結另一方，即被起訴的政府機構的觀點。換言之，教授用第三人稱描述了政府機構對五個州的反駁論點。

　　像這道作文題型，在新托福寫作考試中並不常見。但是這種類型還是會不時出現，因此考生們還是要做好充分的準備。

高分範文　 *Track 014*

People in the Great Lakes states are worried that Asian carp, an invasive species, might invade the Great Lakes and cause great damage to their economies. Hoping to keep that from happening, five of those states filed a lawsuit in order to have the waterway locks closed. The professor talks about the government agencies' objections to the arguments put forth by the States.

First, the agencies question the results of the DNA study cited by the States. They think the methodology of the DNA study was flawed and argue that the study does not prove there are live carp in the Great Lakes. In fact, no one was able to find live Asian carp in the Great Lakes.

For the second argument, the States talk about how fast carp can grow and multiply, inferring they would quickly dominate the Great Lakes. But the agencies hold a contradictory view, believing it is quite difficult for a new species to overtake an ecosystem. They suggest that there are many hurdles facing an invasive species. For example, it needs to have a sufficient number to sustain its population. In ninety percent of the cases, new species fail to establish themselves in the new environment.

Last, the agencies reject the States' claim of potential financial loss as conjecture, making the case that a serious invasion may never take place. In defending their position, the agencies argue that the economy of encompassing commercial shipping and recreational boating, over one billion dollars, would be destroyed immediately if the locks were to be closed.

萬用模板

下面的範本適用於綜合寫作題中關於教授總結反方觀點的題目。如果你遇到的題目是關於兩方之間的糾紛，那麼這個範本正好套用。

[文章第一、二句簡短地介紹背景資訊，指出問題和第一方的觀點]. The professor talks about [第二方] objections to the arguments put forth by [第一方].

First, [第二方] question(s) the results of _____. They think _____ was flawed and argue that _____ does not prove _____.

For the second argument, [第一方] talk(s) about _____, inferring they would _____. But [第二方] hold(s) a contradictory view, believing it is quite difficult for _____ to _____.

Last, [第二方] reject(s) [第一方] claim of _____ as conjecture, making the case that _____.

建立自己的寫作句型庫

寫生命科學方面話題的作文時，下面的句型都可以用上。

• **閱讀好句型，成為我的作文佳句！**

1. **They base their x on several arguments.**
   他們用幾個方面的理由作為……的依據。

   They base their lawsuit on several arguments.

   延伸說法 They base their opinion on several arguments.

2. **To support the claim of…, x cite a research study by x**
   為了支持……的説法，……引證了由某人進行的研究

   To support the claim of urgency, the States cite a research study by a professor who found Asian carp DNA in the water of the canals leading to Lake Michigan.

   延伸說法 To support the claim of imminent danger, the plaintiffs cite a research study by a Biology professor.

3. x is proof that…
……是……的證據

This DNA is proof that live Asian carp are already very close to the Great Lakes system.

延伸說法 The DNA is proof that some Asian carp have already infiltrated the locks.

4. x also claim that once y VERB, they will…
某人還聲稱一旦……

The States also claim that once Asian carp penetrate the locks, they will multiply and overpower the Great Lakes ecosystems.

延伸說法 Fish experts also claim that once invasive species enter a new habitat, they will take over that habitat.

5. Third, x maintain that if x VERB, they could VERB
第三，某人認為如果……，他們就可以……（此處需用虛擬語氣）

Third, the States maintain that if Asian carp enter Lake Michigan, they could have a significant negative impact on the $7 billion Great Lakes fishery industry.

延伸說法 Third, the suit maintains that if they gain access into Lake Michigan, the carp could destroy traditional ways of life on the Great Lakes.

• **講座好句型，成為我的作文佳句！**

1. Yet x reject the assumptions and arguments made by y
然而，……否認了……提出的假設和論據

Yet the agencies responsible for the locks and other waterway functions reject the assumptions and arguments made by the States.

延伸說法 Yet the experts hired by the agencies reject the assumptions and arguments made by the States.

2. First of all, x does not provide adequate information about y
首先，……沒能提供關於……的足夠資訊

First of all, the new DNA methodology cited by the States does not provide adequate information about the number of living Asian carp currently swimming in the lake waters.

延伸說法 First of all, the professor's methodology does not provide adequate information about real live fish swimming in Lake Michigan.

3. x have also rebutted ...s' second claim, …

……還駁斥了第二種說法

The agencies have also rebutted the States' second claim, the imminent hazard to the ecosystem.

延伸說法 The Chicago agencies have also rebutted the second point, the serious threat to the environment.

4. If x were VERBed, y could not take place.

如果……，……無法發生。（該句型用的是虛擬語氣）

If the locks were closed, most of these activities could not take place.

延伸說法 If electric barriers were installed, penetration by Asian carp could not take place.

• 高分範文中，有這些作文佳句！

1. The professor talks about x's objections to the arguments put forth by y

該教授論述了某一方針對另一方提出來的論據的反對意見

The professor talks about the government agencies' objections to the arguments put forth by the States.

延伸說法 The professor talks about the company's objections to the arguments put forth by scientists.

2. First, x question the results of y

首先，一方質疑另一方的結果

First, the agencies question the results of the DNA study cited by the States.

延伸說法 First, the government questions the results of the testing done in Lake Michigan.

3. They think x was flawed and argue that y does not prove…

他們認為……有缺陷，主張……不能證明……

They think the methodology of the DNA study was flawed and argue that the study does not prove there are live carp in the Great Lakes.

延伸說法 They think the research design was flawed and argue that the evidence does not prove that there are carp in Lake Michigan.

4. For the second argument, x talk about…, inferring they would VERB

對於第二個論點，……討論了……，推斷他們會……

For the second argument, the States talk about how fast carp can grow and multiply, inferring they would quickly dominate the Great Lakes.

延伸說法 For the second argument, the States talk about the nature of carp reproduction, inferring they would quickly multiply.

5. But x hold a contradictory view, believing it is quite difficult for y to VERB

但……意見相反，認為……很難……

But the agencies hold a contradictory view, believing it is quite difficult for a new species to overtake an ecosystem.

延伸說法 But the waterway agencies hold a contradictory view, believing it is quite difficult for carp to dominate other species.

6. Last, x reject y's claim of z as conjecture, making the case that...

最後，某一方拒絕另一方……的推測，提出理由證明……

Last, the agencies reject the States' claim of potential financial loss as conjecture, making the case that a serious invasion may never take place.

延伸說法 Last, the agencies reject the lawsuit's claim of future economic disaster as conjecture, making the case that a large-scale invasion is unlikely.

關鍵語塊

- **carp** 鯉魚
- **dominate** 支配
- **be native to...** 原產自……
- **voraciously** 貪得無厭地
- **imported to...** 引進到……
- **disrupting** 擾亂
- **algae** 藻類
- **food chain** 食物鏈
- **aggressive** 侵略性的
- **fishery industry** 漁業
- **watershed** 集水區
- **loss of revenue** 稅收流失
- **the Great Lakes** 北美五大湖
- **navigational locks** 導航水閘
- **filed suit against...** 對……起訴
- **pathway to...** 通向……的通道
- **government agencies** 政府機關
- **waterway functions** 航道功能

- **lawsuit** 訴訟案件
- **imminent hazard** 迫在眉睫的危險
- **urgent** 急迫的
- **invasive species** 入侵物種
- **infiltrate** 潛入，滲透
- **sufficient numbers** 足夠數量
- **locks** 水閘
- **self-sustaining population** 自給自足的族群
- **sewage facilities** 汙水處理工廠
- **exotic species** 外來物種
- **penetrate** 進入
- **recreational boating** 休閒划船
- **overpower** 壓倒
- **security operations** 安全運行
- **ecosystems** 生態系統
- **speculation** 推測

▼再練習一次！

學習了以上這些策略、實用句型、語塊、高分範文和萬用寫作範本之後，返回去看例題。再讀一遍閱讀短文，然後再聽一遍講座。如果還是聽不懂講座內容，就反覆多聽幾遍，或者參考錄音原稿。然後修改你之前寫的作文，或者重新寫一篇作文。修改或重寫作文時，試著運用本章學到的寫作技巧。完成之後，比較一下修改或重寫前後的兩篇作文，注意不同之處。

附錄：錄音原稿

 Track 013

Narrator: Now listen to part of a lecture on the topic you just read about.

(woman) Professor: Five of the Great Lakes states located downstream from Chicago are concerned about the threat of Asian carp. Their joint legal suit seeks an order to close the navigational locks that provide a pathway to the Great Lakes. Yet the agencies responsible for the locks and other waterway functions reject the assumptions and arguments made by the States.

First of all, the new DNA methodology cited by the States does not provide adequate information about the number of living Asian carp currently swimming in the lake waters. Efforts to find living carp have come up empty-handed. Thus, at this time, the government waterway agencies do not believe the DNA methodology is a reliable predictor of live carp in the waters.

The agencies have also rebutted the States' second claim, the imminent hazard to the ecosystem. Their position is supported by the fact that invasive species need to enter the lake waters in sufficient numbers in order to create a self-sustaining population. An expert hired by the agencies explained that, in fact, ninety-percent of invasions by exotic species fail. This expert identified several factors that will stop any invasion, such as the specific habitats carp need to lay eggs in.

Third, the economic threat to the fishery industry. Over a billion dollars is earned each year through activities involving the Chicago locks, including commercial shipping, recreational boating and security operations for the city of Chicago. If the locks were closed, most of these activities could not take place. The States' claim about the potential financial loss to the fishery industry is, at this point, mere speculation. However, the financial loss from closing the locks is real, they argue, and would begin the minute they were shut down.

8 Social Sciences — Advertising
社會科學常考主題 2：廣告

在本章，你將學到……

★如何應對不熟悉的行話與專業術語
★怎麼贊同或反駁某觀點

解讀常考題

討論廣告問題也是綜合寫作題中常見的話題。

▶模擬試題①

閱讀以下的短文並聆聽講座，完成以下這道作文題目。

Narrator: This section measures writing to communicate in an academic environment. There are two writing tasks.

For Writing Task 1, the integrated writing task, you will read a short passage and listen to a lecture and then answer a question. For Writing Task 2, the independent writing task, you will answer a question based on your own knowledge and experience.

Now listen to the directions for Writing Task 1.

For Writing Task 1, you will have three minutes to read a short academic passage. You may take notes. The passage will be removed and you will listen to a lecture about the same topic. Again, you may take notes.

You will have 20 minutes to write a response about the relationship between the lecture and the reading. Try to answer the question as completely as possible using information from the reading passage and the lecture. Do not give your personal opinion. You will be able to see the reading passage again. You may use your notes.

An effective response will be 150 to 225 words. You will be rated on the quality of your writing and on the completeness and accuracy of the content. If you finish your response before time is up, you may go on to Writing Task 2.

Begin reading now.

Strategic advertising is vital for businesses who want to get their names out to customers, along with information about their products and services. The more competitive the market, the more difficult it is to get people to pay attention to an advertising message, making it important for businesses to choose the most appropriate communication medium. Both radio and television advertising can be effective. However, in general, business owners gain better results from purchasing radio airtime.

One of the strongest advantages of radio over TV is that the commercial spots can be better targeted to customer segments. Because they have many different kinds of programs, often with local DJs, radio stations can reach the right people at the right time. That way, companies can run commercials during the time when the most potential customers are tuned in. Moreover, listeners say they are more interested in a product or service when they hear about it on their preferred station, from their favorite radio host.

The costs for producing and airing radio commercials are cheaper than those for TV by a significant margin. For a television commercial, the business has to pay for the services of a video production company in addition to paying for the actual airtime. One reason TV commercials are more expensive is that they involve more, what with script development, multiple shoots and a lengthier editing process.

Finally, radio commercials have a better chance of capturing the full attention of the prospective customer. When, for example, people are in a car, trapped in heavy traffic, or when they are sitting in a bus or subway, they are usually bored and have nothing better to do than listen to commercials. This allows the audience to focus completely on the message.

　　一般情況下，綜合寫作題的講座都是反駁閱讀短文的論點。但是，ETS 出版的《托福考試官方指南》中指出，綜合寫作題的講座也可能贊同閱讀短文中的觀點，因此考生要做好心理准備。本章提供了兩篇講座，一篇贊同閱讀短文中的觀點，另一篇則反駁閱讀短文中的觀點。

　　先來看一個贊同閱讀短文中觀點的講座。

Narrator: Now listen to part of a lecture on the same topic.

 Track 015 在這裡請播放 Track 015。錄音內容全文可在本章結尾找到。

> **Summarize the points made in the lecture, being sure to explain how they strengthen the specific points made in the reading passage.**

Narrator: You have 20 minutes to write Task 1.

下面是反駁閱讀短文中觀點的講座。

Narrator: Now listen to part of a lecture on the same topic.

 Track 016 在這裡請播放 Track 016。錄音內容全文可在本章結尾找到。

> **Summarize the points made in the lecture, being sure to explain how they challenge the specific claims made in the reading passage.**

Narrator: You have 20 minutes to write Task 1.

應對行話與專業術語

行話和專業術語是理解整篇講座和閱讀短文的關鍵因素。考試涉及的學科和分支學科如此之多，考生如何應對這些學科的行話和專業術語呢？

應對行話和專業術語的三個簡單步驟

1）在閱讀短文中，找到定義句，尤其是在第一段中。
2）在閱讀短文和講座中，運用行話或專業術語的情境猜測其大概意思。
3）充分利用閱讀短文和講座中的其他資訊。

在詳細介紹應對專業術語的技巧之前，需要強調一點：除了記住學科詞彙之外，沒有別的方法。此外，由於詞義在不同的情境中會有不同的意思，所以單字和片語應放在特定的情境中去記。

但總會有不熟悉的詞彙和片語，這種情況下怎麼辦？一些學術領域會相對容易懂一些，如描述廣告的語言比描述天文學和基因學的語言更容易一些。但是就算管理學和廣告學之類的「軟科學」也會有自己的專業術語。有時正是諸如 demographics（人口統計學）和 airtime（廣播時間）之類的使用頻率較低的專業術語影響了考生對文章的理解。然而在通常情況下，專業術語的微妙之處在於，一些日常用語在特殊領域會有不同的意思。

例如，本章閱讀短文中的 message 和 shoots。考生知道 message 的意思是 note，在句子 Leave me a message 中的意思是「便條、留言」。shoots 的意思是 small sprouts of plants，在片語 bamboo shoots 中的意思是「竹筍」。但是在這篇短文中這兩個詞是廣告業中的行話，要根據情境判斷詞的意思。現在看看第一句中 message 出現的情境：

The more competitive the market, the more difficult it is to get people to pay attention to an advertising message, making it important for businesses to choose the most appropriate communication medium.

從這個句子可以看出 message 是語塊 advertising message（廣告訊息）中的意思，根據情境（pay attention to the advertising _____），可以推斷出 message 的意思是 the main point that advertisers want customers to receive。此外，除了利用情境之外，考生還應該利用閱讀短文和講座中的其他資訊（文中重複出現的詞語和概念）。例如在這篇閱讀短文中，message 又一次出現在最後一段的最後一行：

This allows the audience to focus completely on the message.

到了閱讀短文最後，只要考生多加注意就可以準確推斷出這些術語的意思。

現在來看另一個例子，也就是本章兩個講座中都出現的專業術語 spots。

For one thing, there are fewer people involved in developing and producing the spots.（錄音原稿 1）

For instance, the claim that radio spots better target potential customers.（錄音原稿 2）

如果考生根據記憶中的意思或直接翻譯 spots 的字面意思，那就可能認為 spots 是「斑點」的意思；但在這個情境下它並不是這個意思。如果考生多注意一下，就會意識到這段講的是面向顧客的 commercial spots。從閱讀短文的情境，考生可以猜出 commercial spots 的意思是 a segment of time reserved for a commercial（廣告插播時段），因此可以猜出這兩處的 spots 意為「（電視、廣播節目的）固定時段」。

應對行話和專業術語的策略

1. 在閱讀短文中，透過觀察詞彙的構成來尋找詞義的線索。例如，在 communication medium 中 medium 看起來與 media 意思相近。
2. 不要根據字面意思推測專業術語的意思，這會浪費時間，而且特殊意義的詞彙很有可能與詞典裡的意思相差很大。
3. 在閱讀短文中找定義句，尤其是介紹主題的第一段。例如，關於市場行銷的一篇短文，第一句有一個很難的術語 viral marketing（病毒式行銷），它被定義為：Viral marketing, the rapid spread of product information through customer interaction, is a powerful way to promote a product.
4. 在閱讀短文和講座中，利用情境猜測行話或專業術語的意思。閱讀短文中尤應如此，因為在閱讀短文中可以看到詞彙的構成，並且可以找到第一次介紹關鍵概念的地方。
5. ETS 會有意設計一些資訊幫助考生理解專業術語。注意那些有目的重複的關鍵字和概念。
6. 在講座中，遇到不熟悉的詞時，不要驚慌。接著往下聽，下面一般會有線索和解釋。

　　兩篇高分範文和萬用寫作範本分別針對支援閱讀短文中觀點和反駁閱讀短文中觀點的講座。這種寫作題要求比較兩種不同的觀點（x 和 y）。支援閱讀短文中觀點的講座認為 x 比 y 好，而反駁閱讀短文中觀點的講座則持相反意見。在這道特殊的寫作題裡，x 指的是收音機廣告，y 指電視廣告。

高分範文（贊同觀點，x is better than y）　 *Track 017*

In order to entice consumers to buy their products and services, businesses need to communicate with consumers regularly. The reading compares two of the ways a business can do this and argues that radio advertising is superior to TV advertising. The professor fully supports the views expressed in the reading.

First, on the question of targeting customers, the professor tacitly agrees with the reading. She gives an example of radio advertising, i.e., tying radio advertising to event marketing. She says companies can sponsor events and have the radio DJ insert their advertising messages while the DJ covers the events live. By taking advantage of the excitement of an event, the company can better influence the radio listeners.

Second, regarding the question of cost, the professor is also in agreement with the reading. She emphasizes the cost savings by characterizing them as "exponential." She goes on to explain how a company can save money on producing radio spots, by using company staff and utilizing the recording facilities offered by radio stations for free. She also notes the benefit of "personal touch" that goes with a company's self-produced commercials.

Finally, the professor supports the reading's view by stating it is possible to attract listeners' attention to radio advertising by the clever manipulation of sound. She further points out a problem that affects TV advertising but not radio. She says consumers are able to skip TV commercials by the use of smart recording devices such as DVRs.

萬用模板（贊同觀點）

　　下面的範本是表示贊同觀點的邏輯框架。顯然，考生需要在每一個分論點後面加一些細節性的陳述，使文章個性化。

[開頭簡潔明瞭地介紹一下收音機廣告和電視廣告的作用和閱讀短文對這兩種廣告所持的觀點]. The professor fully supports the _____ expressed in the reading.

First, on the question of _____, the professor tacitly agrees with the reading. [用三到四個句子陳述教授的說法].

Second, regarding the question of _____, the professor is also in agreement with the reading. [用三到四個句子陳述教授的說法].

Finally, the professor supports the reading's view by stating it is possible to _____ by _____. She further points out a problem that affects _____ but not _____.

高分範文（反駁觀點，x is not better than y）

In order to entice consumers to buy their products and services, businesses need to communicate with consumers regularly. The reading compares two ways of communicating and argues that radio advertising is superior to TV advertising. However, the professor does not agree with the views expressed in the reading.

First, on the question of targeting customers, the professor thinks the reading's argument is based on out-dated information. He says cable TV and advertising tied to cell phones allow companies to target specific market segments. He further mentions that even network TV stations nowadays have developed demographic information for their various TV programs, which can help sponsors decide which programs to place their commercials in.

Second, on the question of cost, the professor finds the reading's argument inadequate. He thinks it is more important to consider the effectiveness of advertising. To support his view, he says people consider TV advertising to be more believable and tend to respect companies that advertise on TV. He concludes by saying radio advertising gives companies a higher return on investment on their TV advertising dollars.

Finally, the professor attacks the reading's assertion that listeners pay attention to contents of radio advertising. He says radio commercials are mere "background noise." He also points out that radio stations play too much advertising, causing listeners to tune to other stations or turn off the radio. Then he says TV does not have as much of this problem because TV programming is generally more engaging and better at attracting viewers' attention.

萬用模板（反駁觀點）

正如上面持贊同觀點的萬用寫作範本，持反駁觀點的萬用寫作範本也要求考生在每個分論點後面加一些細節性的陳述。

[開頭簡潔明瞭地介紹一下收音機廣告和電視廣告的作用]. The reading compares two ways of _____ and argues that _____[x]_____ is superior to _____[y]_____. However, the professor does not agree with the expressed in the _____ reading.

First, on the question of _____, the professor thinks the reading's argument is based on _____ information. [用兩到三個句子陳述教授的說法].

Second, on the question of _____, the professor finds the reading's argument inadequate. He thinks it is more important to consider _____. To support his view, he says people consider _____[y]_____ to be more believable and tend to _____.

Finally, the professor attacks the reading's assertion that _____. He says _____[x]_____ are _____. He also points out that _____, causing _____ to _____.

建立自己的寫作句型庫

下面句型適用於綜合寫作題中有關社會科學的題目。

• 閱讀好句型，成為我的作文佳句！

1. Both x and y can be effective.
……和……都有效。

Both radio and television advertising can be effective.

> **延伸說法** Both broadcast and print media can be effective.

2. However, in general, x gain better results from VERBing
但總體來說，……從……能獲取更好的成果

However, in general, business owners gain better results from purchasing radio airtime.

> **延伸說法** However, in general, small businesses gain better results from local radio commercials.

3. One of the strongest advantages of x over y is that z can be better VERBed
……勝過……最突出的優勢之一是……z 更能夠……

One of the strongest advantages of radio over TV is that the commercial spots can be better targeted to customer segments.

> **延伸說法** One of the strongest advantages of radio advertising over television advertising is that the budget can be better controlled.

4. The costs for x are cheaper than those for y by a significant margin.
……的價格比……的價格要便宜很多。

The costs for producing and airing radio commercials are cheaper than those for TV by a significant margin.

> **延伸說法** The costs for developing radio ads are cheaper than those for television ads by a significant margin.

5. Finally, x have a better chance of capturing the full attention of y
最後，……有更好的機會獲得……的全面關注

Finally, radio commercials have a better chance of capturing the full attention of the prospective customer.

> **延伸說法** Finally, social network sites have a better chance of capturing the full attention of young consumers.

• 講座好句型，成為我的作文佳句！

贊同觀點──

1. The x pointed out in the reading simply cannot be overemphasized.
閱讀中提到的……怎麼強調都不為過。

The advantages pointed out in the reading simply cannot be overemphasized.

> **延伸說法** The importance of education pointed out in the reading simply cannot be overemphasized.

2. **One powerful way that companies can benefit through x is by doing y**
企業能從……獲利的一種有效方法是……

One powerful way that companies can benefit through radio advertising is by doing event marketing.

> **延伸說法** One powerful way that companies can benefit through radio advertising is by doing DJ promotions.

3. **For one thing, there are fewer people involved in VERBing**
首先，……需要的人手要少一些

For one thing, there are fewer people involved in developing and producing the spots.

> **延伸說法** For one thing, there are fewer people involved in labor-intensive activities.

4. **Sure, x is limited to…, but this can be used to an advantage, if y is…**
……在……方面確實有侷限性，但這種侷限性可以變為一種優勢，如果 y 是……

Sure, radio is limited to sound, but this can be used to an advantage, if the message is well crafted.

> **延伸說法** Sure, radio is limited to audio, but this can be used to an advantage, if the music is well chosen.

反駁觀點——

1. **But the points made in the reading passage are not really accurate when you look at x**
但實際上，如果你注意……，閱讀短文中的觀點並不正確……

But the points made in the reading passage are not really accurate when you look at today's media climate.

> **延伸說法** But the points made in the reading passage are not really accurate when you look at all the expenses.

2. **But studies have shown that the public considers x more ADJECTIVE than y**
但研究顯示，公眾認為……比……更……

But studies have shown that the public considers the messages presented on television more authoritative than those presented on the radio.

> **延伸說法** But studies have shown that the public considers television programs more enjoyable than radio programs.

3. Finally, it's simply not true that...

最後，……的説法根本不對

Finally, it's simply not true that radio listeners always focus carefully on the advertisement message.

> **延伸說法** Finally, it's simply not true that radio commercials are cheap to produce.

• 高分範文中，有這些作文佳句！

贊同觀點——

1. The professor fully supports the x expressed in the reading.

該教授完全贊同閱讀短文中表達的……

The professor fully supports the views expressed in the reading.

> **延伸說法** The professor fully supports the opinions expressed in the reading.

2. First, on the question of x, the professor tacitly agrees with the reading.

首先，在……問題上，教授顯然同意閱讀短文中的説法。

First, on the question of targeting customers, the professor tacitly agrees with the reading.

> **延伸說法** First, on the question of market focus, the professor tacitly agrees with the reading.

3. Second, regarding the question of x, the professor is also in agreement with the reading.

其次，關於……的問題，教授也同意閱讀短文的觀點。

Second, regarding the question of cost, the professor is also in agreement with the reading.

> **延伸說法** Second, regarding the question of ROI (return on investment), the professor is also in agreement with the reading.

4. Finally, the professor supports the reading's view by stating it is possible to VERB by...

最後，透過説「……是有可能的」，教授表達了自己同閱讀短文一致的立場

Finally, the professor supports the reading's view by stating it is possible to attract listeners' attention to radio advertising by the clever manipulation of sound.

> **延伸說法** Finally, the professor supports the reading's view by stating it is possible to persuade listeners by choosing charismatic DJs.

5. She further points out a problem that affects x but not y

她進一步指出影響……但並不會對……造成影響的問題

She further points out a problem that affects TV advertising but not radio.

延伸說法 She further points out a problem that affects video production but not audio production.

反駁觀點——

1. The reading compares two ways of VERBing and argues that x is superior to y.

閱讀短文比較了……的兩種方式，認為……要優於……。

The reading compares two ways of communicating and argues that radio advertising is superior to TV advertising.

延伸說法 The reading compares two ways of advertising and argues that a radio commercial is superior to a television commercial.

2. However, the professor does not agree with the x expressed in the reading.

然而，教授並不同意閱讀短文表達的……

However, the professor does not agree with the views expressed in the reading.

延伸說法 However, the professor does not agree with the opinions expressed in the reading.

3. First, on the question of x, the professor thinks the reading's argument is based on y information.

首先，在……的問題上，教授認為閱讀短文裡的論據是基於……的資訊。

First, on the question of targeting customers, the professor thinks the reading's argument is based on out-dated information.

延伸說法 First, on the question of advertising production, the professor thinks the reading's argument is based on biased information.

4. Second, on the question of x, the professor finds the reading's argument inadequate.

其次，在……問題上，教授覺得閱讀短文裡的論據不充分。

Second, on the question of cost, the professor finds the reading's argument inadequate.

延伸說法 Second, on the question of quality, the professor finds the reading's argument inadequate.

5. He thinks it is more important to consider x

他認為考慮……更為重要

He thinks it is more important to consider the effectiveness of advertising.

延伸說法 He thinks it is more important to consider the overall impact of the commercial.

6. To support his view, he says people consider x to be more ADJECTIVE and tend to VERB

為了證實自己的觀點，他說人們覺得 x 比較……而傾向於……

To support his view, he says people consider TV advertising to be more believable and tend to respect companies that advertise on TV.

延伸說法 To support his view, he says people consider what is said on television to be more believable and tend to buy things they see there.

7. Finally, the professor attacks the reading's assertion that...

最後，教授抨擊了短文裡……的斷言

Finally, the professor attacks the reading's assertion that listeners pay attention to contents of radio advertising.

延伸說法 Finally, the professor attacks the reading's assertion that radio listeners believe what they hear on radio programs.

8. He also points out that..., causing x to VERB

他還指出……，致使……

He also points out that radio stations play too much advertising, causing listeners to tune to other stations or turn off the radio.

延伸說法 He also points out that radio DJs talk too much, causing listeners to ignore much of what they say.

關鍵語塊

- **strategic** 戰略（性）的；策略（上）的
- **good cause** 有益的事業
- **be vital for...** 對……很關鍵
- **charismatic** 超有魅力的
- **get... out** 推銷，推廣……
- **in real time** 即時地
- **pay attention to** 注意
- **seamlessly** 無縫地；銜接完美地
- **advertising message** 廣告訊息
- **remote radio broadcasts** 遠端無線電廣播
- **communication medium** 傳播媒介
- **exponentially cheaper** 便宜很多
- **commercial spots** 插播廣告的時間段
- **outsourcing to...** 外包給……
- **targeted to...** 面向……；指向……
- **personal touch** 人情味；溫情
- **customer segments** 客戶細分
- **recording studios** 錄音室
- **DJs** 流行音樂節目主持人
- **for free** 免費地
- **run commercials** 播廣告
- **enfold** 擁抱
- **tuned in** 收聽
- **well crafted** 認真設計的
- **radio host** 電臺節目主持人
- **skip over** 跳過，略過
- **airing** 廣播
- **record... on a DVR** 在數位影像錄影機上燒錄……

- **significant margin** 大幅度
- **media climate** 媒體境況
- **airtime** （無線電或電視廣告等節目的）廣播時間
- **proliferation of...** ……的增長
- **script development** 腳本開發
- **cable TV stations** 有線電視臺
- **multiple shoots** 各種拍攝
- **channeled to...** 引導到……
- **trapped in heavy traffic** 塞在車陣中
- **mainstream television networks** 主流電視網路
- **promotional tool** 行銷工具
- **demographics** （尤指用於市場測算的）人口統計資料
- **makes so much sense** 非常明智的
- **audience profiles** 觀眾情況圖表
- **... simply cannot be overemphasized ......** 極其重要，再怎麼強調都不為過
- **authoritative** 權威性的；可信的
- **event marketing** 事件行銷
- **return on investment** 投資回報
- **sponsor a sports event** 贊助體育賽事
- **brand** 品牌
- **marathon** 馬拉松賽跑
- **background noise** 背景雜音
- **raise money for...** 為……籌資
- **give their full attention to...** 全神貫注於……

▶再練習一次！

學習了以上這些策略、實用句型、語塊、高分範文和萬用寫作範本之後，回頭再看一次例題。再讀一遍閱讀短文，然後再聽一遍講座。如果還是聽不懂講座內容，就反覆多聽幾遍，或者參考錄音原稿。然後修改你之前寫的作文，或者重新寫一篇作文。修改或重寫作文時，試著運用本章學到的寫作技巧。完成之後，比較一下修改或重寫前後的兩篇作文，注意不同之處。

附錄：錄音原稿 1

 Track 015

Narrator: Now listen to part of a lecture on the same topic.

(woman) Professor: In these tough economic times, companies are looking for ways to stay competitive. Of course, without advertising, it's tough for a business to survive. That's why using radio as a promotional tool makes so much sense nowadays. The advantages pointed out in the reading simply cannot be overemphasized.

Let's talk more about targeting customers. One powerful way that companies can benefit through radio advertising is by doing event marketing. For example, a company can sponsor a sports event, like a marathon, to raise money for a good cause. A charismatic DJ broadcasts the race in real time, holding interviews and seamlessly inserting messages about the host company. Remote radio broadcasts on the event day generate excitement, and the company can only benefit.

As for development and production costs, radio advertising is exponentially cheaper than TV. Why is that? For one thing, there are fewer people involved in developing and producing the spots. For small businesses, the advertising script is often written and recorded by staff who work for the company. That's not only less expensive than outsourcing to a media company — it gives the commercial a personal touch. Furthermore, when local companies buy airtime, radio stations will often let them use their recording studios for free.

And let's not forget about how radio can enfold the listener so that he or she truly focuses on the message. Sure, radio is limited to sound, but this can be used to an advantage, if the message is well crafted. And quite frankly, listeners are more likely to listen to radio commercials than TV commercials. Nowadays, there are many software programs that let television viewers skip over commercials when they record them on a DVR. So many people record televisions for later viewing, and those people might very well never hear the commercials that were aired.

Track 016

Narrator: Now listen to part of a lecture on the same topic.

(man) Professor: Of course, there is always the option to advertise on the radio. But the points made in the reading passage are not really accurate when you look at today's media climate.

For instance, the claim that radio spots better target potential customers. While that used to be true, with the proliferation of cable TV stations and the integration of television with mobile phones, TV content — including TV advertising — is increasingly channeled to the right customer segment. And even mainstream television networks, which have broad demographics, have programs with known audience profiles. If you know the ratings of a TV program and its demographics, you can air your advertisement at certain times and target your message to that viewer audience.

And how about the cost of TV advertising? Production costs and airtime are indeed high. But studies have shown that the public considers the messages presented on television more authoritative than those presented on the radio. That means the message will be more influential. A company that advertises on TV has a better chance of having its brand remembered and respected. So the return on investment for a television commercial will be high, since large numbers of people will walk away talking about the product and the brand.

Finally, it's simply not true that radio listeners always focus carefully on the advertisement message. In fact, radio is often heard as "background noise" which people don't really process. And because radio stations often play commercial after commercial, listeners can easily become annoyed. After a while, these ads can cause the listeners to change the channel or even turn off the radio. This happens less often on television, where people tend to give their full attention to the program they are watching — whether it is drama, musical entertainment or news.

Task 2 ▸ Integrated Writing

第二題 獨立寫作全解

　　獨立寫作題的格式基本上和以前的托福寫作題相同。

　　獨立寫作題的題型是：有一個大概兩到三句話的題目，要求考生就既定話題談論自己的看法。一些話題是私人話題，涉及考生或考生的家庭；其他話題的範圍更大一些，諸如教育或租屋買房這類文化和社會問題。題目要求分論點必須要充分展開，表述清晰。考生有 30 分鐘的構思和寫作時間。30 分鐘後，系統會自動保存文章。

▶獨立寫作題的話題

　　ETS 資料表明，新托福考試獨立寫作部分的許多話題和舊托福非常相似。《托福考試官方指南》公佈了 200 個擬真話題，這在其他地方也很容易看到。這些寫作題的措辭會有微小改動，但基本上都是要求考生回答 agree or disagree（同意或者反對）、 compare and contrast（對比和對照）相關觀點或看法。經常會出現新題目，所以考生要做好各種準備。

　　有趣的是，新托福考試口語第二題中出現的許多題目也會出現在獨立寫作題中，只是會有一些微小的改動。因此，在複習獨立寫作題時，考生可以利用口語第二題中的題目；反之亦然。

▶獨立寫作題的八類題型

　　要真的「押中」寫作題，猜到自己會碰上哪一題，可能機率不是很高。但是只要瞭解了獨立寫作題的特點，考生看到作文題目的時候便可以迅速抓住題目的核心，信心十足地開始寫。基於其題目中的措辭和邏輯，每一道獨立寫作題都可以歸入一個「情境」下。這些情境框架就像地圖，可以告訴考生應該寫什麼內容以及如何構思。

　　獨立寫作題可以分為八個情境框架（可以理解為八類題型）。根據它們在考試中出現的頻率高低來排序的話，是以下八種：

1. Choose one from two: Do you agree or disagree / Do you support or oppose
   二選一題型 1（同意或不同意）

2. Choose one from two: Either x or y, which do you choose / Some people prefer x, others prefer y
   二選一題型 2（兩者中偏好哪一個）

3. Explicit compare and contrast / Advantages and disadvantages
   「比較與對比」和「利弊」題型

4. "What"
   What 題型

5. "Why"

　　Why 題型

6. "How"

　　How 題型

7. Hypothetical "if"

　　假設性題型

8. Open-ended describe and discuss

　　開放型題型

　　每一種題型，本書都將會用一章的篇幅來講解，告訴考生如何根據每一種題型的語言和邏輯要求寫出優秀的作文。

▶獨立寫作題如何評分？

　　獨立寫作題的評分準則比綜合寫作題的評分準則更重視話題的展開和連貫性。這是因為在獨立寫作題中，考生無從獲得閱讀短文和講座設定好的結構和內容。更確切地說，考生必須寫出全新的內容，把幾個觀點串聯起來。

　　考生的作文同時由評分人和自動評分軟體來評分。每篇作文由幾個評分人評閱，然後決定作文的分數。

▶獨立寫作題如何拿到高分？

　　ETS 告訴考生，作文的字數應不少於 300 個字。當然，如果超過 300 個字也不會扣分。在我看來，300 ～ 400 個字是個合適的長度。但許多考生認為作文寫得長就可以讓評分者給他們打高分，所以他們經常翻來覆去地重複一個觀點，千方百計地寫成長文章。這並不是明智之舉！ETS 的評分人不會去數作文的字數，而且作文長度也不是高分的標準。

　　要想作文得高分，需要做到：

1. 結構清晰
2. 觀點明確
3. 文法大部分正確
4. 句型豐富

　　在給獨立作文評分時，評分人看的是內容的展開、篇章結構和語言運用。但評分人是根據整體來評分，並不會專門針對這三個方面單獨評分。評分人看整篇作文時，如果發現這篇作文在某個方面欠佳，他們會留意，但在打分數時會綜合考慮其他因素。

　　就內容的展開而言，考生需要有恰當的論據和例子用來論證論點。清晰和準確的寫作思路至關重要。具體、有針對性的例子是加分點！

　　就篇章結構而言，考生的作文要有連貫性，銜接得當。加入 First 和 Second 這樣的語篇敘述特徵會有幫助，但這些尚不足以讓考生取得高分。考生還需要做到句與句、前後觀點之間緊密連接，而且觀點要表達得非常流暢。

　　就語言的運用而言，考生需要有很強的對詞彙及文法結構的把握能力。這並不是說你要用上花俏的 GRE 詞彙；也不是讓你機械地設計 10 個不同的句型結構。評分人當然不會去算你用了幾個句型，他們看的是整體的多樣性。因此，考生只需多寫些不同類型的句型，用詞自然、流暢就行了。考生應提出自己的觀點和例子。參加新托福考試的人很多，久而久之，模仿的痕跡就會暴露無遺。如果評分人或評分軟體發現很多作文裡都有大量抄襲的花俏語言，他們自然不會給這些作文打高分。如果模仿情節嚴重，他們甚至會要求考生重考。評分人每天都會看到很多背模板的作文，因此，一定不要一字不漏地背作文模板。寫作個人化才是關鍵！

讓人欣慰的是，在新托福寫作考試中，即使考生在文法、用詞和拼寫上出現幾個小錯誤，並不影響得高分。這樣的要求讓考生的壓力會小一些。

Choose one from two 1
如何應對二選一題型 1

在本章，你將學到……

★獨立寫作題如何構思
★獨立寫作題如何設定最理想的篇章結構

解讀常考題

　　獨立寫作題的第一種題型是二選一：Do you agree or disagree；do you support or oppose。顧名思義，「二選一題型」就是給考生兩個具體的選擇，要求他們從中選擇一個。在新托福寫作題的八類題型中，有兩種「二選一」題。第一種是目前出現頻率最高的：Do you agree or disagree with the following statement? 然後給出一個陳述。

　　另外一種是先陳述一件事，然後問：Do you support or oppose this [policy, rule, etc.]? 這種題目很容易辨別，因為它可以用 yes 或 no 來回答。

　　現在先來看看第一類「二選一題型」的例子。

▶模擬試題①

　　閱讀以下的短文並聆聽講座，完成以下這道作文題目。

Directions:

Read the question below. You have 30 minutes to plan, write, and revise your essay. Typically, an effective response will contain a minimum of 300 words.

> Do you agree or disagree with the following statement?
> **Students are influenced more by their teachers than they are by their classmates.**
> Use specific reasons and examples to support your answer.

　　這道寫作題要求考生回答學生受老師的影響多一些，還是受同學的影響多一些。簡化一下題目就是：Do teachers influence students more? 簡單的答案是：Yes, they are influenced more. 這是肯定原說法。另一個合乎邏輯的回答是：No, students are influenced more by their classmates. 這個回答否定了原說法。當然，考生討論這個話題也可以分情況來處理。從下面的高分範文和萬用寫作範本可以看到處理方法。我們會發現，只有運用相對高的語言技能，才能得到高分，但如果處理得好，這種 Do you agree or disagree / do you support or oppose 話題是可以寫出非常優秀的作文的。

▶ **Exercise 1**

根據上面例題的題目要求寫一篇作文。初稿完成後，繼續學習下部分的內容。仔細研讀高分範文、萬用寫作範本、高分策略和寫作句型庫，運用所學的新知識完成 Exercise 2。

高分範文 *Track 019*

All creatures on earth have to learn skills that allow them to compete and stake out a place for themselves in their environment. Humankind is no exception. Our first lessons are taught to us by our parents. However, as we grow older, more people come into our life and we start to learn from them. From the people who surround us, we can absorb new knowledge and skills, but we also develop values and character. In this regard, teachers and classmates can influence us. Generally speaking, I agree that teachers and other authoritative figures influence students more. However, there are a number of factors at play, as I shall discuss below.

One of these factors is a student's age. Young children tend to be very curious. They ask a lot of questions, and they also are very observant. At certain stages of child development, children will consciously model themselves after people they look up to, usually their parents. In high school and college, young people have developed a stronger sense of self, but they are still looking for role models. Although we are influenced by our peers, deep down inside we have a natural tendency to learn from and be influenced by people we perceive to be authoritative or respectable because we want to become like them when we go out into society. This is one reason why teachers have more influence over us than classmates do.

Obviously, what is said above presupposes that we spend an equal amount of time with both teachers and classmates. In reality, a person might spend so little time with his or her teachers that most of the influence comes from classmates or friends. A typical example of this phenomenon is a troubled student who spends considerable time with classmates who don't study or who lack moral fiber. Thus, time is another important factor in determining the source of a young person's influence.

In sum, I think most of us are influenced more by our teachers than by classmates because we gravitate, consciously or subconsciously, towards people of authority. From infancy we look for role models to help us do well in society. This principle will hold true unless there are unusual factors such as time or negative social settings.

萬用模板

[在文章開頭，用兩三個句子交代背景資訊]. Generally speaking, I agree that _____. However, there are a number of factors at play, as I shall discuss below.

One of these factors is _____. [用兩三個句子解釋第一個因素，為總論點提供論據]. This is one reason why _____.

Obviously, what is said above presupposes that we [承認總論點不成立的一兩個要素或情況]. In reality, [解釋前一句]. A typical example of this phenomenon is _____ . Thus, _____ is another important factor in _____.

In sum, I think most of us [改述總論點]_____ because we [改述理由]. This principle will hold true unless there are unusual factors such as [提及例外情況] or [提及例外情況].

獨立寫作題的構思和篇章結構

1. 完成獨立寫作題的三個簡單步驟

1）先識別題型（即情境框架），弄清題目的邏輯，構思幾分鐘之後，列表或提綱。

2）不要考慮文法和拼寫，迅速寫下初稿。注意觀點和行文的流暢性。可以多寫一些，甚至超過題目要求的字數也沒關係，只要記得一定要留下檢查作文的時間就好。

3）修改初稿，刪去錯誤和重複的片語，確保文章銜接自然、前後連貫。

需要說明的是，獨立寫作題得高分的關鍵之一便是文章觀點明確，論據（例子或原因）充足。

2. 構思步驟

進行寫作構思時，考生要先決定自己是贊同還是反對寫作題中的論點。在上面這篇例文中，該考生贊同「老師對學生的影響比較大」這一觀點，但也談到了例外情況：和同學相處的時間長了，有些學生受同學的影響會多一些。

構思時，考生可以寫下老師更有影響力的原因：

> Good teachers
> **Authority, respectability**
> **Role model**
> **Time spent**
> Experience
> Student clubs
> **Age of the student**

不一定非要很有條理地寫下這些觀點。為了節省時間，最好用縮寫形式。構思時最先出現的想法應該快速用英語寫下來，以便於迅速擴展思路形成一篇完整的文章，這是文字處理的好處之一。然後，列提綱時，選擇你想要側重的兩個或三個方面。

高分範文選擇的論述點是上述加粗的部分。一些點可以安排在第一段；其他則可以作為分論點。在實際寫作中，考生可以不提列出來的某些「點」，選擇自己想要用的觀點或片語就可以。在構思過程中，如果考生想不出足夠多的例子來支持自己的立場（agree），那麼可以試著從相反立場（disagree）來寫。

3. 獨立寫作題最理想的篇章結構

一篇文章的理想開頭會用一個有趣的句子介紹話題，設定基調。在作文第一段，考生應該緊扣作文題提出鮮明的觀點。以上面這道寫作題為例，考生的陳述應該明確表明贊同或否定該論述。

第一段之後，應該有兩到三段的論證段落。論證可以是真人軼事、事實或其他形式的邏輯論證，但必須緊扣作文主題，這樣文章才有「統一性」和「連貫性」。考生需把分論點分成幾個段落，透過連接詞、重複的關鍵字、指示詞和邏輯使文章做到銜接自然、前後連貫。

最後，考生可以再換句話說一次論點，作為文章的結論。

4. 寫作時間分配

因為許多考生擔心 30 分鐘寫不完作文，所以他們看完題目就馬上動手寫，希望一下筆就有觀點出現在腦海中。如果這樣的話，考生會遇到「寫作障礙」，即考生想不到夠多例子或原因。這就是我強調考生要花幾分鐘去構思的原因。

那麼，在寫作過程中如何做好時間分配呢？

步驟	做什麼	時間分配
1	理解題目	1/2 minute
2	構思	2 minutes
3	列提綱	1/2 minute
4	寫作文	20 minutes
5	檢查和修改	7 minutes

5. 從哪個角度去檢查和修改作文

修改和潤飾文章時，要檢查片語和句子的流暢性，確保使用的連接詞恰當。同時也要檢查前後連貫性，確保每一句的觀點符合前後邏輯，沒有邏輯上的漏洞。

同時考生需要修改文法錯誤。每一個考生都有可能出某類錯誤，最常見的錯誤如下所示：

托福考生作文中常見錯誤	
1	第三人稱單數形式的動詞應該有「s」 如：He supports me.
2	性別前後不一致 I am grateful to my mother because he always helps me.☒

3	主詞與動詞不一致 He like to go swimming. ☒ He likes to go swimming. ☑
4	時態錯誤（如果講一個故事作為例子，整個故事都要用一般過去式。）
5	單複數錯誤 People need many informations in the modern world. ☒ People need a lot of information in the modern world. ☑
6	分詞作形容詞表示主動和被動錯誤 We are interesting in him because he is an interested person. ☒ We are interested in him because he is an interesting person. ☑
7	定冠詞和不定冠詞混淆 The good health is a blessing. ☒ Good health is a blessing. ☑
8	間距與空格問題（段與段之間空一行，段首縮進五個字母的空格，這種形式會使文章一目了然。）
9	標點符號錯誤（例如英文逗號的用法，應該是標在詞彙的最後一個字母後，與下一個單字空一個字元。）

要想寫出一篇出色的文章，可運用以下策略

1. 考試前，要多練習打字。熟練的打字能力有利於在電腦上寫作。

2. 考試時，要認真看題目要求，弄清題目意思。確定該題目是什麼題型（即情境）之後，再根據題型來運用不同的寫作策略。

3. 用一兩分鐘時間構思，寫下一個簡短的提綱。提綱可以寫在紙上，也可以寫在電腦上。

4. 在第一段迅速寫下一個論點。接下來，寫第一個分論點的段落（第二段）。至少需要寫兩個分論點段落作為文章的主體。然後寫一段簡短的結尾段。最後，回到開始處完成第一段，並開始修改和潤飾。

5. 初稿可以多寫，修改時再根據邏輯刪掉一些內容。

6. 如果考生套用模板範本，那麼作文內容一定要個性化，不要直接抄寫他人的作文。評分人和評分軟體都有可能會識破。

7. 寫作思路展開之後，一定要圍繞中心論點來寫。不要漫談或偏離主題。

8. 考試時不要嘗試以高於自己真實能力的語言水準寫作。要使用自己慣用的語言，這樣寫出來的觀點才易於理解並且更「個性化」。

9. 不要在文章主體部分一再重複論點。結論部分可以重複論點，但應該用別的詞彙換句話說。

10. 想「大改」前要先看時間。除非有足夠的時間，不然不要對作文進行大改動。

建立自己的寫作句型庫

1. Generally speaking, I agree that x influence students more.

總之，我認同……影響學生比較多。

Generally speaking, I agree that teachers and other authoritative figures influence students more.

延伸說法 Generally speaking, I agree that our friends influence us more.

2. However, there are a number of x at play, as I shall discuss below.

但是有許多……在起作用，我會在下面討論。

However, there are a number of factors at play, as I shall discuss below.

延伸說法 However, there are several circumstances at play, as I shall discuss below.

3. One of these factors is x.

其中一個因素是……

One of these factors is a student's age.

延伸說法 One of these factors is time.

4. This is one reason why x have more influence over us than y

這是……比……對我們更有影響力的一個原因

This is one reason why teachers have more influence over us than classmates do.

延伸說法 This is one reason why parents have more influence over us than teachers do.

5. Obviously, what is said above presupposes that…

顯然，上面所說的先決條件是……

Obviously, what is said above presupposes that we spend an equal amount of time with both teachers and classmates.

6. In sum, I think most of us are influenced more by x than by y because we…

總而言之，我認為我們大部分人受……影響比受……的影響多一些

In sum, I think most of us are influenced more by our teachers than by classmates because we gravitate, consciously or subconsciously, towards people of authority.

延伸說法 In sum, I think most of us are motivated more by grades than by a desire to learn.

▶再練習一次！

學完高分範文、萬用寫作範本、高分策略和寫作句型庫，運用所學的技能修改你的初稿，並認真看修改之處。然後用學到的新句型去練習下面五道模擬試題的寫作。

寫作模擬試題

1. Do you agree or disagree...

Do you agree or disagree with the following statement?
Rich people who do not work will be unhappy.
Use specific reasons and examples to support your answer.

寫作構思（粗體條目是高分範文中用到的。）

Rich people profile
Millionaires
Rich have nothing to worry about
Can spend time with grandchildren
The need to feel useful
Maslow
Idle rich = boredom
May think they can do anything

高分範文 1　 *Track 020*

Because I am not rich, I cannot be sure whether rich people will ever be unhappy. Most people work hard all their lives to make some money and have a better quality of life. One would think that, if we reach our goal of accumulating a little money or even exceed our goal by amassing a great fortune, we will live very happy lives. This said, my guess is that wealthy people will not be happy if they do not work. Let me elaborate.

First, all humans have needs, from physiological needs to self-actualization. Most of us are familiar with them as defined by the psychologist Maslow. While his arrangement of needs in a hierarchy is controversial, most people would agree that work is the thing that can satisfy the most needs. Consequently, when a person is deprived of work, his or her needs will no longer be met. The person will then probably become unhappy.

Second, all play and no work is boring. When we have too much of one thing, we get bored. One may say they can try to create variety by pursuing different leisure activities such as playing cards and golf. But play is play; the nature of leisure activity is the same, no matter what form it takes. After a while, boredom sets in. A bored person cannot be a happy person.

The third factor that might be responsible for unhappiness is that wealth breeds trouble. Many of today's rich have become wealthy by building successful businesses. In the process of battling their competitors or leading their subordinates at work, these individuals become accustomed to the use of power. As a result, many of them develop a bloated ego and think they can get anything they set their eyes on. If they stop working, they might use their power and wealth in pursuit of the wrong things. You only need to read the tabloids to see the kind of trouble that the idle rich can get into.

To summarize, work is vital to our health and wellbeing. It gives our life purpose and meaning, which helps us be content, regardless of how much money we have. Without work, even rich people will sense that something is missing and feel unhappy.

托福總監評析

　　這道寫作題要求考生對「不工作的有錢人是否快樂」談談自己的觀點。這篇範文的第一段非常吸引人。考生說因為自己不是有錢人，所以不知道不工作的有錢人是不是快樂。但接下來考生說有人認為透過一點一點的財富積累達到自己的人生目標是快樂的，根據這種說法，自己猜測如果有錢人不工作就不會快樂。然後，從第二至第四段，考生闡述了有錢人可能不快樂的原因。

　　在第二段，考生提到美國著名的心理學家馬斯洛（Maslow）。馬斯洛曾提出過需求層次理論，文中考生引用了此理論，但並沒有繼續說明。

....

2. Do you agree or disagree...

Do you agree or disagree with this statement?
Nowadays the extended family (grandparents, cousins, aunts and uncles) is less significant than it was in previous times.
Use specific reasons and examples to support your answer.

寫作構思

Ext vs. nuclear family
Nowadays can talk to family by phone
Fight when under one roof
Industrial Age
Chinese culture
Division of labor
Insurance systems

高分範文 2　　 *Track 021*

Across different cultures, society follows a common pattern. When the means of production changes, it brings with it changes in society. A family is an organizational unit in society; therefore, it is subject to change when the structure of society changes. Without a doubt, the extended family in most developing countries has lost much of the importance it had in an earlier age.

Before the Industrial Revolution, production was generally small-scale and agriculture was considerably more important than other industries. Families usually supplied the labor required by small businesses and family farms. A larger family was thus more advantageous in such an environment. With the Industrial Revolution came a new means of production which required the establishment of large businesses. As these large businesses gradually replaced the small businesses, people would leave their hometowns in search of work. As a result, families were broken up. Members of a family would relocate to different cities where the factories were located, and a new and smaller family, the nuclear family, was born.

At the same time, the nature of work changed. Some of the most important work traditionally done by the extended family is now handled by service workers. For example, rearing the young and caring for the old used to be done by family members. Uncles and aunts would pitch in to help raise young children, and it was unthinkable to have old parents live apart from their adult children. Nowadays, it is not uncommon to send children to childcare centers and old parents to senior homes.

Yet another factor that has diminished the importance of the extended family is the insurance systems common in many countries. In the past, when a person was struck with a financial crisis such as a bodily injury that required lengthy care, members of the extended family would often help. Now, more often than not, medical insurance takes care of this.

As we can see from the above, new ways of production and the establishment of new institutions typical of the market economy have brought profound changes to human societies. The importance of the extended family has been greatly diminished in the process. We currently live in a world where we increasingly rely on commercial, social and governmental institutions rather than the extended family.

托福總監評析

　　這道寫作題要求考生就當今社會大家庭的作用表明自己的看法。考生要嘛選擇贊同觀點：Yes, the extended family is less important. 要嘛持否定觀點，認為大家庭和以前同樣重要（或者更重要）。高分範文用的是經典的「五段論」方法。第二至第四段分別從社會和經濟發展的角度來論證，認為生產方式的改變使大家庭的重要程度降低了。注意，考生並沒有直接引用題目裡的用語，說：I agree that the extended family is less significant nowadays. 而是用巧妙的方式表達了相同的意思：Without a doubt, the extended family in most developing countries has lost much of the importance it had in an earlier age. 在總結段，考生透過換句話說再次強調了論點：The importance of the extended family has been greatly diminished in the process. 這種寫作手法非常吸引評分人。

---

3. Do you agree or disagree...

> **It is often said that it is unwise to borrow money from a friend since the friendship can be damaged. Do you agree? Why or why not?**
> Use reasons and specific examples to explain your answer.

寫作構思

> **Demise of a friendship**
> Difficult to say no
> Friend in need is friend indeed
> **Really in need?**
> Limited amount of cash
> **Examples of friendship destroyed**

高分範文 3　 *Track 022*

Borrowing money from a friend is something that I would never do. In fact, if a friend ever wants to borrow money from me, he had better have a compelling reason. I am relieved to say I don't think any of my friends would even attempt to ask me for money. Money borrowing is one of the most often cited causes for the demise of a friendship.

We live in a modern society where the lending and borrowing of money is facilitated by large institutions catering to the needs of businesses and individuals. As long as a person is creditworthy and has the ability to repay a loan, he or she can generally borrow money from a financial institution. Thus, there is really no need to borrow from one's friends unless you are not able to meet the bank's lending requirements.

Stories abound about how friendships were ruined because of borrowing. In a typical situation, the friend who has borrowed money cannot keep his or her promise to repay the money. At first, the debtor will try to provide excuses. Familiar excuses include "I thought I was going to receive a sum of money this month," "My friend owes me some money and he did not pay me back," or "My mother got sick." As time drags on, the debtor will get comfortable with the idea of not repaying the loan — angering his creditor friend in the process. Or, the borrower may feel guilty and start avoiding the creditor friend. At this point, the friendship between the two is basically destroyed.

With the exception of emergencies, most problems of borrowing stem from the lack of discipline on the part of the borrower. If one abides by the principle of living within one's means, there is little need for borrowing from a friend. However, once the borrower starts to think he or she can take advantage of the friendship, trouble is on its way. The relationship is likely to become damaged or totally destroyed.

托福總監評析

這道寫作題要求考生針對借錢給朋友好不好這一問題談談自己的看法。第一段，考生提出自己鮮明的觀點：Borrowing money from a friend is something that I would never do. 第二段談現代人可以從金融機構貸款，沒有必要向朋友借錢。第三段舉例說明朋友之間借錢會出現的結局。總結段重複了之前段落的觀點，指出導致很多友誼破裂的主要原因是借錢的一方缺乏自律。

4. Do you support or oppose...

In many countries, people are no longer permitted to smoke in public places and places of work. Do you support or oppose this rule?
Use specific reasons and details to support your position.

寫作構思

People don't really obey smoking rules
Damage to health
Dedicated "smoking sheds"
Freedom and equality
Children and second-hand smoking
Define public place
Rights of business owners

高分範文 4　 *Track 023*

The destructive effects of smoking on our health have been thoroughly researched and proven beyond any doubt. Second-hand smoke likewise has been well studied and is clearly just as harmful to non-smokers as it is to smokers themselves. There is no argument here; both opponents and proponents of a smoking ban in public places agree that smoking is bad for health. Nevertheless, I find the rule to ban smoking in public places problematic. Once we start arbitrarily setting rules to ban things, where will we stop? Alcoholic beverages? Fast foods? This does not seem like a coherent way to set policy.

To make a fair rule, we need to find a way to balance the rights of smokers and non-smokers. Traditionally, non-smokers have felt their rights to clean air have been trampled by the smokers. Assume you are not a smoker. If you went to a famous restaurant, only to find the room is filled with cigarette smoke, wouldn't you be annoyed? Wouldn't you want all those smokers to put out their cigarettes? When there is no ban on smoking in restaurants, the rights of the smokers are protected. But this is not fair to non-smokers.

Perhaps the best way to resolve the issue is to make sure that, as part of the smoking ban rule, there is a far way to define "public place." For example, is a restaurant considered a public place? Isn't it more reasonable to consider privately owned restaurants "private establishments"? Moreover, if we include private businesses in the "public" category, aren't we trampling on the property rights of business owners? My own feeling is that we should not encroach upon business owners' rights; that is to say, we should exclude private businesses from the ban. This way, restaurant owners and other private establishments will have the freedom to choose what kind of clientele to serve. I'm fairly confident there will always be "smoke-free" places for non-smokers to enjoy.

In summary, I agree that we should institute a ban on smoking in truly public places; however, we have to be careful not to define "public" too broadly. In my opinion, public places should include government properties and office buildings, but not private bars and restaurants.

托福總監評析

　　這道寫作題要求考生就公共場合禁菸這條法規表達自己的觀點。這篇範文開篇即承認吸菸有害健康。但是，公共場合禁菸的這條法規有問題。然後，第二段指出禁菸問題成為平衡吸菸者和不吸菸者權利的問題。不吸菸者一直處於不利地位。第三段提到，解決這個問題得看怎麼界定「公共場所」，如果公共場合禁菸令範圍過於廣泛，那麼就侵犯了私人企業的權利。考生在總結段提出自己的觀點：公共場合禁菸是一件好事，但公共場合不應包含私人酒吧和私人飯店。

....

5. 需要回答「yes / no」的題目：

> **When famous people such as actors, athletes and pop stars give their opinions, many people listen. Do you think we should pay attention to these opinions?**
> Use specific reasons and examples to support your answer.

寫作構思

> Jackie Chan
> We are persuaded by people we like
> **Celebrity advertising**
> **Promote a movie**
> **Charity causes**

高分範文 5　　 *Track 024*

Celebrities are everywhere nowadays. They dominate the media, and so when they speak, we listen. Actors use their fame to extol the virtues of products; professional athletes speak out to galvanize support for a social cause. It is easy for these famous people to gain our attention; however, it is not easy to persuade us. This is a good thing, because we should be able to form our own opinions.

Furthermore, more often than not, famous people on television aren't even saying what they really think. It is no secret that companies often pay hefty sums to engage a celebrity to endorse their products. In advertisements the opinions expressed by these celebrities are literally "bought" opinions. Consequently, we cannot assign any weight to such opinions.

In addition, celebrities are surrounded by people who are trying to manage their image. Publicists and agents create media opportunities so the celebrity they represent looks good to the public. They manufacture opportunities for celebrities to make comments. Yet these "opinions" are scripted in advance and made as part of a PR effort, to promote a movie or a sports event.

With the above said, it is true that many celebrities give time and money to charity. Some famous people raise funds for medical research to help cure certain diseases. If we wanted to be cynical, we could say they do this just for the image. However, it seems that some actors and athletes actually believe in the causes they represent. One famous example is the actor Paul Newman, who with his wife, created many foundations and has given hundreds of millions of dollars to charity. In cases like these, "Actions speak louder than words." We can be influenced by the opinions of Paul Newman because of his generosity.

In general, however, we should not pay too much attention to what celebrities say. Actors and sports stars may have strong emotional appeal to us, but much of what they say is driven by business and PR concerns. Substituting their opinions for our independent thinking does not seem like a wise thing to do.

托福總監評析

　　這道寫作題要求考生對是否應該重視名人的觀點表達自己的想法。文章第一段提到，名人佔據了媒體，他們説什麼，大家都會聽。考生的觀點是：No, we should not pay attention to their opinions; we should form our own. 第二段以名人代言產品作為例子，説明我們不必認真對待名人的觀點。第三段承認也有例外情況；例如，那些真正做慈善事業的名人，他們的觀點代表自己的心聲。總結段把論點換句話説，重述我們不應該受名人觀點的影響。

建立自己的寫作句型庫

1. Because I am not x, I cannot be sure whether…

因為我不……，所以我不確定是否……

Because I am not rich, I cannot be sure whether rich people will ever be unhappy.

延伸說法 Because I am not a technology expert, I cannot be sure whether technology nowadays is creating a common culture.

2. One would think that, if we VERB, we will live very happy lives.

有人會認為，如果我們……，我們就能過幸福的生活。

One would think that, if we reach our goal of accumulating a little money or even exceed our goal by amassing a great fortune, we will live very happy lives.

延伸說法 One would think that, if we have a strong family, we will live very happy lives.

3. This said, my guess is that x will not VERB if they do not VERB

根據這種說法，我猜測……如果不……就不會……

This said, my guess is that wealthy people will not be happy if they do not work.

延伸說法 This said, my guess is that intelligent people will not become teachers if they do not get paid much.

4. A(n) x person cannot be a happy person.

……的人不可能快樂。

A bored person cannot be a happy person.

延伸說法 A lazy person cannot be a happy person.

5. The third factor that might be responsible for x is that…

……的第三個相關因素可能是……

The third factor that might be responsible for unhappiness is that wealth breeds trouble.

延伸說法 The third factor that might be responsible for poor customer service is that complaints are not clearly explained.

6. To summarize, x is vital to our y

總而言之，……對……很關鍵

To summarize, work is vital to our health and wellbeing.

延伸說法 To summarize, diverse courses are vital to our undergraduate education.

7. Without a doubt, x in most developing countries has VERBed
毫無疑問，大部分發展中國家的……已經……

Without a doubt, the extended family in most developing countries has lost much of the importance it had in an earlier age.

延伸說法 Without a doubt, economic growth in most developing countries has been a priority.

8. x was thus more advantageous in such an environment.
因此，在這種環境裡，……更有優勢。

A larger family was thus more advantageous in such an environment.

延伸說法 Economies of scale were thus more advantageous in such an environment.

9. Nowadays, it is not uncommon to VERB
當今，……很常見

Nowadays, it is not uncommon to send children to childcare centers and old parents to senior homes.

延伸說法 Nowadays, it is not uncommon to wear stylish designer clothes.

10. The importance of x has been greatly diminished in the process.
在這一過程中，……的重要性驟減。

The importance of the extended family has been greatly diminished in the process.

延伸說法 The importance of the Humanities has been greatly diminished in the process.

11. VERBing is something that I would never do.
我絕不會做……

Borrowing money from a friend is something that I would never do.

延伸說法 Playing video games is something that I would never do.

12. VERBing is one of the most often cited causes for…
……是最常被人們提到的原因之一

Money borrowing is one of the most often cited causes for the demise of a friendship.

延伸說法 Burning fossil fuels is one of the most often cited causes for the demise of the environment.

13. Stories abound about how…

關於……的故事舉不勝舉

Stories abound about how friendships were ruined because of borrowing.

延伸說法 Stories abound about how a good neighbor saved the life of the person next door.

14. Nevertheless, I find x problematic.

但是，我發現……有問題。

Nevertheless, I find the rule to ban smoking in public places problematic.

延伸說法 Nevertheless, I find most television programs problematic.

15. In summary, I agree that we should VERB; however, we have to be careful not to VERB

總之，我贊同……，但是我們必須……

In summary, I agree that we should institute a ban on smoking in truly public places; however, we have to be careful not to define "public" too broadly.

延伸說法 In summary, I agree that we should let children spend some time learning music; however, we have to be careful not to let them neglect their studies.

16. Furthermore, more often than not, …

此外，多半情況下，……

Furthermore, more often than not, famous people on television aren't even saying what they really think.

延伸說法 Furthermore, more often than not, parents spoil their children.

17. With the above said, it is true that…

雖如上述所說，但還是確實存在……的情況

With the above said, it is true that many celebrities give time and money to charity.

延伸說法 With the above said, it is true that many concerts are inspiring events.

Choose one from two 2
如何應對二選一題型 2

在本章，你將學到……

★ 如何準確且有說服力地表達自己的偏愛

解讀常考題

第二種「二選一」的題目也很常見，如：

Some people prefer to [eat in restaurants], while others prefer to [eat at home]. Which do you prefer?

這類「二選一」作文題目是讓考生表達自己的偏愛。例如，題目會說一些人喜歡做這件事，而其他人則喜歡做別的事情。考生需要在這兩件事情中挑選自己喜歡做的一件事。

除了這類表達自己個人偏愛的題目，另一種題目是 either x or y，如：

Your school has enough money to buy either computers or books. Which should your school choose to buy?

這類題目很容易辨別，因為它們通常會含有 which 或 which one，要求考生二選一。換句話說，考生不需要對一個陳述表示同意或反對，而只需在兩項中選擇其一。當然，也可以不陳述自己的觀點，只說自己不知道應該選擇哪個，但這樣做是有風險的。

這種作文題型的常見題目有：
1. Do you **prefer** x or y?
2. Which **do** you **prefer**, x or y?
3. Which [of the two] **would** you **prefer**?
4. **Would** you **rather** do x or y?
5. **Would** you **prefer** to x or y?
6. **Which** [of the two] is better?
7. **Which** [of the two] is more important?

在寫「偏好」或「要嘛……要嘛……」的作文時，考生要在兩處說清楚自己的選擇：第一段和最後一段。而在文章的主體，即分論點段落，則要解釋你選擇的原因。

先來看一個例子：

▶ 模擬試題①

閱讀以下的短文並聆聽講座，完成以下這道作文題。

Directions:
Read the question below. You have 30 minutes to plan, write, and revise your essay. Typically, an effective response will contain a minimum of 300 words.

> **Some students prefer to study alone. Others prefer to study in a group. Which do you prefer?**
> Use specific reasons and examples to support your answer.

　　這道寫作題給了考生兩個選擇：獨立學習或者小組學習。考生可以非常簡單地回答：I prefer to study alone 或 I prefer to study in a group. ，但考生也可以這樣寫：I usually prefer to..., although there are times that..., 然後說明例外的情況。

▶ Exercise 1

> 　　根據上面例題的題目要求寫一篇作文。初稿完成後，繼續閱讀下部分的內容。仔細研讀高分範文、萬用寫作範本、高分策略和寫作句型庫，運用所學的新知識完成 Exercise 2。

寫作構思

Regular study schedule
Discipline or lack of it
Alone is quiet
Questions need answering
Perspective
Learn more

高分範文 *Track 025*

Studying alone certainly has its advantages. Being by yourself in your room allows you to move at your own pace and to enjoy the peace and quiet. For me, however, studying with a group of people is definitely my preference. If one is careful about including only conscientious people in the group, the study experience can be surprisingly productive.

The benefits of group study all revolve around the ability for students to talk with one another about course material. One individual can ask a question, and another can answer it. When a learner talks out loud about what he or she has read in a textbook or heard in a lecture, the learner is able to reinforce the new ideas. Moreover, a motivated group can give individuals who have questions positive feedback and moral support, so that each individual keeps working hard.

In a similar vein, I like the fact that group study provides each group member with new perspectives on the course material being discussed. When I study alone, I have only one point of view on a subject. However, in a group situation, each of the participants has different perspectives. We can quickly assess each of these viewpoints and advance our own thinking in the process. This is not only an efficient way of learning, it is interesting.

Yet another reason to work in study groups is that a student is more likely to find out the best sources of information when he or she is networking with a number of people. Very often, we may think we have found some interesting articles or reference works, and we may think these materials suffice. But as soon as you start asking around, your friends might have found other materials that are equally useful, if not even better. The truth is that there is a vast amount of information out there, and when you tap into a "search party" looking for specific information and good resources, you are more likely to end up with better and more up-to-date useful materials.

To summarize, there are many benefits associated with group study. Even though it is timeconsuming to get everybody in the same place, overall, I think the study group experience is worth the trouble. I prefer to learn together with my friends.

萬用模板

[你不喜歡的活動] certainly has its advantages. [改述不喜歡的活動] allows you to _____ and to _____. For me, however, [你喜歡的活動] is definitely my preference. If one [必要的條件], the _____ experience can be surprisingly [正面表述的形容詞].

The benefits of [改述喜歡的活動] all revolve around [第一個好處]. [用兩三個句子來闡釋該好處].

In a similar vein, I like the fact that [你喜歡的活動] provides [第二個好處]. [用兩三個句子來闡釋該好處]. This is not only [正面表述的形容詞], it is [正面表述的形容詞].

Yet another reason to [動詞 + 你喜歡的活動] is that [第三個好處]. Very often, we may think _____, and we may think these suffice. But _____. The truth is that [改述第三個好處].

To summarize, there are many benefits associated with [你喜歡的活動]. Even though it is [改述你喜歡的活動的不足之處], overall, I think the [你喜歡的活動] is worth the trouble. I prefer to [動詞 + 你喜歡的活動的改述].

　　在這篇範文中，考生先說獨立學習有其優點，然後說自己喜歡小組學習。這種呈現形式使第一段顯得非常有趣。第二至第四段分別陳述自己為什麼喜歡小組學習。注意總結段，考生並沒有詳細複述上文提到的小組學習的利處，相反地，考生提到小組學習的問題：耗時（time-consuming），並把該活動的名稱換句話說（the study group experience）。這種手法不再使文章顯得繁瑣單調。文章最後一句用簡單且個性化的語言改述了論點，顯得簡潔而有力。

表達偏愛

1. 表達偏愛的四大規則

在新托福考試的口語和寫作部分，考生必須會表達自己的偏愛。那麼表達個人偏愛有沒有規則可循呢？我為大家總結了四條規則。只要大家在寫作過程中記住這四條規則，這類題型便能輕鬆應對。

規則一：

以相對正式的方式去表述自己的偏愛。如果只是簡單地寫：I prefer to study alone. 評分人不會被打動。考生需要把這些句子嵌入複雜的長句中，例如：There is a lot of pressure at my school, and so in general, I prefer to study alone.

規則二：

在文中兩個地方正式表明自己的偏愛：

1）第一段（論點陳述）

2）最後一段（改述論點）

規則三：

因為在最後一段需要用自己的語言來重述論點，所以考生要學會用不同的方式來說明同一件事情。這樣不論遇到什麼寫作話題，都可以做到靈活運用。

表達偏愛的句型

❶

I prefer to study in groups.

I prefer studying in groups.

I prefer studying in groups to studying alone.

My preference is to study in groups.

My preference would be to study in groups.

❷

I like handmade items better.

I like handmade items better than machine-made ones.

My preference would be handmade items.

Handmade items are more to my liking.

Handmade items suit me better.

Handmade items are more to my taste.

❸

I would rather choose my own roommate.

I would rather choose my own roommate than have one assigned.

❹

I would prefer to live some place where the weather changes.

I prefer to go at a slow pace instead of rushing around.

I choose to be outdoors whenever I can.

> I tend to prefer staying in one place.
> I vastly prefer eating out, at small restaurants.
> I somewhat prefer small towns, although cities are certainly exciting places.
> Working on one project at a time is my first choice.

下面是高分範文裡的兩個段落，看看它們是如何表達偏愛的（表達偏愛的句型用粗體表示）。

第一段：

> Studying alone certainly has its advantages. Being by yourself in your room allows you to move at your own pace and to enjoy the peace and quiet. **For me, however, studying with a group of people is definitely my preference.** If one is careful about including only conscientious people in the group, the study experience can be surprisingly productive.

最後一段總結段：

> To summarize, there are many benefits associated with group study. Even though it is time-consuming to get everybody in the same place, overall, I think the study group experience is worth the trouble. **I prefer to learn together with my friends.**

注意上述兩個表達偏愛的句子有什麼不同。一個較長，一個較短；一個用名詞 preference，另一個用動詞不定式 prefer to。

規則四：

另一個重要的規則是如果作文題目裡有情態動詞 would，作文裡應該用相同的情態動詞。例如，一道作文題 Would you prefer to live in a traditional house or in a modern apartment? 考生的回答應該是：I would prefer to live in a traditional house. 但如果作文題目是：Do you prefer handmade items or machine-made items? 考生應該寫：I prefer handmade items.

2. 考生表達偏愛時常見的文法錯誤

因為表達形式多樣，所以考生很難做到文法完全正確。現在來看看考生表達偏愛的句子中經常出現的一些錯誤以及正確的表達。用底線畫出的內容是不正確的。

考生作文中表達偏愛時常見的文法錯誤

有文法錯誤的句子	改正的句子
Given a choice, I <u>will</u> prefer to keep a pet.	Given a choice, I would prefer to keep a pet.
I <u>prefer to</u> be self-employed <u>other</u> than work for an employer.	I would prefer to be self-employed rather than work for an employer.

I would rather <u>a trip</u> to Seoul than to Tokyo.	I would rather take a trip to Seoul than to Tokyo.
I would prefer to <u>living</u> in a city.	I would prefer to live in a city.
I <u>prefer</u> working for a large company <u>than</u> a small one.	I would rather work for a large company than for a small one. or I prefer working for a large company to working for a small one.

考生應該儘量避免犯上述錯誤，記住正確的用法。

表達偏愛的策略

1. 措辭和句型要正確，記住本章中表達偏愛的句型和片語。特別注意何時用不定式（prefer to VERB），何時用動名詞形式（prefer VERBing），以及何時用動詞原形（I would rather VERB）。

2. 表達偏愛的作文中，要有兩個表達偏愛的句子，一個在第一段，另一個在最後一段。這兩種句型應該有所不同。

3. 如果寫作題目中包含情態動詞，例如：Would you prefer to be outdoors or indoors on vacation? 作文中就應該使用相同的情態動詞，即：On vacation I would prefer to stay indoors.

建立自己的寫作句型庫

1. VERBing certainly has its advantages
……確實有它的優勢之處。

Studying alone certainly has its advantages.

延伸說法 Living in the city certainly has its advantages.

2. For me, however, VERBing is definitely my preference.
但對我而言，我絕對比較喜歡……

For me, however, studying with a group of people is definitely my preference.

延伸說法 For me, however, working for myself is definitely my preference.

▶再練習一次！

學完高分範文、萬用寫作範本、高分策略和寫作句型庫，運用所學的技能修改你的初稿，並認真看修改之處。然後用學到的新句型去練習下面五道預測題的寫作。

1. Would you prefer to x or would you prefer to y...

> **Some people prefer to spend their free time outside. Other people prefer to spend their free time indoors. In your leisure time, would you prefer to be outdoors or would you prefer to be inside?**
> Use specific reasons and examples to explain your choice.

寫作構思

Energetic personalities
Indoors more chance to learn
Student life
Stress
Badminton
Hiking
Exceptions

高分範文 1 *Track 026*

As a university student, I spend most of my time indoors, taking classes and studying. These indoor activities can be very stressful, and so in the rare free time that I have, I choose to be outdoors whenever my schedule permits. No matter how busy I am, I try to find a way somehow to get fresh air.

During the week, I go to classes during the day and do homework in the evening. Still, I can usually squeeze in an outdoor activity before dinner. Sometimes, for example, I play badminton on the lawn just outside my dorm with a classmate. We hit birdies back and forth for about 45 minutes, even if the weather is cold or a little rainy. Afterwards, we feel more relaxed and can enjoy our cafeteria meal.

On weekends, when I have more time, I like to do outdoor activities like hiking and mountain climbing. Less than two hours away from Beijing by bus are many small mountains that one can climb. Not long ago I went with other members of my university's hiking club to a mountain near the Great Wall. The path was a little rough and it was hot outside, but I enjoyed looking at the scenery, and thinking about what it would have looked like thousands of years ago, when the Great Wall guards were there. By the time we got back to campus, even though we were all physically tired, we felt revitalized and ready to get back to our studies the next day.

Of course, I also have some indoor hobbies, such as reading novels and playing chess. However, during the school semester, because I spend so much time indoors, and am constantly reading books and articles for school, I don't really feel like reading during my spare time, even interesting novels. Perhaps after I finish my semester, I will change this way of thinking and do more indoor leisure activities.

托福總監評析

　　這道寫作題要求考生回答個人問題：In your leisure time, would you prefer to be outdoors or would you prefer to be inside? 這篇範文的結構非常完整。在第一段，考生描述了自己的個人情況，提供了背景。考生是一名大學生，大部分時間都在教室和圖書館裡唸書，因此在休閒時間，考生比較喜歡戶外活動。第二段和第三段分別講述了不同時間段的活動：平時和週末。在這兩段中，考生不僅描述了戶外活動，還描述了自己從事這些活動的感受（第二段中 more relaxed 和第三段中 revitalized）。因為平時和週末之間的邏輯聯繫，這幾段的承接非常流暢。在最後一段，考生提到其他幾項室內活動，先說 Of course, I also... ，但緊跟其後的是一個重新強調論點的論述：因為我在室內唸書的時間太多，所以休閒時間不太願意再呆在室內看書（However, during the school semester, because I spend so much time indoors... ）。以這種概述形式來總結非常不錯。最後一句談放假後自己的打算，這種多角度的陳述使全文的結構非常完整、緊湊。

---

2. Do you prefer x or do you prefer y...

> **Do you prefer to work on one project till it is finished or do you prefer to work on several projects at one time?**
> Use specific reasons and examples to support your answer.

寫作構思

> Achievement
> **Loose ends**
> **Anxiety**
> **Multi-tasking**
> Team projects
> Job assignments usually multiple projects

高分範文 2　　*Track 027*

In the interests of efficiency, I have tried to work on several projects simultaneously, but always found it difficult, if not impossible. I am accustomed to working on one project at a time. I don't know if I understand all the reasons why this is, but I will try to explain below.

For one thing, when I devote myself totally to one project, I can enjoy each little step I make towards its completion. I pay a lot of attention to detail and make sure I do each step correctly. In my eyes, each milestone is a small achievement. As time passes, I can see the project gradually taking shape and moving toward completion. I don't know that I would say "the process" is more important than the "outcome" of a project, but I am certainly a person who enjoys the process.

Another possible reason for my wanting to focus is that I am not very good with loose ends. I become anxious when I think about several projects waiting for me to do. Even a single project takes up much of my energy, because once a project is started, I tend to think about it all the time. I reflect on how to resolve the problems that have already presented themselves, how to approach the next step and what I need to do in terms of further research. These are the kind of unresolved "loose ends" that I face for one open project. With multiple open projects, there would just too many issues for one person to address.

In my heart, I know that it is good to be able to "multitask," to work on several projects at the same time. For example, if you hit a roadblock with a particular project, and work on something else for a while, when you go back to the original project, a solution becomes easier. In theory, I see the logic of this approach, which is why I have tried doing several projects at once. However, perhaps because I am a perfectionist at heart, working on one project at a time is still my first choice.

托福總監評析

因為這道寫作題問的是「你」（Do you prefer to work on a project...），所以範文中考生採用了自我反思的口吻，例如用到了如下句子：I don't know if I understand all the reasons why this is, but I will try to explain below. 這種句子非常適合這類寫作題。這種自我反思的口吻與客觀描述不同，後者更適用於非個人問題的話題，例如關於網際網路之類的社會問題。在第二段和第三段，考生從心理因素的角度陳述喜歡一次做一個項目的原因，解釋詳細且有説服力。從第一段提出論點直接過渡到原因，符合獨立寫作題評分準則中「統一性、漸進性和連貫性」的標準。最後一段呼應第一段：嘗試過同時做幾個項目，但還是傾向一次做一個項目。最後一句重申論點（working on one project at a time is still my first choice）和原因（perhaps because I am a perfectionist at heart），使結尾顯得生動有趣。

3. Do you think x or do you think y...

> Some people use Internet to gain information, while others think using it will lead to problems. Do you value the information on the Internet a lot or do you think the information on the Internet has problems?

寫作構思

Problems with inaccurate information
Self-publishing
Traditional sources
Who has responsibility?
Smart phones with Internet link
Depends on nature of information

Many people criticize the Internet for having bad information. Yet one might well ask, is there any source of information that will not lead to problems? I sincerely doubt it. In fact, it is not fair to say that a random piece of information on the Internet is of poorer quality than information in newspapers, or even many books. Consequently, we should not spend energy finding fault with this or that information source. Rather, we should train information users to make sure they are not misinformed, regardless of the source. Let us look at a few examples.

In centuries past, most technical information came to us from publishing organizations. Arguably, the most reliable sources of academic information have been professional journals, where articles have to go through blind reviews by experts in the same field. However, these publications tend to focus narrowly on new issues at the forefront of a discipline. The quality of this information is high, but the language is very technical. When reporters try to summarize these research findings, there are often distortions in fact. Indeed, for everyday people, the most common source of information has traditionally been news organizations. Yet people tend to forget that print media may not be accurate either. For example, at one time in United States history, newspapers were funded by political parties and were heavily biased in their political views. It was only in the last century that major newspapers realized that maintaining a relatively unbiased position was good for business. Even so, one can still argue that most newspapers are not entirely neutral.

Of course, the Internet is somewhat unique in that it is so easy for any individual to publish information. As a result, the world wide web is filled with information that is self-published. One can access academic journals and online newspapers on the Internet; however, the vast majority of information online has not been fact-checked by news editors or reviewed by experts.

In sum, the Internet is a valuable resource, but users must remember that the quality of information published by website hosts, bloggers and forum participants can range from excellent to garbage. Consequently, an information seeker using the Internet should exercise caution by consulting multiple sources and checking the background of the information provider. However, this information seeker should exercise this kind of rigorous approach, no matter what the information source is.

托福總監評析

　　該考生以質疑寫作題中的説法著手：Yet one might well ask, is there any source of information that will not lead to problems? 考生用這種方式表明自己的立場：我們應該擔心的不是資訊源頭。這一觀點反覆出現在第一段和最後一段。為了論證這一觀點，第二段和第三段指出專業雜誌和報紙等其他資訊源頭的問題。第四段轉向網際網路這一話題。考生認為網路比較特殊，一般情況下網際網路上的內容沒有經過編輯和專家的審核。最後一段重申論點，即網際網路是重要的資訊源頭，但資訊使用者要明白，資訊是否可靠是由資訊提供者決定的，所以使用網際網路資訊時要慎重。

---

4. Which would you do...

> **Your school has enough money to purchase either laptops for students or books for the library. Which should your school choose to buy — computers or books?**
> Use specific reasons and examples to support your recommendation.

寫作構思

> **Uses for laptops**
> **Uses for books**
> **Personal items**
> **Library**
> **Lab computers**
> Need to develop computer literacy
> Young people like computers

高分範文 4 *Track 029*

These days, the laptop computer has become a sort of personal item, similar to iPods and PDAs. Students expect to purchase their own laptops and do not need the university to provide them. Consequently, if my school had sufficient funds, it should acquire new books for the library.

The benefit of books is vast. No wonder, then, that the library collection is one of the defining characteristics of a great institution of learning. Because it is challenging to keep up with the pace of new scholarship, a school should do whatever it can to continually enlarge its collection. Moreover, there are few things more inspiring to students than a richly furnished library. Who can forget the first time he or she walked into a good university library? I, for one, clearly remember the awe I felt inside the large stone building filled with shelves and shelves of books. I made a vow then and there that before I graduated, I would spend a significant amount of time soaking up those books.

Granted, schools need computer facilities where students can go to do certain classroom tasks or research. Lab computers are a convenience for certain classes or for quick Internet sessions. For example, for a Fine Arts or Architecture class, the school may wish to purchase Mac laptops. In general, however, there is no real need for the university to purchase laptops now that most people have at least one laptop or tablet.

Books, on the other hand, are desperately needed to reflect ongoing scholarship in all sorts of disciplines. Reference works and professional journals are expensive, but serve as invaluable resources. In short, weighing the benefits of books versus computers, I think most people would agree that buying more books represents a better use of the available money.

托福總監評析

這道題要求考生談談自己學校應該為學生購買筆記型電腦還是購買書籍充實圖書館。可以有幾種論證方法：一種是論證某種投資為什麼是必要的或有價值的。第二種是論證另一項投資為什麼沒有必要或沒有價值。在上面這篇範文中，這兩種論證方法都用到了。第一段考生提出自己的觀點：手提電腦是私人物品，應該由學生自己購買。按照常規邏輯，考生接下來應該説書籍是更好的投資方式，而考生也真的就這麼做了。第二段描述圖書館藏書的現實意義，列舉了剛上大學時圖書館留給自己的深刻印象，以及自己在圖書館看過的書。第三段談到，某些情形下應該由學校購買電腦設備，但這些是屬於特殊情況。最後一段把論點換句話説，即學校很有必要購買不同學科的書籍來展現學術成就，並提到工具書和專業雜誌，使全文的論點更為完整。

5. Is it more important to x or to y...

Is it more important for students to understand general concepts or to learn specific facts?
Use specific reasons and examples to support your answer.

寫作構思

What are concepts?
How different from facts
Need facts in order to understand concepts
Inferences and judgments
Time and complexity
Example — Physics

高分範文 5　 *Track 030*

Both general concepts and specific facts are vital to human existence; we cannot live our lives without learning them. Facts are easily memorized and can be picked up by individuals throughout their lives. Concepts, on the other hand, are more complex and are better learned in a structured and systematic environment, such as a school. This essay will demonstrate what concepts are and why learning concepts is a priority for students.

We can define concepts loosely as mental representations of what things are and how things work. Conceptual frameworks are based on facts. Let us look at an example of a concept taken from Physics. The concept of gravity states that there is an attraction force between any two objects with mass. We can learn this concept by noting several facts. I will mention just two of these. Fact one: If we let go of a ball from our hand, it will fall to the ground. Essentially, one object, the ball, is pulled toward the other object, the Earth. Fact two: The Earth can maintain a stable orbit around the Sun because the Earth's centrifugal force (which would otherwise cause Earth to fly into space) is balanced by gravity (which pulls the Earth toward the Sun). To some people, such a discussion of gravity may seem complicated and a bit difficult to comprehend. Indeed, this illustrates my point. Concepts are not easily absorbed. Learning them requires time, practice and many examples to see how the concepts can be applied.

This is why most of the fundamental concepts, especially those in basic sciences such as Physics and Chemistry, are taught in school. Yet there are other many important concepts as well; for example, concepts related to Philosophy and Ethics. We do not wait till we have finished our formal education to start studying these. Moral concepts and the ideals of the Humanities are first taught to us at home, and reinforced in elementary school and beyond.

As we can see, it is more important for students to spend time learning concepts than memorizing isolated facts. Concepts are complex and are probably more important to our success in the workplace and in life. As for facts, we should not worry too much about memorizing hundreds of them in school, because there is always time to acquire more facts later on.

托福總監評析

　　為了說明概念和事實哪個對學生更重要這個問題，這篇文章匠心獨具，提出概念的定義，並舉了一個詳細的物理概念為例。第一段先對事實和概念進行了比較，而在該段最後一句，考生陳述了自己的觀點，並告知讀者下文接下來要講的內容：This essay will demonstrate what concepts are and why learning concepts is a priority for students. 第二段介紹了概念的定義並以重力這一概念為例。第三段講述學校教授基礎學科的原因。最後一段把論點換句話說（As we can see, it is more important for students to spend time learning concepts than isolated facts.），並指出生活和職場中掌握概念的重要意義。

....

建立自己的寫作句型庫

1. **[TIME PHRASE], when I have more time, I like to do x like VERBing and VERBing.**
   時間充裕的話，我喜歡做……，例如……和……

   On weekends, when I have more time, I like to do outdoor activities like hiking and mountain climbing.

   延伸說法 In the evening, when I have more time, I like to do sports like swimming and running.

2. **I don't know if I understand all the reasons why this is, but I will try to VERB below.**
   我不確定自己是否明白這件事的所有原因，但我會在下文中嘗試……

   I don't know if I understand all the reasons why this is, but I will try to explain below.

   延伸說法 I don't know if I understand all the reasons why this is, but I will try to give some examples below.

3. **Another possible reason for my wanting to VERB is that I am not very good with x**
   我想做……的另一個原因可能是我不太擅長……

   Another possible reason for my wanting to focus is that I am not very good with loose ends.

   延伸說法 Another possible reason for my wanting to work for myself is that I am not very good with bureaucracy.

4. **In theory, I see the logic of this approach, which is why I have tried VERBing**
   從理論上講，我明白這種方法的合理性，這也是我之所以嘗試……的原因

   In theory, I see the logic of this approach, which is why I have tried doing several projects at once.

   延伸說法 In theory, I see the logic of this approach, which is why I have tried spending time in a large group.

5. **Yet one might well ask, is there any x that will not lead to problems?**
   但很可能有人會問，有哪個……不會引發問題嗎？

Yet one might well ask, is there any source of information that will not lead to problems?

延伸說法 Yet one might well ask, is there any means of transportation that will not lead to problems?

6. Of course, x is somewhat unique in that it is…
當然，因為……，所以它有點獨特

Of course, the Internet is somewhat unique in that it is so easy for any individual to publish information.

延伸說法 Of course, a foreign movie is somewhat unique in that it is able to take you on a distant trip.

7. Consequently, if my school had sufficient funds, it should VERB
因此，如果我的學校有充足的資金，它應該……

Consequently, if my school had sufficient funds, it should acquire new books for the library.

延伸說法 Consequently, if my school had sufficient funds, it should invest in state-of-the-art computers.

8. The benefit of x is vast.
……大有裨益。

The benefit of books is vast.

延伸說法 The benefit of travel is vast.

9. No wonder, then, that x is one of the defining characteristics of y
那麼，……成為……的明顯特徵不足為奇

No wonder, then, that the library collection is one of the defining characteristics of a great institution of learning.

延伸說法 No wonder, then, that the ability to plan well is one of the defining characteristics of a good leader.

10. In general, however, there is no real need for x to VERB now that most people VERB
然而，一般來說，現在既然絕大多數人都……，對……就沒有真正需求

In general, however, there is no real need for the university to purchase laptops now that most people have at least one laptop or tablet.

延伸說法 In general, however, there is no real need for teachers to write on the blackboard now that most people have access to the PowerPoint notes.

11. In short, weighing the benefits of x versus y, I think most people would agree that VERBing x represents a better use of the available money.

總之，在權衡……和……的優勢時，我認為絕大多數人會認同……

In short, weighing the benefits of books versus computers, I think most people would agree that buying more books represents a better use of the available money.

> **延伸說法** In short, weighing the benefits of a museum versus a sports gymnasium, I think most people would agree that building a gymnasium represents a better use of the available money.

12. This essay will demonstrate what x are and why learning x is a priority for students.

本文會說明……的概念，學生優先要學習……的原因。

This essay will demonstrate what concepts are and why learning concepts is a priority for students.

> **延伸說法** This essay will demonstrate what the Internet is and why learning how to use the Internet is a priority for students.

13. As we can see, it is more important for x to spend time VERBing than VERBing

正如我們所見，花時間……比……花時間……更為重要

As we can see, it is more important for students to spend time learning concepts than memorizing isolated facts.

> **延伸說法** As we can see, it is more important for teachers to spend time motivating students than giving exams.

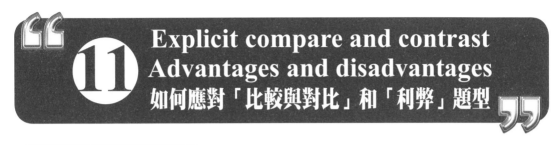

Explicit compare and contrast
Advantages and disadvantages
如何應對「比較與對比」和「利弊」題型

在本章，你將學到……

★ 如何有條理地表述事物的利弊

解讀常考題

　　「比較與對比」題型和「利弊」題型的相似之處在於它們都明確要求考生比較或對比兩種不同的事物。題目有時要求考生比較兩個事物的優點，有時要求考生比較某個事物的利弊。有些題目要求考生談自己的觀點。有時則不作要求。

　　要想取得這類作文題的高分，考生需要有條理地論述被比較的事物。在比較題中，不論題目要求是什麼，考生都得一步一步進行有條理的比較。這類作文相對比較正式，但結構更複雜。

　　要求進行比較或對比的題目有多種形式，下面是出現頻率最高的形式：

1. Compare the advantages of x with the advantages of y.
2. Compare the contributions of x to society with the contributions of y to society. Which type of contribution is valued more?
3. Compare the different kinds of x you could use to travel. Which one is best?
4. Compare these two choices: ... Which one do you prefer?
5. Compare your friend's two choices and explain which one you think your friend should choose.
6. Compare the advantages of these two different ways of VERBing. Which one do you prefer?
7. Compare the advantages and disadvantages of VERBing.
8. Compare and contrast x [knowledge] gained from experience with x gained from books. Which is more important?

　　現在看一則例子，該題明確要求考生比較事物的優點和缺點。

▶模擬試題①

　　閱讀以下的短文並聆聽講座，完成以下這道作文題目。

Directions:

Read the question below. You have 30 minutes to plan, write, and revise your essay. Typically, an effective response will contain a minimum of 300 words.

> The government has announced that it plans to build a new multilane highway near where you live. Compare the advantages and disadvantages of living near this project. What is your view of this project? Give details to support your opinion.

這道寫作題要求考生比較住在多車道公路邊的利弊。考生可以寫自己的個人偏愛；也可以保持中立，給出客觀的分析。但為了保證上下文的連貫，考生需要把自己提到的幾方面利弊融合到作文的論點中。

▶ Exercise 1

根據上面例題的題目要求寫一篇作文。初稿完成後，繼續學習下部分的內容。仔細研讀高分範文、萬用寫作範本、高分策略和寫作句型庫，運用所學的新知識完成 Exercise 2。

寫作構思

Advantages:
Good when region gets government money
Can visit friends in other part of city
Convenient if commuting to other towns
Convenient to get to airport
Profitable if near exit and zoning allows you to run a business — gas station or restaurant
Disadvantages:
Encourages people to use private cars instead of subway (gridlock)
Easier for dangerous people to come by
Noise from cars and trucks moving at fast speeds at all hours
Pollution from exhaust pipes
Property values may go down if you are residential

高分範文　 *Track 031*

Cities and towns must routinely upgrade their road systems. As part of that upgrade, the road authorities in rapidly developing areas often construct multilane highways that cut through or nearby the city itself. For city residents, there are advantages and disadvantages to living near a new multilane highway.

Among the benefits of living near a large highway is the convenience of being able to hop onto a main road right away, without having to spend time in local traffic. This is a distinct advantage if a person commutes by car to another town because the commuter can quickly access the highway and get going. Being near to a major highway is also very convenient when the person is going to the airport, since most highways connect to the airport highway. Finally, if one owns property on land that is near a future highway, and if the zoning laws permit commercial establishments, it might be possible for a person to open a restaurant or a gas station that would attract travelers.

Of course, there are significant disadvantages to having a multilane highway near one's home. The noise made at all hours of the day and night by speeding cars and trucks harms the quality of life. Even if noise walls are built along the road, the sounds are still very annoying to residents. A related problem caused by highways is the pollution that comes from exhaust pipes and the litter that gets thrown out of moving vehicles. If a person owns a home in a residential area bordering the new highway, it is likely that the property value of that residence will go down, since no one will want to buy a home near a noisy highway.

My point of view on this issue would depend on whether I was a renter or a homeowner. If a highway was planned to run by my area where I was renting, I might not mind. The construction process for the highway would probably be a nuisance, however, and so I might choose to move away from the construction area. If, however, I owned property and a highway was planned, I would be extremely unhappy. Although the government usually pays residents when the highway goes right through where their house is, the government does not compensate a property owner if the highway is just "nearby." That would be very unfortunate.

萬用模板

[用兩三個句子介紹背景資訊]. For [涉及的人], there are advantages and disadvantages to _____.

Among the benefits of _____ is the convenience of being able to _____, without having to _____. This is a distinct advantage if a person _____. _____ is also very convenient when the person is _____, since _____.

Finally, if one _____, and if _____, it might be possible for a person to _____.

Of course, there are significant disadvantages to having _____. [用一個句子來陳述第一個「弊」]. Even if [處理第一個「弊」的措施], _____ are still very annoying to [涉及的人]. A related problem caused by _____ is [第二個「弊」]. If a person _____, it is likely that [第三個「弊」], since _____.

My point of view on this issue would depend on whether I was _____ or _____. If _____, I might not mind. If, however, [一個不利因素], I would be extremely unhappy. [用一個句子來解釋上面的問題]. That would be very unfortunate.

　　這篇範文的開頭先是多車道公路的背景資訊：As part of that upgrade, the road authorities in rapidly developing areas often construct multilane highways that cut through or nearby the city itself. 考生還敘述了題目要求：For city residents, there are advantages and disadvantages to living near a new multilane highway. 這有助於幫助讀者（評分人）理解論點的展開。這篇範文分層次來比較利和弊。第二段是第一個層次，考生列舉了住在多車道公路附近的三個優勢。第二個層次在第三段，考生列舉了住在多車道公路附近的三個弊端。在第四段總結段，考生陳述了自己的觀點：住在多車道公路附近的利弊取決於自己是房客還是房主。這一觀點非常明確，評分人一看便知，因為在談利和弊的段落中考生已經提到了公路會影響房產所有權和房產價值。

　　這篇範文將近 400 個單字，比較型寫作題的長度通常是如此，因為進行有條理的比較，其步驟相對複雜，寫作時間也會長一些。

有條理地進行比較

1. 寫作中進行有條理的比較需要三個簡單的步驟

　　1）認真閱讀題目，準確理解題目要求比較的內容，看清楚題目是否要求陳述自己的觀點。
　　2）確定作文結構是用模組法還是逐點法（下面會說明），並列表或畫圖。
　　3）先寫一篇連貫的作文，包括所有的比較點，如有要求，再陳述自己的觀點。

2. 進行比較的兩種寫作方式

　　比較事物的作文，如果想做到條理清晰，可以有兩種組織分論點的方法：
　　模組法（A block approach）
　　逐點法（A point-by-point approach）
　　兩種方法都可以用來強調相同點、並對比不同點或相同點。這兩種方法各有優點，但我們要記得，新托福考試獨立寫作題是一篇不超過 400 個單字的文章，寫作時間是 30 分鐘，所以通常模組法比較實用。當寫作題涉及考生個人觀點時，模組法更有利於寫作，因為考生需要迅速涵蓋各種觀點以寫出有說服力的總結段。

模組法

　　在模組法中，考生通常把所有特點都歸到一個段落裡。如果想強調某一論點，考生可以另起一段。右頁的例子摘自前面的範文，兩個「模組」分別是住在多車道公路附近的利與弊。

第一段	提出論點，陳述或暗指自己的想法。
利（第二段）	1. Quick access for commuters to other towns 2. Quick access to the airport 3. Property owners can open a restaurant or a gas station

	1. Noise 2. Pollution 3. Depreciation of house value
弊（第三段）	
總結段	以換句話説的方式重申論點。

逐點法

在逐點法中，考生選擇事物的兩個特點（如果時間充裕的話，可以多選一些特點）。有了這些特點才能逐一比較兩個事物，每一個特點自成一段。下面的例子摘自下文預測題的第五篇範文，文中對比了虛擬網路課程和真實課程，兩個特點是 efficiency 和 soft skills。

第一段	提出論點，陳述或暗指自己的想法。	
	Online Virtual Lectures	**Lectures in Classroom**
Efficiency （第二段）	① Don't have to go to class; takes less time ② Better retention of facts due to focus	① Classes sometimes large, distracting ② Have to spend time going to class in all sorts of weather
Soft Skills （第三段）	① Not easily developed through virtual lecture ② "Hard skills" more of a strength of virtual lectures	① Interactions promote interpersonal skills, communication ② Teachers inspire students
總結段	以換句話説的形式重申論點。	

3. 並列比較

不論作文運用哪種組織方法，考生一定要進行並列比較。但一些考生在進行並列比較的時候，句子會出現文法錯誤。最常見的錯誤有：

Life in the country is different from the city.

The speed of trains is faster than cars.

為了讓比較並列，句子應改正為：

Life in the country is different from life in the city.

The speed of trains is faster than the speed of cars.

或者，在第二處，用 that 來代替：

Life in the country is different from that in the city.

The speed of trains is faster than that of cars.

為了使比較事物的作文顯得有條理，可運用以下策略

1. 認真閱讀寫作題目，知道要比較什麼內容。
2. 注意是否需要給出自己的觀點。
3. 確定使用模組法還是逐點法。一般而言，出於時間考慮，模組法效果更好。
4. 當考生確定自己選擇的事物更具有整體優勢後，直接運用模組法進行比較。如果考生想對比兩件事物時，使用逐點法，但該方法比較耗費時間。
5. 迅速列出論點或特點，例如優缺點、利弊等。
6. 要比較的事物在句型結構上是並列的。
7. 如果對比兩個事物，可以先提一提相似之處，這樣的表述更有說服力。
8. 在模組法中，先寫不同意觀點，這會使下文包含同意觀點的段落更有說服力。
9. 如果使用逐點法，一定不要多次重複論點。重複過多，評分人會給低分。
10. 不論使用哪種方法，結論都要簡短有力，不要逐一重複所有的論據。相反，要選擇最突出的點進行總結。

建立自己的寫作句型庫

1. For x, there are advantages and disadvantages to VERBing
對於……而言，……有利也有弊

For city residents, there are advantages and disadvantages to living near a new multilane highway.

延伸說法 For commuters, there are advantages and disadvantages to having a car.

2. Among the benefits of x is the convenience of being able to VERB, without having to VERB
……的好處之一便是有……的便利，無須……

Among the benefits of living near a large highway is the convenience of being able to hop onto a main road right away, without having to spend time in local traffic.

延伸說法 Among the benefits of e-mail is the ability to give someone a message, without having to interrupt him or her.

3. Of course, there are significant disadvantages to having x
當然，……也會有明顯的缺點

Of course, there are significant disadvantages to having a multilane highway near one's home.

延伸說法 Of course, there are significant disadvantages to having a large group of tourists with you all the time.

4. My point of view on this issue would depend on whether I was x or y
我對此事的觀點則要看我……

My point of view on this issue would depend on whether I was a renter or a homeowner.

延伸說法 My point of view on this issue would depend on whether I was traveling to a city or the countryside.

▶再練習一次！

學完高分範文、萬用寫作範本、高分策略和寫作句型庫，運用所學的技能修改你的初稿，並認真看修改之處。然後用學到的新句型去練習下面五道預測題的寫作。

▶寫作預測題

1. Compare the advantages and disadvantages of...

There are many modes of transportation that carry people from one destination to another. Compare the advantages and disadvantages of traveling by train.
Use specific details in your discussion.

寫作構思

Advantages:
Comfort
Fewer check-in, security and boarding procedures
Scenic views
Dining car
More civilized
Disadvantages:
Slow for long distances
Not possible for travel of oceans
May get seated in cars with loud people
Too bumpy
No flexibility

高分範文 1 *Track 032*

In the modern world, there are many ways to get from one place to another. All forms of transportation seek to leverage new technologies, and rail travel is no exception. Nonetheless, like all modes of travel, train travel has advantages and disadvantages.

On the positive side, train travel is extremely comfortable compared to other forms of travel, including car and plane travel. The seats are large and passengers can get up and walk around. During long trips, if a traveler can reserve a sleeper car, it is possible to get a good night's rest. Another advantage of train travel is the relatively easy boarding procedure. Unlike train passengers, airplane passengers need to report very early and go through lengthy security checks.

Perhaps the best part of riding on trains is the ability to look out the windows at the scenery. Depending on the route, a train may pass through mountains, rivers and farmland. Many people think this aspect of train travel is very soothing, and even romantic.

Yet train travel is not well suited for all trips. The most obvious drawback of trains is the inability to cross large stretches of water. Although trains can travel on bridges across large rivers and even bays, there is no way to go across oceans. Another downside to train travel is that it can take a very long time, especially if one is traveling a great distance. This length of time is due to the fact that trains often stop in roundabout places. For example, a train from New York to Chicago can take anywhere from nine hours to twenty hours, depending on the route. A plane takes less than three hours.

Additionally, one of the most annoying characteristics of train travel is the possibility of being confined in a train car with loud and obnoxious people. If you are unlucky, you may end up spending hours and hours in close proximity to some very rude people, who keep talking or singing. If this situation arises, it won't matter how comfortable the seats are or how beautiful the scenery is.

托福總監評析

　　和多車道公路的寫作題一樣，這道寫作題要求考生比較火車旅行的利與弊。注意這道題沒有要求考生陳述個人偏愛及原因。搞清楚這一點非常重要，因為考生可以集中時間在作文主體部分進行詳細的比較。

....

2. Compare the advantages of... with... Which would you choose?

> **Some students like to live on campus in dormitories, while others like to rent apartments off campus. Compare the advantages of living in a dormitory with the advantages of living in an off-campus apartment. Which would you choose? Give reasons for your preference.**

寫作構思

On-campus dormitory:
Closer to classrooms; can sleep late and get to class on time
Can eat buffets
Cafeteria is nearby
Being part of social events on campus
Resident Assistant looks out for you
Off-campus apartment:
More freedom and privacy
Less gossip
Can make decor cozier

> **More living space for less money**
> **Quieter atmosphere**

高分範文 2　 *Track 033*

Nowadays, many college students are considering staying in housing off campus, especially at universities where dormitory space is limited. The decision is not always an easy one, since there are advantages to both dormitories and apartments.

One advantage of living in a campus dormitory is convenience. Most dorms are located very close to classroom buildings, which means students can sleep in later in the morning. They also will be able to save time and money on transportation to and from class, since they won't need a bicycle, a bus or a car. In dormitory living, meals are also more convenient as most dorms are located right next to student dining halls. Finally, students who live in dormitories, especially underclassmen, have a richer social life because dorms are the hub of social activity, sponsoring quite a few formal and informal events every week.

Yet, as mentioned above, living off campus in a rental apartment also has perks. First and foremost, the atmosphere in an apartment is quite calm. There are fewer people coming and going; this allows a student to have more privacy. Moreover, because there are fewer interruptions, students can focus on their reading and their term papers, and so can be very efficient.

My personal choice would be to live in a university dormitory during my freshman year, and to live off campus in an apartment from my second year on. That way, I could make many new friends in the dormitory, not have to worry about cooking meals and become familiar with university activities. Then, for the next three years, I would rent an inexpensive apartment with a few classmates. Hopefully, the apartment would not be too far away from my classrooms; otherwise, I would have to use my bicycle or come up with some other transportation. At that point, I could work hard in my own space instead of having to find someplace else to study. If I wanted to socialize, my roommates and I could always invite people over to parties on the weekend. Whether the apartment was quiet or full of people would be up to me, as I would have control over my living environment.

托福總監評析

　　這道題要求先比較兩個事物的優點，再談自己的選擇。不論在內容還是語言上，比較學生兩種住宿形式的「利」並不是很難。和第 10 章許多寫作題一樣，這道題目包含 Some people like to VERB, while others like to VERB 這類片語。但這道題目明確要求考生比較兩種事物的「利」，因此考生應關注「利」，而不是「弊」。當然，順便提一提「弊」也是可以的。

該範文的第一段使用了新聞式的引導句，説越來越多的學生傾向住在校外。第二段寫住校內宿舍的優點；第三段則説明住在校外公寓的優點。總結段總結了第二段和第三段的要點，提出自己的觀點：第一年住在校內宿舍，接下來的三年住在校外公寓。

....

3. Compare two choices and explain which one your friend should choose.

> **Your friend has received some money and plans to use all of it to take a trip or to buy a car. Your friend asks you for advice. Compare your friend's two choices and explain which one you think your friend should choose.**
> Use specific reasons and details to support your recommendation.

寫作構思

> **Negatives of car:**
> **City traffic**
> **Parking**
> Friend doesn't know how to drive
> **Positives of car:**
> Friend wants car for commuting
> **Positives of vacation:**
> **Learn new things**
> **Experiences will shape individual**

 高分範文 3 *Track 034*

Whenever we give advice, it is a big responsibility. To counsel my friend about whether to use his gift money for a car or a trip, I would first try to understand his situation. Barring any special circumstances, I would recommend that he take a trip and persuade him with the following arguments.

On the surface, a car may seem like a better investment: It is a material possession and a status symbol. Perhaps he might be able to use it on weekends. Yet the reality is that buying a car just doesn't seem practical for my friend, and so is a poor choice. For one thing, my friend is a student and doesn't need a car to get to class. Moreover, driving a car within the city is not efficient because the traffic is always a nightmare. On the other hand, if my friend puts the money he has received toward a special trip, he will be investing in himself.

Why is this true? For one thing, during his excursion he will be able to see distant places first-hand and learn about the people and customs there. For example, if he chooses to travel to Southern Europe, he can learn about the rich Mediterranean culture and the people there. He will be able to taste fresh ocean fish seasoned with olive oil. No doubt he will also learn some expressions in French, Spanish, Italian and Greek.

In addition, my friend will accumulate unforgettable experiences and memories. These will all integrate into his identity. That is to say, for the rest of his life, these experiences will open his horizons, influencing how he thinks and how he perceives the world.

I would present the above arguments to my friend and encourage him to quickly choose a great destination for the coming summer. For a long trip, it is important for him to go now, before he gets tied up with a full-time job.

托福總監評析

這道寫作題要求考生比較一個朋友的兩種選擇，並給出建議。第一段先說需要全面瞭解朋友的情況後方可提出建議，然後說若沒有特殊情況，建議朋友去旅行。第二段寫得非常好，先陳述擁有轎車的好處，然後說朋友目前並不需要車，最後，談完朋友不需要車的原因後，建議選擇旅行。第三段和第四段詳述旅行對朋友的益處。總結段非常簡短，因為作文主體部分已經給出了非常有說服力的論據。為了讓結論更有趣，考生還提了一個建議：For a long trip, it is important for him to go now, before he gets tied up with a full-time job.

....

4. Compare two views. Which view do you agree with?

Some people believe that young people spend too much time trying to plan things that are out of their control. Other people believe that careful planning is essential for people who want to control their professional lives. Compare these two views on life planning. Which view do you agree with?

Use specific reasons to support your answer.

寫作構思

Anti-planning view:
World is changing, can't predict
Obsession with control creates stress
Depends on personality of person
Pro-planning view:
Many professions, so research needed
Don't know what skills needed
Only irresponsible people don't plan

高分範文 4 *Track 035*

I recently spoke to a retired man who told me there were lots of opportunities for his generation, but few for my generation. This man never created a master career plan. He started several businesses and became very wealthy. After talking to him, I began to wonder whether careful planning was necessary to succeed in one's professional life.

Long-term career planning seems almost impossible in this day and age because there are so many unexpected developments. Every time the economy goes up and down, certain jobs are added or eliminated. For example, manufacturing jobs, finance jobs, and IT jobs are in flux. If one cannot predict the future, why plan for it?

Another reason young people might not want to spend time on detailed planning is that they can easily become obsessed about developing the "perfect" plan. Trying to achieve complete control over one's career through planning is impossible and causes stress. Young people should realize that there will always be "surprises" in life.

Yet there are also people who say planning has become indispensable in this era. There are many diverse careers available these days, with new fields and jobs emerging every day. Thus, unless students spend time researching various professions, they won't know which opportunities suit them best. The chances of us stumbling onto the right career are slim.

A related argument for life planning is the need for young people to know what skills will be needed for their chosen profession. Different careers require different skill sets. While some skills can be acquired on the job, many take a long time to develop. Communication skills are one such example. In today's highly competitive job market, successful job candidates need to start identifying and honing career skills early on.

It is not easy to plan because of the unknowns in our lives. However, my personal view is that nowadays young people should plan carefully. Even though we cannot know exactly what will happen, the core skills of many jobs are predictable. Those who can plan ahead will be much better equipped to meet the requirements of their chosen field and rewarded with a better future.

托福總監評析

　　這道寫作題要求考生比較兩種觀點並表達個人意見。在第一段，考生用一個退休人士的故事引出話題：After talking to him, I began to wonder whether careful planning was necessary to succeed in one's professional life. 這個句子很自然地引出下面幾段贊同及反對職業規劃的論據。在總結段，考生表達了自己的觀點：儘管生活中充滿了不確定的因素，但年輕人還是應該提前做好職業規劃。

5. Compare and contrast... with... Which is better?

> **Compare and contrast the education gained through online virtual lectures with the education gained through lectures in a physical classroom. Which is better?**
> Use reasons and specific details to explain your choice.

寫作構思

Virtual lectures:
Efficiency
Retention of information
Lower tuition
Traditional classroom lectures:
Interactions
Personal bonds with teachers
Relationships that help us after school
Teachers like traditional classroom better
Online courses get watered down so not respected

高分範文 5 *Track 036*

Webcasts and other virtual lectures delivered to one's home or dormitory through computers have become increasingly common at universities. In fact, many first-year classes are offered only through virtual lectures. Studies have examined student learning in virtual lectures and traditional classroom lectures and have found that both types of lecture have positive effects on learning. Moreover, in many ways, the new online virtual lectures are better than traditional lectures. Even so, virtual lectures cannot replace all the benefits of traditional classroom lectures, as I will explain below.

In terms of efficiency, virtual lectures are clearly superior to traditional classroom lectures. For one thing, students taking virtual courses do not have to get up early to go to class. Whereas students attending a lecture in a physical classroom have to navigate through rainy and snowy weathers, virtual lecture students can simply log onto their computers. Another way in which virtual lectures are relatively efficient is the fact that students are usually more focused while they are looking at the online lecture. This is in contrast to the relatively lax focus of the students sitting in large traditional lecture halls, where they can easily become bored or distracted by other students.

However, one way in which virtual lectures cannot compete with classroom lectures is in the ability to teach students "soft skills." Soft skills include interpersonal skills and critical reasoning skills, all very important for a student's career success. Students can't learn these important skills on a computer because a virtual lecture does not readily accommodate interaction among students, or between students and the teacher. In contrast, a traditional classroom enables a teacher to literally reach out to learners in real time. Furthermore, in the classroom, it is easier for teachers to be a source of inspiration, to diagnose potential problems and to foster personal growth.

From the above, it is clear that both modes of lecturing can be effective teaching platforms. Nevertheless, I personally believe that education in the traditional classroom is superior. While virtual lectures may be more efficient for teaching "hard skills," classroom lectures enrich a student by offering opportunities for social and intellectual interaction. Education is not just learning facts, it is also learning about people.

托福總監評析

　　因為寫作題要求考生進行比較和對比，所以這篇作文採用的是逐點法。在第一段，考生說虛擬網路課程和傳統實體課程都各有優點。從某些方面來說，虛擬網路課程比較好一些，但它不能代替傳統實體課程。這基本上就是本文的論點。第二段比較虛擬網路課程和傳統實體課程的效率。第三段則在學生「軟技巧」（soft skills）的學習方面對兩種課堂進行比較。在總結段，考生重述論點，聲明自己更傾向於傳統實體課堂。

建立自己的寫作句型庫

1. **Nonetheless, like all modes of travel, x travel has advantages and disadvantages.**

   但是，……旅行跟其他所有旅行模式一樣，也是有利有弊的。

   Nonetheless, like all modes of travel, train travel has advantages and disadvantages.

   延伸說法 Nonetheless, like all modes of travel, air travel has advantages and disadvantages.

2. **On the positive side, x travel is extremely ADJECTIVE compared to other forms of travel, including y and z travel.**

   從正面來看，同其他方式的旅行（包括 y 和 z）相比，……旅行非常……

   On the positive side, train travel is extremely comfortable compared to other forms of travel, including car and plane travel.

   延伸說法 On the positive side, car travel is extremely flexible compared to other forms of travel, including bus and train travel.

3. **Unlike x passengers, y passengers need to VERB**

   與……乘客不同，……乘客需要……

   Unlike train passengers, airplane passengers need to report very early and go through lengthy security checks.

   延伸說法 Unlike air passengers, car passengers need to stop and get gas.

4. The most obvious drawback of x is the inability to VERB
……最明顯的劣勢便是它無法……

The most obvious drawback of trains is the inability to cross large stretches of water.

延伸說法 The most obvious drawback of living in a dorm is the inability to cook.

5. Another downside to x is that…, especially if one is...
另一個不便之處就是……，尤其如果你……

Another downside to train travel is that it can take a very long time, especially if one is traveling a great distance.

延伸說法 Another downside to buying a car is that there are many additional costs, especially if one has to pay for parking.

6. The decision is not always an easy one, since there are advantages to both x and y
因為……和……各有優勢，從中做出決定並非易事

The decision is not always an easy one, since there are advantages to both dormitories and apartments.

延伸說法 The decision is not always an easy one, since there are advantages to both virtual online lectures and classroom lectures.

7. One advantage of VERBing is….
……的優勢之一是……

One advantage of living in a campus dormitory is convenience.

延伸說法 One advantage of building a new museum is the ability to attract tourists.

8. Yet, as mentioned above, x also has perks.
但是，如上文所述，……也有好的地方。

Yet, as mentioned above, living off campus in a rental apartment also has perks.

延伸說法 Yet, as mentioned above, traveling abroad also has perks.

9. To counsel my friend about whether to VERB, I would first try to understand his situation.
為了給朋友提供……建議，我要先瞭解他的情況。

To counsel my friend about whether to use his gift money for a car or a trip, I would first try to understand his situation.

延伸說法 To counsel my friend about whether to buy a car, I would first try to understand his situation.

10. On the other hand, if my friend puts the money he has received toward x, he will be investing in himself.

另一方面，如果我的朋友將自己的收入用於……，那麼他便是在自我投資。

On the other hand, if my friend puts the money he has received toward a special trip, he will be investing in himself.

延伸說法 On the other hand, if my friend puts the money he has received toward overseas travel, he will be investing in himself.

11. I would present the above arguments to my friend and encourage him to VERB

我將用上述觀點來勸說朋友，鼓勵他……

I would present the above arguments to my friend and encourage him to quickly choose a great destination for the coming summer.

延伸說法 I would present the above arguments to my friend and encourage him to find an internship position at a bank.

12. x seems almost impossible in this day and age because…

在現代，……似乎是幾乎不可能的，因為……

Long-term career planning seems almost impossible in this day and age because there are so many unexpected developments.

延伸說法 Restoring historic buildings seems almost impossible in this day and age because of the demand for prime real estate.

13. However, my personal view is that nowadays x should VERB

可是，我個人認為在現在……應該……

However, my personal view is that nowadays young people should plan carefully.

延伸說法 However, my personal view is that nowadays city planners should preserve historic buildings.

14. In terms of x, y are clearly superior to z

……在……方面明顯優於……

In terms of efficiency, virtual lectures are clearly superior to traditional classroom lectures.

延伸說法 In terms of cost, bus travel is clearly superior to air travel.

15. This is in contrast to x in y, where they can easily become ADJECTIVE

這與……的……相反，……很容易就……

This is in contrast to the relatively lax focus of the students sitting in large traditional lecture halls, where they can easily become bored or distracted by other students.

延伸說法 This is in contrast to the long hours of a high-paying job in a corporation, where they can easily become exhausted.

16. However, one way in which x cannot compete with y is in the ability to VERB
可是，在……方面，……與……無法相提並論

However, one way in which virtual lectures cannot compete with classroom lectures is in the ability to teach students "soft skills."

延伸說法 However, one way in which the old generation cannot compete with younger generation is in the ability to use new technologies.

17. Nevertheless, I personally believe that x is superior.
但我個人認為……更好。

Nevertheless, I personally believe that education in the traditional classroom is superior.

延伸說法 Nevertheless, I personally believe that handmade items are superior.

"What": What changes What skills 如何應對 What 題型

在本章，你將學到……

★如何組織 What 題型作文的篇章結構
★怎麼寫好作文第一段

解讀常考題

獨立寫作題中會有很多 What 題型。這種題型大多會考你一些人事物應該具有什麼樣的特徵或特點，例如好老闆、好鄰居、好朋友、好父母、好兒子或好女兒等應具有什麼樣的特徵。還有一種 What 題型是問從事某些職業的人群需要哪些技能。

另一種 What 題型會問考生一些抽象的問題，例如考生如何看待某一類話題或者為了實現某個目標他們會怎麼做。這種題目和 agree / disagree 寫作題型有相似之處，但有一個很大的區別：What 題型是開放性的，考生不需要二選一，而是要進行自由闡述。

大部分 What 題型都是開放性的，但有一小部分 What 題型會包含幾個和話題相關的例子來幫助闡明語境，例如：

What quality is most important for success in life (for example, honesty, a sense of humor, intelligence)?

在給出例子的 what 題中，考生可以不從給出的例子裡挑選寫作素材。考生可以選擇自己想討論的任何特點，例如毅力。給出例子只是為了幫助考生理解題目意思，並不是給出一個寫作範圍。

某些開放性的題目會有難度，有些考生可能不知道該寫什麼內容。如何解決這一難題呢？

1. 看題目，列提綱（用母語或者英語都可以）。例如，你個人可能認為「朋友」需要具備以下特徵：loyal、understanding、generous、a good-listener 和 sensitive。然後，選其中幾個特徵來寫，看看哪一個特徵更容易寫出來。

2. 不要逐字背誦別人寫的範文，一定要加入自己的經歷。沒有個性化的作文是得不到高分的。

3. 要自信，還要有想像力！切記，在這種寫作類型裡，沒有標準的答案或寫法。

包含 what、why 或 how 的開放性寫作題的篇章結構可以按照以下來組織：
Specific（具體的）→ **General**（概括的）→ **Specific**（具體的）→ **General**（概括的）

利用這種方法，考生應在第一段給出問題的具體答案，例如可以說：To me, the most important quality in a friend is that she be generous. 在概括部分，要概括說明 generosity 對自己表示什麼，為什麼它很重要，例如：In give-and-take relationships, such as friendships, and even marriage, generosity of spirit is the foundation. 在接下來的分論點段落，考生可以給出有關慷慨（或缺乏慷慨）的具體例子來說明其重要性。最後，總結段概括並總結觀點，補充其他特徵，例如：As I have described above, when people are willing to make sacrifices for one another, it is a true sign of friendship. Selfish people are not going to keep friends very long.

另一種篇章結構的組織方式是：

General（概括的）→ **Specific**（具體的）→ **General**（概括的）

在這種結構中，考生在第一段陳述自己的觀點前，要先總體概述。下面這篇關於植物的高分範文就是用這種方法。

▶ 模擬試題①

閱讀以下的短文並聆聽講座，完成以下這道作文題。

Directions:

Read the question below. You have 30 minutes to plan, write, and revise your essay. Typically, an effective response will contain a minimum of 300 words.

> **Plants can be used for many things. What is one kind of plant that is important to you or your country?**
> Use specific reasons and details to explain your choice.

這道寫作題要求考生寫一種對自己或其國家具有特殊意義的植物，並說明理由。寫作文前，考生必須迅速進行構思，選定一種植物。然後，寫下該植物對自己或國家意義重大的兩三個原因。這兩三個原因就是作文的分論點段落。

▶ Exercise 1

根據上面例題的題目要求寫一篇作文。初稿完成後，繼續學習下部分的內容。仔細研讀高分範文、萬用寫作範本、高分策略和寫作句型庫，運用所學的新知識完成 Exercise 2。

寫作構思

Bamboo
Gardens
Poetry
Trees
Food chain
Raw materials
Landscaping
Deforestation

高分範文 Track 037

All plants are valuable resources; it is not a coincidence that plants are at the bottom of the food chain. Through photosynthesis, they produce carbohydrates, the basic energy source for our bodily functions. Besides this fundamental use, humans have learned to use plants in different ways, so we can live more comfortably. Of all plants, the one that I think is most important to China is the tree.

One way in which trees contribute to our standard of living is as a source of material. Trees can be used to make a variety of things. Nice homes are built with lumber; most furniture is made of wood. Paper can be made from several different plants, but it is made primarily from tree pulp. The fabric rayon, a man-made silk, is made mostly of tree fibers. These fibers make fabrics shiny and allow them to hang well.

And who can deny that trees in landscaping add value to our lives? Trees that are strategically planted around a house can provide shade that cools us and helps save energy in the summer. They also add to the beauty of a space, whether it is where a person lives or works. In cities, people love to have tree-lined boulevards and parks with lots of flowers and trees. In fact, our sense of natural beauty in landscape design depends, to a large extent, on the presence of attractive trees.

Yet as significant as trees are as resources for materials and landscaping, these uses pale next to our need for trees to supply us with a healthy planet. Large-scale tree felling creates a host of environmental problems. In our country, large areas of land have been cleared for agricultural use to feed the ever-growing human population. Crops cannot hold topsoil the way trees can. As a result, floods have been a problem throughout our country's history as soil accumulation changed the course of waterways. In addition, increased human activity beginning with the Industrial Revolution has increased the amount of carbon dioxide in the atmosphere by thirty percent, causing global warming and unpredictable climate change. Because forests absorb carbon, deforestation makes climate problems even worse.

Fortunately, China has a large land mass which can support a lot of trees. If we learn how to live with trees, we can enjoy many tree products and live in a beautiful and healthy environment.

萬用模板

[開頭用兩三句介紹植物的重要性]. Of all _____, the one that I think is most important to _____ is _____.

One way in which _____ contribute to our standard of living is as _____. _____ can be used to [第一種用途]. [舉兩三個具體例子].

And who can deny that _____ in _____ add value to our lives? [舉兩三個具體例子].

Yet as significant as _____ are as resources for [第一種用途] and [第二種用途], these uses pale next to our need for _____ to supply us with [第三種用途]. [舉兩三個具體例子].

Fortunately, _____ has _____ which can support a lot of _____. If we learn how to live with _____, we can enjoy [改述第一種用途] and [改述第二種和第三種用途].

　　這篇範文的開頭先概述：植物是寶貴的資源，處於食物鏈金字塔的最底層，是人體的能量來源。然後，為了引出下面的觀點，説人類學會了很多利用植物的方法。第一段最後一句，考生提出：自己認為最重要的植物是樹木。第二段和第三段闡述了樹木的兩種用途：人類重要的生產和生活原料，以及景觀美化。第四段描述了樹木和森林對環境的保護作用。注意本文是如何在最後説明樹木最重要的用途的！這是一種有效的修辭策略。總結段沒有補充內容，但總結得非常好。

如何寫出漂亮的第一段

1. 第一段寫什麼內容

　　第一段應包含三項內容：
　　1）為讀者提供有用的並且有趣的背景資訊。
　　2）讓讀者瞭解話題，例如，對題目進行換句話説。
　　3）就該話題進行清晰的陳述或者「暗示」自己的觀點。

2. 讓第一段吸引人的寫作方法

　　雖然這是考試作文，但是開頭寫得吸引人對考生有好處。評分人要看成百上千篇作文，一天下來會非常疲憊。如果考生的作文吸引人，尤其在開始段落，評分人往往會給高分。

　　第一段打造有趣的句子有很多種方法：
✓ 總體概述
✓ 開門見山陳述觀點（中心句）
✓ 為一個術語或問題下定義
✓ 陳述一件驚奇的事
✓ 強調一個需要解決的問題
✓ 講述一個解説性的軼事
✓ 描述一個相關的趨勢
✓ 提出一個核心問題

　　以上有些方法是可以同時運用的。例如，一道要求討論飲食習慣的寫作題，考生可以提綱挈領地提出一個問題作為開頭，如下頁所示：

Is the fast food industry making our children sick?

提出問題之後，考生再給出背景資訊，提出論點。如：

Is the fast food industry making our children sick? For years, researchers have been telling us that the fats and sugar in fast food are harmful to the health of customers, including children. There are many harmful effects of eating out at fast food restaurants, as I will explain below.

再看看本章中範文第一段的寫法，它們展示了不同的寫作技巧。

下面的開頭句包含一個總體概述和一個有趣且重要的科學事實：

All plants are valuable resources; it is not a coincidence that plants are at the bottom of the food chain. Through photosynthesis, they produce carbohydrates, the basic energy source for our bodily functions. Besides this fundamental use, humans have learned to use plants in different ways, so we can live more comfortably. Of all plants, the one that I think is most important to China is the tree.

下面這一首段的開頭句講述了相關趨勢：

Over the years, each generation has embraced a different style of parenting. One generation advocates a strict approach, while the next generation tells us to "follow the child's personality." Certainly, it is easier to be a parent in theory than in practice. Yet despite the differences in parenting trends, I think most people agree that certain characteristics are necessary for young people who seek to raise loving and responsible children.

在下面這個開頭段，考生先描述趨勢，然後給 adulthood 下定義：

Ever since the Industrial Revolution, human beings have spent relatively more time in "childhood," perhaps because the complex world forces us to spend more time learning the skills we need to prosper. **In my view, "adulthood" is defined as the time when a person is ready to deal with the world without parental help.**

寫出漂亮第一段的策略

1. 給出背景資訊，為讀者提供充足的語境。
2. 不要用 Yes, I agree 等類似的簡短評論開頭。至少寫一句可以讓評分人理解話題或論點的句子。
3. 改述題目中的用詞。
4. 陳述自己的觀點或者至少表明你對該話題的想法。
5. 觀點句可以在總體概述之前也可以在總體概述之後。只要充分表達，每一種方法都可以引起讀者的興趣。
6. 第一段最後一句和第二段第一句的銜接一定要自然、連貫。

　　作文第一段寫得有趣有很多種方法，上述開頭段落的寫法只是其中的幾種。想要瞭解更多寫好第一段的方法，考生應該認真研讀本書所有的高分範文。

建立自己的寫作句型庫

1. Of all x, the one that I think is most important to y is the z

所有……之中，我認為……對於……最重要

Of all plants, the one that I think is most important to China is the tree.

延伸說法 Of all plants, the one that I think is most important to South Korea is the chrysanthemum.

2. One way in which x contribute to our standard of living is as a source of material.

……作為一種材料來源，有助於我們生活水準的提升。

One way in which trees contribute to our standard of living is as a source of material.

延伸說法 One way in which bamboo contributes to our standard of living is as a source of material.

3. x creates a host of environmental problems.

……引發許多環境問題。

Large-scale tree felling creates a host of environmental problems.

延伸說法 Using too much fertilizer creates a host of environmental problems.

4. If we learn how to VERB, we can enjoy many x products and live in a beautiful and healthy environment.

倘若我們學會如何……，我們就能享用……的產品，並生活在美麗、健康的環境之中。

If we learn how to live with trees, we can enjoy many tree products and live in a beautiful and healthy environment.

延伸說法 If we learn how to garden organically, we can enjoy many organic products and live in a beautiful and healthy environment.

▶再練習一次！

　　學完高分範文、萬用寫作範本、高分策略和寫作句型庫，運用所學的技能修改你的初稿，並認真看修改之處。然後用學到的新句型去練習下面五道預測題的寫作。

寫作預測題

1. What are some of the characteristics...

What are some of the characteristics of a good parent?
Use specific details and examples to explain your answer.

寫作構思

Parenting trends
Sense of humor
Invest in children
Values education
Role model
Encouraging
Firm

高分範文 1　　 *Track 038*

Over the years, each generation has embraced a different style of parenting. One generation advocates a strict approach, while the next generation tells us to "follow the child's personality." Certainly, it is easier to be a parent in theory than in practice. Yet despite the differences in parenting trends, I think most people agree that certain characteristics are necessary for young people who seek to raise loving and responsible children.

One of the indisputable requirements for good parenting is being a good role model. Children learn from imitating adults. They observe parents dealing with their friends and colleagues, obeying laws and regulations, taking care of animals and the environment, as well as keeping house and reading books. Working and playing, our offspring learn and copy what they see. It is said that children are genetically wired to learn from their parents without asking questions. If this is true, then there is no better way to teach children than to be a good example. Through modeling, parents teach their children even though no explicit language is used.

Being firm is another important quality for a parent. Too often you will see unruly children in public places, and you will see their parents by their side and doing nothing about it. Children by nature are curious and like to try out new things; they also like to see what they can get away with. Rule-obeying citizens are the foundation of a civic society. If the children are to grow up to be law-abiding citizens, they need to be taught to respect rules from an early age. When you see children displaying unacceptable behavior in public, you can be sure their parents do not teach them at home. I am not against loving and doting parents, but I think they have a duty to society when they bring a life into this world. They should be responsible for making sure children grow up to be good citizens. They have to be firm and teach them the value of obeying rules.

Other characteristics that are helpful for parents include being responsive to children's needs, being patient and being supportive. Many best-selling books about parenting have been published, but raising children is not as easy as the books suggest. Still, if we strive to be good role models and work hard to teach our children the difference between right and wrong, we have a better chance to become good parents.

托福總監評析

　　這篇範文先說不同時代有不同的教育方式，接下來說儘管有不同的教育方式，但是優秀的父母具備某些共同特點。第二段和第三段分別講述了一個特點：以身作則和嚴格要求。最後一段先列舉了優秀父母具備的其他幾種特質，然後重申只要父母以身作則，教孩子明辨是非，就是好父母。

---

2. What events...

> **People make a distinction between children and adults. What events (experiences or rituals) make someone an "adult"?**
> Use specific reasons and examples to explain your answer.

寫作構思

> **Coming of age**
> **Legal age**
> Puberty and physical maturity
> Get married
> **College age**
> Working age
> **Rituals**

高分範文 2　 *Track 039*

Ever since the Industrial Revolution, human beings have spent relatively more time in "childhood," perhaps because the complex world forces us to spend more time learning the skills we need to prosper. In my view, "adulthood" is defined as the time when a person is ready to deal with the world without parental help.

Although every society is unique, there are several commonly shared events that mark the passing of childhood into adulthood. First is the legal age. The legal age varies in different countries; it could be 18, or 21 or some other age. In addition, different legal ages are set for different purposes; for example, the minimum ages set for driving, voting and drinking. The rationale behind this delineation is that when one reaches that particular age, one is no longer a child and can be held legally accountable for one's acts.

The "college age" is another demarcation between children and adults. Students are treated more or less as children prior to entering university, but once they are enrolled, they tend to be treated as adults. It is not surprising that most people go to college at the age of 18, also the legal age for voting in many countries. Nothing speaks more strongly about a person's acceptance into the world of adults than when he or she is granted the right to vote for the election of public officials.

Oftentimes rituals are held to celebrate an individual's induction into adulthood. In France, young women are introduced to society when they reach a certain age. The young ladies are called debutantes, signifying their first appearance on the public stage. In Jewish culture, Bar and Bat Mitzvah ceremonies are held for young men and women coming of age. In relatively remote societies such as the one found in Papua New Guinea, there are elaborate ceremonies marking the coming of age of young men.

It is important to remember that the biological age at which one is considered an adult varies from one society to the next. What is comparable in all societies is the expectation that upon "coming of age," the individual will bear the responsibilities that come with being an adult.

托福總監評析

　　在第一段，考生先給 adulthood 下定義，即一個人離開父母的保護，可以獨立處事的時期。第二段談論成人的法定年齡。第三段把上大學作為成年的一個標誌。第四段談論幾個國家的成人禮儀式。總結段最後一句重述論點：不論年齡或儀式，「成熟」就是要有能力、責任作為社會的一員。

3. What is one thing you will do...

> **You have decided to volunteer some time each month to improve the community where you live. What is one thing you will do to improve your community? Why?**
> Use specific reasons and details to explain your choice.

寫作構思

> **Wuhan**
> Clean up litter on campus
> Spend time with senior citizens
> Read to the blind
> **Help children of migrant workers**
> **They seem to be the ones most in need**
> **I enjoy teaching children**

高分範文 3   *Track 040*

Because my university is located in Wuhan, China, that is the community where I would work as a volunteer. Wuhan is a big city. Not surprisingly, there are many things needed to be done in order to improve the lives of local people. Many social initiatives are best carried out by the city government, but there is always a need for volunteers in the private arena. If I had a few hours to spare, I would spend them teaching the children of migrant workers.

Some people might not regard migrant workers as members of our "community" since they are not technically permanent residents. The fact is, however, that the migrant workers here spend all their time working in metropolitan Wuhan, with the exception of 10 or so days a year, when they go back to their hometowns for the Spring Festival. To me, that qualifies them as members of our community and deserving of social support.

A sense of fairness drives my desire to help these children. Many migrant families come from agricultural backgrounds, and so the parents are often not really qualified to tutor them at home. Moreover, it seems particularly appropriate for me to "give back" to society in the specific area of education. Like other college students, I pay a relatively low tuition fee, thanks to a heavy subsidy from our fellow countrymen. It is only right that we give back some of our time and energy to people in need.

Not all my reasons for volunteering are altruistic, since I know I will be rewarded for my work in the form of enjoyment and fulfillment. Teaching children can be a wonderful experience. Every time you work with them, you can see how the human mind is developing. Moreover, these children, along with their parents, are especially appreciative of every hour invested, which will make my job as tutor all the more gratifying.

In sum, if I had to choose one area in which to contribute my time, I would definitely choose to teach the children of migrant workers. Many of these children are very bright and hard-working, and I know that even a little time spent with them will yield tangible results.

托福總監評析

　　這道寫作題要求考生選擇做一件事來完善社區生活。有幾種開頭方法：一種是描述幾種志願工作，從中選擇一種；另一種是簡單陳述自己的選擇並說明理由。這篇範文用到的是第二種方法。考生先介紹自己所居住的城市，然後陳述選擇的志願活動。第二段陳述農民工的生存狀況，說他們是社會的成員，應該得到社會的支助。第三、第四段解釋為什麼想幫助農民工的孩子。總結段重申論點（I would definitely choose to teach the children of migrant workers.）並補充說農民工的孩子都很聰明，而且也很努力，我的付出會有很大的成效。

4. What have you learned...

Films can tell us a lot about the country where they were made. What have you learned about a country from watching movies?

Use specific examples and details to support your response.

寫作點題

Foreign films
Borat
US
Learn colloquial English from movies
See beautiful scenery without traveling
Everyday people
Domestic films

高分範文 4 Track 041

Unlike many of my friends, I am not passionate about movies, especially foreign ones. Nevertheless, from the few foreign films I have watched, I think I have learned quite a bit about other countries.

In the comedy "Borat," for example, I was exposed to everyday culture in the US. The title character, Borat, played by an English comedian, is supposedly a government worker from Kazakhstan. Borat's mission is to produce a video that can introduce the American way of life to his countrymen. As Borat goes around the country, he gets involved in all kinds of situations, all the time asking Americans how they do things. He often makes a fool of himself, pretending to be ignorant, even to the point of rudeness. In one scene, a nice man patiently teaches Borat how to drive a car. In another, Borat hitches a ride with a group of rowdy young men. Very few of the Americans photographed during the production knew "Borat" was really a comedian producing a feature film.

Upon viewing this movie, what I learned was how open Americans were and how willing they were to help strangers, even "crazy" ones. In one scene where Borat is invited to join a dinner among friends, he deliberately tries his hosts' patience by asking ridiculous questions and acting in impolite ways. The movie audience sees how these ordinary people got pulled into pranks like these unwittingly, all the while being gracious and helpful, until it was just too weird for them to continue. I have not been to the US, but I do have a few American friends. Like the real people shown in "Borat," my friends seem very willing to help people, even people they have never met before.

Actually, I usually learn something new even when I watch movies made in my own country. For example, I become more familiar with the geography and local culture where the story is set. In especially good movies, the social setting and regional dialect play a prominent role, making me understand even more about that particular time and place. Thus, no matter whether I am watching foreign or domestic movies, my horizons are broadened in one way or another.

托福總監評析

　　範文第一段雖然簡單但很有作用。考生說自己並不喜歡看電影。看過幾部國外影片，從中瞭解到不少其他國家的知識。第二段和第三段講述影片 **Borat** 的故事情節，並說自己透過觀看這部影片瞭解了美國文化和美國人熱情開放、樂於助人的性格特徵。總結段補充了一點：觀看本國電影也學到了新東西。最後一句重申論點：中外影片擴展了自己的視野。

5. Which x would you like...

You have won a prize that allows you to visit a foreign country of your choice for two weeks. Which country would you like to visit?
Use specific reasons and details to explain your choice.

寫作構思

> **Japan**
> US
> Italy
> Singapore
> **Differences**
> **Similar history**
> **How they became modern**
> **Cleanliness**
> Am studying the language

高分範文 5 *Track 042*

There are many countries I would like to visit, including Italy, the United States and Singapore. But the country I would most like to explore is Japan. We Chinese have mixed feelings about Japan. We admire it because of the phenomenal technical and economic achievements the Japanese have made in the last hundred years, yet we remember the atrocities committed in China by Japanese forces during the war. These contradictory images come together in my mind, making me eager to see how Japanese live now. At the same time, I want to gain more insight into how China and Japan compare.

One area of difference relates to the pace of modernization in each of our countries' histories. About a hundred and fifty years ago, both Japan and China were relatively undeveloped. Both countries were forced to sign unequal treaties with Western powers. Reformers in both countries were trying to transform society from a feudal system to a more modern system. For Japan, modernization came swiftly, with the Meiji Restoration. However, for China, modernization did not take place until well over a hundred years later. Many historians blame our problems on the imperial court politics of the late Qing dynasty, but to me this does not explain why Japan was so successful. I believe that part of Japan's success can be attributed to the character of the Japanese people, one reason I want to see Japan first-hand.

I have to confess that I also want to see if Japan is really as spotless as everyone says it is. Friends who have visited Japan are always raving about the cleanliness of Japan. I know from television programs that this is true, but I still want to go there and see for myself. I am hoping to understand how big cities, full of people, can remain so clean.

In short, though Chinese and Japanese cultures are similar, there are many differences. It is these differences, particularly in our everyday lifestyles, that pique my interest. I am confident that a two-week visit to Japan will provide insights into some of these issues and answer a lot of my questions.

托福總監評析

　　這篇範文的第一段非常有趣，考生先表明自己想去旅遊的國家是日本。接下來談原因：對日本持有複雜的感情—永遠不會忘記第二次世界大戰中日本在中國犯下的罪行，同時很欽佩日本在科技和經濟上取得的巨大成就。這種矛盾的心理讓「我」對這個國家產生了好奇心。同時，也想瞭解中日兩國的差異。第二段對兩國的差異進行了舉例論證，即日本和中國在現代化的實現方式上有所不同。這一段也非常有趣，因為考生提出了一個假設並且想證實該假設：part of Japan's success can be attributed to the character of the Japanese people。第三段很引人入勝，描述了想去日本旅遊的第二個動機：想看日本的 cleanliness。總結段重述考生觀點，即中國和日本有很多相同點和不同點，但進一步論述說，正是這些不同引起「我」對日本的興趣。最後一句論述了這次擬定的行程能讓「我」深入瞭解兩國的差異，並解開「我」心中的許多疑問（在第二段和第三段中概述的疑問），因此結尾很出色。這篇範文優秀地展現了在寫作中如何做到前後連貫。

建立自己的寫作句型庫

1. **Over the years, each generation has embraced a different style of x**

多年來，每一代人都有不同的……方式

Over the years, each generation has embraced a different style of parenting.

延伸說法 Over the years, each generation has embraced a different style of communicating.

2. One of the indisputable requirements for x is…
……其中一個不容爭辯的必要條件是……

One of the indisputable requirements for good parenting is being a good role model.

延伸說法 One of the indisputable requirements for a good teacher is having an inquisitive mind.

3. x is another important quality for a parent.
……是家長的另一個重要品質。

Being firm is another important quality for a parent.

延伸說法 A sense of humor is another important quality for a parent.

4. Other characteristics that are helpful for parents include x, y and z
其他有益於家長的性格特點是……

Other characteristics that are helpful for parents include being responsive to children's needs, being patient and being supportive.

延伸說法 Other characteristics that are helpful for parents include patience, enthusiasm and a willingness to listen.

5. Although every society is unique, there are several commonly shared x that mark the passing of childhood into adulthood.
雖然每個社會都是獨一無二的，但一個人從童年步入成年時有一些相通的……。

Although every society is unique, there are several commonly shared events that mark the passing of childhood into adulthood.

延伸說法 Although every society is unique, there are several commonly shared ceremonies that mark the passing of childhood into adulthood.

6. x is another demarcation between children and adults.
……是兒童與成人的另一個分界線。

The "college age" is another demarcation between children and adults.

延伸說法 The onset of puberty is another demarcation between children and adults.

7. A sense of x drives my desire to help y
一種……的感覺，驅使我想幫助……

A sense of fairness drives my desire to help these children.

延伸說法 A sense of empathy drives my desire to help these senior citizens.

8. It is only right that we give back some of our time and energy to x

抽出一部分時間和精力用於⋯⋯是正確的

It is only right that we give back some of our time and energy to people in need.

延伸說法 It is only right that we give back some of our time and energy to victims of natural disasters.

9. In sum, if I had to choose one area in which to contribute my time, I would definitely choose to VERB

總之，如果必須選擇在某一領域投入時間，我一定會選擇⋯⋯

In sum, if I had to choose one area in which to contribute my time, I would definitely choose to teach the children of migrant workers.

延伸說法 In sum, if I had to choose one area in which to contribute my time, I would definitely choose to help build new homes for earthquake victims in China.

10. Nevertheless, from the x I have VERBed, I think I have learned quite a bit about other countries.

但我認為我已經從我曾⋯⋯的⋯⋯中瞭解到許多關於其他國家的知識。

Nevertheless, from the few foreign films I have watched, I think I have learned quite a bit about other countries.

延伸說法 Nevertheless, from the books I have read, I think I have learned quite a bit about other countries.

11. In [MOVIE TITLE], for example, I was exposed to everyday culture in [COUNTRY].

以⋯⋯為例，我從中瞭解到了⋯⋯的日常文化

In the comedy "Borat," for example, I was exposed to everyday culture in the US.

延伸說法 In "Amelie," for example, I was exposed to everyday culture in France.

12. There are many countries I would like to visit, including x, y and z

我想遊覽許多國家，包括⋯⋯

There are many countries I would like to visit, including Italy, the United States and Singapore.

延伸說法 There are many countries I would like to visit, including Spain, Italy and France.

13. But the country I would most like to explore is x

但我最想探索的國家是……

But the country I would most like to explore is Japan.

延伸說法 But the country I would most like to explore is Sweden.

14. One area of difference relates to x

其中一個差異和……有關

One area of difference relates to the pace of modernization in each of our countries' histories.

延伸說法 One area of difference relates to the fact that England is an island.

15. I have to confess that I also want to see if x is really as y as everyone says it is.

我不得不承認我也想對人們傳說中的……一探究竟。

I have to confess that I also want to see if Japan is really as spotless as everyone says it is.

延伸說法 I have to confess that I also want to see if Thailand is really as fun as everyone says it is.

16. I am confident that a two-week visit to x will provide insights into some of these issues and answer a lot of my questions.

我相信在……為期兩週的遊覽會讓我對一些事情有深入的瞭解,並解開我心中的許多疑問。

I am confident that a two-week visit to Japan will provide insights into some of these issues and answer a lot of my questions.

延伸說法 I am confident that a two-week visit to India will provide insights into some of these issues and answer a lot of my questions.

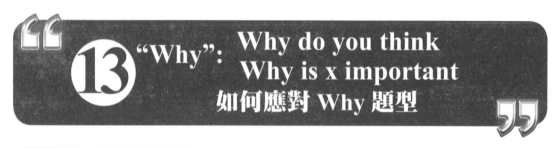

13 "Why": Why do you think Why is x important 如何應對 Why 題型

在本章，你將學到……

★作文中如何透過解釋原因來達到論證目的

解讀常考題

因為作文中需要給出原因，分論點需要圍繞主論點進行論證，所以幾乎所有的獨立寫作題目都要求考生解釋原因，儘管沒有明確說明。但有些寫作題目會直接出現 why，要求考生解釋某個現象，問考生為什麼認為……，或問某事物為什麼重要等。本章要說明的就是這類題目。

考生解釋原因或說明潛在動機時，表達應清晰，語言要有說服力。

常見的題目有：

1. People often VERB. Why?
2. People VERB for different reasons. Why is x important to many people?
3. Many students choose to VERB. Why do some students VERB?
4. Why do you think people VERB?

下面來看一個例子。

▶ 模擬試題①

閱讀以下的短文並聆聽講座，完成以下這道作文題目。

Directions:

Read the question below. You have 30 minutes to plan, write, and revise your essay. Typically, an effective response will contain a minimum of 300 words.

> **Some gifts that we receive are particularly special to us. Why?**
> Use specific reasons and examples to support your answer.

▶ Exercise 1

根據上面例題的題目要求寫一篇作文。初稿完成後，繼續學習下部分的內容。仔細研讀高分範文、萬用寫作範本、高分策略和寫作句型庫，運用所學的新知識完成 Exercise 2。

寫作構思

Bicycle from father
Money from grandmother
Old photos
Few gifts
Occasion commemorated
Significance

Nowadays, people receive gifts for birthdays, Valentine's Day, the Spring Festival, school graduation and other special occasions. In days past, gifts were much rarer. When I look back on the years I spent growing up in a poor family, I see very few gifts in my young life. There was one special present, however, that I will never forget.

In my third year of elementary school, my father gave me a bicycle after I placed first in the whole class. At that time, we didn't have much money and so a bicycle to ride for fun was really a luxury item. From the first day of kindergarten I was a good student, and I consistently ranked in the top three, semester after semester. Still, my family never bought me a "prize" because they could not afford it. For reasons unknown to me, that spring was an exception. My father told me he would get me a gift if I did well again. Actually, I had never really thought about getting a present. It was enough for me to know my parents were proud of me; that was all the motivation I needed. I was happy I could please them with my good grades.

Once again, I ranked top of my class at the end of the semester. Not long after grades were posted, as I was returning home, I noticed there was a brand new bike standing in front of our small apartment. Running inside, I found my father sitting in a lounge chair fanning himself in the summer heat. I could see a smile on his usually serious face, but I rushed out to try the bike. From that day, that smiling face has been deeply etched in my memory, serving to encourage me during tough times.

Without a doubt, this bicycle was a special childhood gift, a tangible symbol of my achievements and my parents' approval. Yet now that I am grown, I realize that the memory of that day is an even greater gift.

萬用模板

Nowadays, people receive gifts for _____ and other special occasions. In days past, gifts were much rarer. When I look back on _____, I see very few gifts in my young life. There was one special present, however, that I will never forget.

In [時間片語], _____ gave me _____ after _____. At that time, [用兩三句來描述事件].

[用兩到三個句子來描述當時的感觸，贈送禮物者的感觸]. From that day, that ADJECTIVE face has been deeply etched in memory, serving to encourage me during tough times.

Without a doubt, [具 體 禮 物] was a special childhood gift, a tangible symbol of _____ and _____. Yet now that I am grown, I realize that the memory of that day is an even greater gift.

在這篇範文中，考生透過講述故事來說明原因。講述故事的方法對於 Why is x important to you? 這種寫作題尤其有效，因為故事更容易表達事件的重要性。

第一段陳述故事的背景資訊，說現在人們經常收到禮物，但像「我」這樣來自貧困家庭的孩子，記憶之中很少有禮物。這是種鋪陳，有助於讀者理解下文要提及的禮物的重要性。第二段告訴讀者這件特殊的禮物是什麼，然後開始講述故事。第三段繼續講述故事，但側重描述這件禮物對「我」的重要意義。總結段很簡潔，總結了這份特殊禮物的意義以及留給「我」的美好記憶。

解釋原因

在新托福考試的口語和寫作部分，透過具體原因和細節來支持自己觀點的能力是考生一項很重要的能力。如果獨立寫作想得 5 分，考生一定要在作文中詳細地解釋原因。

口語考試中，考生可以用非正式的語言來陳述原因，例如 That's because... 或 That's why I...。但在寫作部分，考生則要用正式的語言陳述原因，即用結構複雜的長句來呈現銜接和連貫。

在作文中解釋原因，必須包括：
1. 為話題提供背景知識及闡明話題的幾個具體細節或事實
2. 原因信號詞

寫 Why 題型的作文時，考生應該先提供一些背景知識，然後說明原因。因為原因可能非常複雜，所以考生必須得詳細解釋；例如，上篇高分範文中的最後一句：Yet now that I am grown, I realize that the memory of that day is an even greater gift. 這個句子告訴讀者：這份禮物喚起的是對父親的回憶，但是直到長大成人之後「我」才意識到那一天對「我」的意義。

　　另外，沒有必要總是列出原因一、原因二和原因三。考生可以給出有意思的細節來解釋原因和目的。當然，這些細節要一目了然，其前後組織要有序，還要有恰當的信號詞。下表中是常用的信號詞，可以用在獨立寫作題中解釋原因。

解釋原因的句型

• The reason I... • I hold this belief because... • Thus, because I VERBed..., • I went on to VERB • It was x that made me VERB • There are x reasons why... • The reason for me doing x was... • The reason this experience was so meaningful to me is that... • For one thing,... • Another factor was... • My interest in x was due to...	• Due to my interest in x • ... for the reason that... • My motivation for VERBing • It was only because... • If x had not y, I would never have VERB • As a result, I... • Without the influence of x, I would never have VERB • x made me realize... • x caused me to VERB • x led me to VERB

　　許多考生解釋原因時經常寫出錯誤的句子。先看看下面考生作文中常見的錯誤句，再看看正確的表達。不正確的單字或片語標有底線。

常見錯誤表達	正確表達
<u>Here come</u> the reasons.	The reasons are listed below.
<u>Reasons</u> as follows.	The reasons for this are as follows.
I choose to avoid risks for <u>some</u> reasons.	I choose to avoid risks for several reasons.
There are <u>some</u> reasons to support my point of view.	There are several reasons to support my point of view.
I do not agree with the city's proposal <u>with</u> the following reasons.	I do not agree with the city's proposal for the following reasons.
There are several reasons <u>influence that</u> how many years people can live.	There are several factors that influence how many years people can live.
The reason <u>for scientists to invent things</u> is that they do the research over and over again.	The reason that scientists are able to invent things is that they do the research over and over again.

解釋原因的策略

1. 解釋原因的措辭和句型要恰當。記住本章整理的句型和「建立自己的寫作句型庫」裡的相關表達，這樣就可以運用自如。

2. 要想表述清晰，在第一段就要說明接下來會列舉原因；例如：Even in the 21st century, music is all around us and continues to play an important role in our lives, for many reasons.

3. 解釋原因一定要具體。例如，簡單地說 I like popular music because it is lively 並不能把原因解釋清楚。要想得高分，原因需要用具體、緊隨其後的例子來闡明。如：I like popular music because it is lively; for example, I listen to upbeat music like Rihanna's *Don't Stop the Music.*

4. 在大多數情況下，一個段落講述一個原因。該段的中心句是原因，其餘內容便是例子、解釋和特殊情況。

5. 為了使表達清晰，一次講述一個原因。如果同時講多個原因，在文章中要說明。以本章寫作預測題第三篇高分範文為例。第二段集中講發展中國家學生的留學原因；第三段集中講發達國家學生的留學原因。這兩個原因分開來講。但第四段提到的原因是包括這兩類人在內的，即 seeking prestige。這種情況下，考生應該指出前面提到的兩類人都有追求聲譽的動機，如：Aspiring young people from both developing and developed countries seek to enhance their resumes by obtaining degrees from worldclass universities. 這會使文章的表述更清晰，邏輯更連貫。

6. 有些題目可以透過講述故事來給出原因。這種策略對 Why is x of special importance to you? 的寫作題尤其有效。

7. 把最重要的原因放到最後講。

8. 總結段不需要詳細地重述所有原因，只需總結及換句話說。最好在結論部分補充一條原因，這會達到更好的寫作效果。

建立自己的寫作句型庫

1. There was one x, however, that I will never forget
然而，我永遠不會忘記……

There was one special gift, however, that I will never forget.

延伸說法 There was one occasion, however, that I will never forget.

2. Without a doubt, this x was a special childhood gift, a tangible symbol of y
毫無疑問，這個……是我童年的一份特殊禮物，是……的有形象徵

Without a doubt, this bicycle was a special childhood gift, a tangible symbol of my achievements and my parents' approval.

延伸說法 Without a doubt, this antique necklace was a special childhood gift, a tangible symbol of my great-grandmother's love.

▶ Exercise 2

學完高分範文、萬用寫作範本、高分策略和寫作句型庫，運用所學的技能修改你的初稿，並認真看修改之處。然後用學到的新句型去練習下面五道預測題的寫作。

寫作預測題

1. Why is this?

Groups and organizations are an essential part of some people's lives. Why is this?

Give specific reasons and examples to explain your answer.

寫作構思

Motivations
Sharing experiences
Volunteer groups
Loneliness
Have to pay dues
Informal, formal
Deal with emotional issues
Expand knowledge of their profession
New developments in the field

高分範文 1   *Track 044*

We live in a world with many different kinds of groups and organizations. Some groups are informal; for example, a circle of friends who get together every week to play cards. Other groups are formal in nature, such as professional and trade organizations. Associations exist for every occupation from doctors to plumbers; the list goes on and on. No matter whether informal or formal, each group and organization holds purpose for the individual members.

The primary motivation for people to join informal groups is social. Many informal support groups, for example, exist so that members can sit together and talk. In these small, relatively private settings, people can let off steam and discuss problems of common interest. There are, for example, support groups for parents of children with special needs such as learning disorders and autism. Other informal support groups are made up of people trying to lose weight. These groups provide an important function that even medical professionals are unable to provide. Sharing experiences, even painful ones, can have a healing power. In addition to receiving moral support, group members are able to get timely practical advice from people in circumstances similar to their own.

Compared to informal group members, people who choose to become members of formal organizations have a wider range of reasons for their affiliations. For one thing, large associations allow members to expand their knowledge of their profession or industry by taking classes, listening to lecturers and gaining professional certification. At regularly scheduled regional and national meetings, people can network with other members about new developments in the field and job opportunities. In short, there are many practical benefits of large organizations.

From the above, we can see how both informal and formal groups and organizations offer utility to their members. Informal groups tend to be smaller and more private, and so individuals who seek personal help would be more likely to join one of these. Formal organizations have more resources and hold more prestige, and so individuals seeking professional advancement would have incentives to join these. Of course, the social element is common to all types of groups and organizations; the people who join up usually like to be with other people.

托福總監評析

　　這道寫作題並不太容易寫，因為 groups 和 organizations 的概念比較模糊。為了簡化該寫作題，考生從 informal 和 formal 兩個角度為 groups 和 organizations 分類。這讓話題更具體，也更容易理解，還為下文的論證提供了一個組織框架。第二段集中講述非正式團體。考生列舉了幾個非正式團體，然後解釋人們為什麼加入這些團體。第三段集中講述正式團體。注意考生是如何運用信號詞 Compared to informal group members,... 來連接兩個段落，同時，還比較了非正式團體和正式團體會員的入會動機。這種寫作手法增強了文章的銜接性和連貫性。總結段總結了人們加入非正式和正式團體的原因。在最後一句，考生強調了這些會員相同的動機，在修辭上稱得上是一個不錯的結尾。

2. Why is this x important...

Almost everyone listens to music, but not for the same reasons. Why is music important to people?
Use specific reasons and examples to support your answer.

寫作構思

Classical music
Soothing
Releases stress
Boring job, passes time
Expressing emotion
Love songs
Dance
Digital music is everywhere

高分範文 2 *Track 045*

The ancient Greek philosopher Plato once said that music was the soul of the universe. What Plato actually meant was that music adds value to humanity. Even in the 21st century, music is all around us and continues to play an important role in our lives, for many reasons.

First and foremost, music makes us feel good. Like songbirds, human beings like to pour their hearts out in song. We have evolved into a species that can create diverse and sophisticated music to express different emotions. There is music for every occasion; for celebrations, for funerals, for memorials and for expressing love. We respond to the kind of music that addresses our emotional needs of the moment. Love songs, for example, are universally popular because people are happy when they think about love.

In addition to making and listening to music, people love to move to music. Dance is inseparable from music. Toddlers start dancing as soon as they can stand on their two feet. Teenagers usually like dancing to loud music with a strong beat. Ballet dancers and dance skaters are athletes who need music to perform. In all of these cases, physical movements follow the sounds. In fact, many people move their bodies to music by clapping their hands or snapping their fingers.

Yet another reason that music is integral to so many people's lives is that it is so accessible. There is a seemingly endless supply of music because so many musicians are hard at work creating it. Basic laws of supply and demand affect prices; music is a relatively affordable consumer product. Furthermore, nowadays one can download digital files of songs for very little money and enjoy this music right away. There are many types of music playing devices, from fancy audio equipment to the portable mp3 players. Whether people are working out at the gym or relaxing with friends at a party, digital music has become a staple.

To be sure, there are many art forms of value to us, such as cinema and literature. However, as we have seen from the examples above, the unique emotional impact of music and its widespread availability in digital format give music special importance.

托福總監評析

　　這道寫作題的題意非常清晰，但討論 why music is important 的文章並不好寫，因為它屬於審美層次上的賞析，這類話題本質上是很抽象的，不論用哪種語言都很難寫。在這篇高分範文中，考生引用柏拉圖「音樂是萬物的靈魂」這一名言作為開頭。然後從概括過渡到具體，說明音樂在人類生活中扮演重要角色是有其原因的。第二至第四段分別敘述不同的原因：音樂讓人心情愉悅，人們喜歡伴隨音樂的節奏跳舞或做其他肢體動作。在總結段，考生說還有許多其他重要的藝術形式，然後總結了前文提到的音樂對人們重要的原因，並增加了一個新觀點，即音樂有特殊意義。

3. Why do some students study...

> **Many students attend schools or universities far away from home. Why do some students study abroad?**
> Use specific reasons and details to explain your answer.

寫作構思

> **Better education**
> Broader horizon
> Life is an adventure
> Learn a foreign language
> Types of students
> **Culture**
> **Prestige**

高分範文 3　　 *Track 046*

Given a chance, most students would welcome an opportunity to study abroad, regardless of what their home country is. Students from developed nations who have relatively good educations might choose to study abroad for reasons different from students in developing countries, but the idea of going overseas is equally appealing to students of both groups.

Getting a better education is probably the most often cited reason for students in developing Asian nations to go overseas. It is true that higher education in the West is generally more rigorous, and that there are a large number of world-class scholars working at the research universities there. We all want to go to a school where we can study with the top minds in our field. Besides this, most great universities in the West have unparalleled research facilities which are hard to find in some developing nations. It is obvious that this combination of top scholars and great facilities is a strong draw for students from other parts of the world.

For students from developed countries, culture is the reason given most often for overseas study. A college education is not only about the specific subjects one studies, it is also about broad exposure to people and ideas, looking at the world from different perspectives and shaping one's character. Thinking along these lines, a student will often feel that exposure to a different culture is a useful complement to the education he or she is receiving at home. The junior-year abroad experience is a typical example of this in an undergraduate education.

Aspiring young people from both developing and developed countries seek to enhance their resumes by obtaining degrees from world-class universities. Thus, another reason why students go abroad is prestige. It seems having one degree from a top university in their own country is not enough, so they go to another top university in a different country and earn another degree there.

In general, then, it seems the experience of spending some of one's learning years in a foreign country has a positive effect for various student groups. In this global era, I think more and more people will take advantage of these overseas opportunities.

托福總監評析

　　表面上，這道寫作題好像比較容易。可能所有考生都比較瞭解出國留學這個話題，因此也較熟悉該情境的單字和片語。然而，正是因為該話題可說的內容有很多，所以從某些方面來說，這道寫作題又很難寫。大學生和研究生的出國原因是不同的，不同科系和不同經濟背景的學生的出國原因也是不同的。

　　為了讓這個話題更容易處理，考生透過發展中國家和已發展國家的差異來對留學目的進行分類（注意該方法和前面範文中有關正式團體和非正式團體的寫作手法有何相似之處）。作文主體部分一直在講留學目的的差異，第二段講述亞洲發展中國家學生出國留學的原因，第三段轉而討論已發展國家學生的出國留學原因。第三段開頭的過渡很突出：For students from developed countries, culture is the reason given most often for overseas study. 這是一種增強作文前後連貫的好方法。第四段講述了發展中國家學生和已發展國家學生出國留學的一個共同原因：透過拿國外學位獲得聲譽。因為作文主體部分非常詳細，總結段可以簡短一些：總結一下兩個出國學習的好處便足夠了。

4. Why do they do this...

Many people enjoy visiting museums when they take trips. Why do they do this? Use specific reasons and examples to support your answer.

寫作構思

Curiosity
Educational value
Imagine ancient times
Art museums inspire us
More time to appreciate museums when on vacation
Shops
Priority of the host city or country

高分範文 4 Track 047

Museums, particularly the most famous ones, are major tourist attractions. A large amount of money and time have been invested in great museums, and so people generally accept that visiting them is a worthwhile exercise. There are many reasons why different individuals choose to go to a museum while traveling, but I will pick three in my discussion below.

Museums display items that people are curious about. In fact, early museums were often private collections of wealthy individuals, even monarchs. In previous eras, it was not easy for everyday people to obtain access to those collections. Then, as museums gradually opened their doors to the public, people became accustomed to exploring various museums to see what interesting artifacts they would find. Travelers want to take the time to see things that they can't see at home.

Another obvious reason why people are attracted to museums is the educational value associated with them. Science museums are popular among science lovers, art museums attract art aficionados and history museums draw in history buffs. This profile of a museum visitor is a motivated learner who will not pass up an opportunity to learn more about something they are already interested in.

Gift items at museum gift shops are yet another reason why museums are popular. Some travelers buy souvenirs for their personal use, and others may feel they are obligated to give gifts to friends and family back home. Since museums tend to be viewed as part of the identity of their local city, people feel items bought at a particular museum represent the city or the country they have visited. Visiting a museum's gift shop is often a traveler's primary motive to visit a museum.

Any combination of these reasons could compel a traveler to pay a visit to a museum. Good museums offer visitors a wealth of opportunities to explore new vistas in art, history and science. And while learning about new things is probably the primary driver for museum visits, everyone likes to get museum store souvenirs as well.

托福總監評析

　　本文緊扣題目，陳述了不同人群參觀博物館的不同原因。第二、三和四段分別陳述了參觀者不同的心理驅動因素：好奇心、學知識、去博物館禮物店購物。總結段總結了之前陳述的觀點：Any combination of these reasons could compel a traveler to pay a visit to a museum. 這個句子增強了文章的連貫性，因為它提到了前文說的原因，但沒有一一列舉。如果在此處再列舉會使文章顯得無趣，不能打動評分人。所以考生用自己的語言總結了上文提到的原因。

5. Why do you think...

Why do you think some people engage in dangerous sports and other risky activities?

Use specific reasons and examples to support your answer.

寫作構思

Psychological need for adrenaline rush
Desire to push oneself
Crave media attention
Confident people
Lengthy training so well prepared

高分範文 5 *Track 048*

To me, the people who take part in dangerous, potentially life-threatening athletic activities are somewhat crazy. Even though I admire their courage and their physical abilities, it is hard for me to understand why they continually put themselves at risk. However, there are clearly factors that cause certain people to pursue these activities.

One reason people do things like climb steep mountains and jump out of airplanes is that they enjoy the rush of adrenaline they get. They know the level of risk, and they may even be a little afraid. When they actually do these dangerous tasks, they overcome their fears, which is psychologically satisfying. Additionally, in certain extreme sports, athletes crave speed and become addicted to it. They say that dangerous speeds make them feel more "alive."

Another reason individuals engage in "extreme" sports is the desire to keep pushing the limits. Many athletes and explorers have a burning need to keep getting better and better. A swimmer wants to break the world record by swimming a faster race. To improve, there is little risk, just hard work. However, when an extreme skateboarder wants to break records, he or she jumps higher and does more twists, even though bones may get broken. Both the swimmer and the skater want to reach higher levels of achievement; it's just that the skater doesn't mind the risk.

Finally, we can probably all agree that many people involved in dangerous sports enjoy the attention they get from the media. In recent years, television programs have broadcast extreme sports events, which are very popular. The top athletes can become celebrities. Some fans go to the competitions to cheer on each athlete as he or she does more and more challenging jumps or runs. The athletes, who must work hard to be in good physical shape, probably enjoy the reward of having the public cheer their efforts. In addition, companies advertising sportswear or health drinks often ask top athletes to endorse their products. This leads to even more fame and a lot of money.

Although we cannot know for sure what drives individuals to engage in challenging physical ventures, it is obvious that their personalities are different from ours. They are willing to take risks that the average person is not, and that is why we watch them on television.

托福總監評析

在這篇範文中，考生一開始便說自己並不理解為什麼有些人會去參加危險的活動。很顯然，人們從事危險的活動是有原因的。第二、三和四段分別論述了不同的原因：興奮、挑戰極限的慾望和追求成名。最後一段重述第一段的觀點，即自己不太理解為什麼一些人喜歡從事危險活動。但顯然，這些人的個性不同於普通人；這也就是我們會在電視上看到這些人的原因。

建立自己的寫作句型庫

1. The primary motivation for people to join x is…
人們加入……的最初動機是……

The primary motivation for people to join informal groups is social.

延伸說法 The primary motivation for people to join industry associations is professional develoment.

2. In addition to VERBing, group members are able to VERB
除了……外，組織成員還能……

In addition to receiving moral support, group members are able to get timely practical advice from people in circumstances similar to their own.

延伸說法 In addition to getting information, group members are able to spend time with people just like them.

3. Compared to x members, people who choose to become members of y have…
與……的成員相比，選擇成為……的成員會……

Compared to informal group members, people who choose to become members of formal organizations have a wider range of reasons for their affiliations.

延伸說法 Compared to volunteer group members, people who choose to become members of industry organizations have economic incentives.

4. In short, there are many practical benefits of x
總之，……有諸多實際好處

In short, there are many practical benefits of large organizations.

延伸說法 In short, there are many practical benefits of group membership.

5. **Even in the 21ˢᵗ century, x is all around us and continues to play an important role in our lives, for many reasons.**

   即便在 21 世紀的今天，……仍然伴隨我們左右，並且基於多種原因，它將在我們的生活中繼續發揮重要作用。

   Even in the 21ˢᵗ century, music is all around us and continues to play an important role in our lives, for many reasons.

   > **延伸說法** Even in the 21ˢᵗ century, face-to-face communication is all around us and continues to play an important role in our lives, for many reasons.

6. **First and foremost, x makes us feel good.**

   首先，……使我們心情愉悅。

   First and foremost, music makes us feel good.

   > **延伸說法** First and foremost, being outdoors makes us feel good.

7. **Yet another reason that x is integral to so many people's lives is that it is so ADJECTIVE**

   然而，……對絕大多數人的生活必不可少的另一個原因是……

   Yet another reason that music is integral to so many people's lives is that it is so accessible.

   > **延伸說法** Yet another reason that technology is integral to so many people's lives is that it is so addictive.

8. **However, as we have seen from the examples above, the x of music and its y give music special importance.**

   可是，正如上文中的例子所示，音樂的……以及……特性使其變得極為重要。

   However, as we have seen from the examples above, the unique emotional impact of music and its widespread availability in digital format give music special importance.

   > **延伸說法** However, as we have seen from the examples above, the emotional content of music and its ability to make us dance give music special importance.

9. **Given a chance, most students would welcome an opportunity to study abroad, regardless of…**

   如果有可能，絕大多數學生會樂於接受出國留學的機會，不管……

   Given a chance, most students would welcome an opportunity to study abroad, regardless of what their home country is.

   > **延伸說法** Given a chance, most students would welcome an opportunity to study abroad, regardless of what they are studying.

10. x is probably the most often cited reason for students in developing Asian nations to go overseas.

……可能是亞洲發展中國家的學生出國留學最常提到的原因。

Getting a better education is probably the most often cited reason for students in developing Asian nations to go overseas.

延伸說法 Getting a degree in technology probably the most often cited reason for students in developing Asian nations to go overseas.

11. For x, y is the reason given most often for overseas study.

對於……來說，……是最常被提到的出國留學原因。

For students from developed countries, culture is the reason given most often for overseas study.

For many students, getting an MBA is the reason given most often for overseas study.

12. Thus, another reason why students go abroad is x

因此，學生出國留學的另一個原因在於……

Thus, another reason why students go abroad is prestige.

延伸說法 Thus, another reason why students go abroad is job insurance.

13. There are many reasons why different individuals choose to VERB, but I will pick three in my discussion below.

不同人選擇……有很多原因，但我下面只列舉其中的三種來討論。

There are many reasons why different individuals choose to go to a museum while traveling, but I will pick three in my discussion below.

延伸說法 There are many reasons why different individuals choose to study abroad, but I will pick three in my discussion below.

14. x are yet another reason why museums are popular.

博物館之所以如此受歡迎的原因，還有……

Gift items at museum gift shops are yet another reason why museums are popular.

延伸說法 Guided tours are yet another reason why museums are popular.

15. x is often a traveler's primary motive to visit a museum.

……經常是人們遊覽博物館的主要動機。

Visiting a museum's gift shop is often a traveler's primary motive to visit a museum.

延伸說法 Seeing ancient relics is often a traveler's primary motive to visit a museum.

16. Even though I admire their x, it is hard for me to understand why they VERB

雖然佩服他們的⋯⋯，但我很難理解他們為什麼⋯⋯

Even though I admire their courage and their physical abilities, it is hard for me to understand why they continually put themselves at risk.

延伸說法 Even though I admire their determination, it is hard for me to understand why they devote themselves to these particular activities.

17. However, there are clearly factors that cause certain people to VERB

可是，促使人們⋯⋯顯然是有原因的

However, there are clearly factors that cause certain people to pursue these activities.

延伸說法 However, there are clearly factors that cause certain people to listen to music.

18. Many x have a burning need to keep VERBing

許多⋯⋯急需要持續地⋯⋯

Many athletes and explorers have a burning need to keep getting better and better.

延伸說法 Many composers have a burning need to keep creating music.

19. Finally, we can probably all agree that many people involved in dangerous sports VERB

最後，大家可能都同意，許多從事危險運動的人⋯⋯

Finally, we can probably all agree that many people involved in dangerous sports enjoy the attention they get from the media.

延伸說法 Finally, we can probably all agree that many people involved in dangerous sports live each day for the moment.

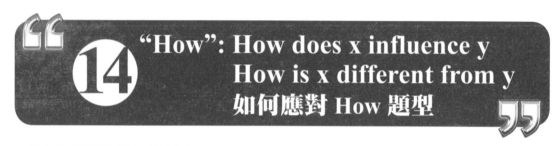

14 "How": How does x influence y
How is x different from y
如何應對 How 題型

在本章，你將學到……

★如何利用指示詞使文章銜接自然

解讀常考題

這類題的典型題目是：How does x influence y 和 how is x different from y。

在獨立寫作部分，How 題型並不是很多，但考生也應該做好充分的準備。這類題型一般都比較簡單，例如：How have views changed? 在該情境中，how 相當於 In what way(s)。How 題型一般要求考生描述一個過程、結果或者比較變化。考生需要給出一些細節。

最常見的 How 題型如下：

1. People often VERB. **How** does this influence their ideas about x?
2. Nowadays many people VERB. **How** have attitudes toward x changed?
3. x is a problem. **How** can people improve this situation?
4. Imagine that you were given x technology. **How** would you use this technology on your campus?

在寫 How 作文時，經常需要用上 by VERBing 和 through x 這樣的片語，如：
How can we help new students?
By counseling new students, we could put them at ease.
How can we best travel in the country?
Through train travel, we can appreciate the scenery.
How do clothes reflect a person's personality?
Clothes often represent a certain personality or style through their color; for example, bright red would probably be worn by an outgoing person.

有些 How 作文題要求討論影響或結果。這些題可以用因果模式，如：
How have video games influenced children?
Some video games have caused young people to become violent.

還有一些 How 作文題要求對比兩個事物，如：
How is a rural community different from an urban community?
People who live in the countryside tend to be easy-going, whereas city dwellers, crowded together, are often unfriendly.

▶模擬試題①

閱讀以下的短文並聆聽講座，完成以下這道作文題目。

Directions:

Read the question below. You have 30 minutes to plan, write, and revise your essay. Typically, an effective response will contain a minimum of 300 words.

> **Young children often enjoy watching television. How does television influence children's thoughts and behavior?**
>
> Use specific details to explain your answer.

這篇作文題要求考生談論電視對孩子的影響。考生既可以談論正面影響，也可以談論負面影響，或者兩者都討論。這道題目的難點是能不能提供夠多的問題和例子。同時，不要因為寫得太多而失去了「流暢性」，或因為時間不夠而無法完成寫作。

▶ Exercise 1

根據上面例題的題目要求寫一篇作文。初稿完成後，繼續學習下部分的內容。仔細研讀高分範文、萬用寫作範本、高分策略和寫作句型庫，運用所學的新知識完成 Exercise 2。

寫作構思

> **Negative influences:**
> Vulgar language
> **Violence**
> **Commercials**
> **Waste time**
> **Positive influences:**
> Cartoons make kids laugh
> Selective viewing
> **Educational programs**
> **Gain skills**
> **Parent explanations**

Some children spend many hours a day in front of the television. Because these young people are still in their formative years, television watching is believed to have a great deal of influence on their development. Research studies have been conducted to understand the effects of various programs on children; for example, on cognition and personality. The results show that television is indeed a powerful influence, with many negative impacts.

For example, there are adverse effects when children view programs containing violence and sexual content. Movies shown on television, like their counterparts on the big screen, contain violent behavior, including fist-fights, guns and rude language. Some children imitate this behavior, consciously and unconsciously. Other children have nightmares, worrying about terrorist bombs.

Another negative impact of television on children comes from commercials. The constant advertisements that show children eating unhealthy foods and playing with expensive toys make young viewers want these foods and toys. They often pressure their parents to buy these things, even when they are harmful.

Perhaps the most regrettable influence is the time wasted when children mindlessly sit in front of the screen. When they do this, they are not getting any exercise, nor are they engaged in meaningful activities such as homework or club projects.

Of course, there are some programs which exert a positive influence on children. Examples are *Sesame Street* and the science programs found on the Discovery Channel. From these, children can acquire practical skills, develop cognitive abilities and gain basic facts about nature, general science and culture. Even programs that target broad audiences can be beneficial to children if parents discuss the content with children in an appropriate way. For example, parents might sit with children to watch a news program and explain what is happening.

Interestingly, studies have shown that children's intellectual abilities are positively correlated to the number of hours of television watched, up to a certain point. On the other hand, excessive television deprives young children from physical exercise, leading to obesity, and violent content clearly influences behavior in harmful ways.

萬用模板

[開頭用一個句子引出話題]. Because these young people are still in their formative years, television watching is believed to have a great deal of influence on their _____. Research studies have been conducted to understand the effects of various programs on children; for example, _____. The results show that television is indeed _____.

For example, there are [形容詞] effects when _____. [用兩三個句子描述不良影響，添加一些細節資訊].

Another [形容詞] impact of television on children comes from _____. [用兩三個句子描述不良影響，添加一些細節資訊].

Perhaps the most [形容詞] influence is _____. [用兩三個句子描述不良影響，添加一些細節資訊].

Of course, there are some programs which _____. Examples are _____and _____. From these, children can acquire _____. [用兩三個句子描述正面影響，添加一些細節資訊].

Interestingly, studies have shown that _____. On the other hand, _____clearly influences behavior in [形容詞] ways.

　　第一段談到有些兒童一天看好幾個小時的電視。研究表明，電視對兒童有諸多負面影響。接下來的三段分別講述負面影響：充滿暴力的內容、大量不健康食品和昂貴玩具的商業廣告和缺乏運動。第五段從優秀兒童節目的積極影響角度來寫。總結段給出的事實讓人吃驚：看電視的時間長度和兒童的智力直接相關！但考生緊接著說只有看電視時間達到一定的量後才會出現影響兒童智力這種情況。在這一要點後，考生重述了電視對兒童的兩個負面影響。

利用指示詞來銜接

　　一篇銜接自然、前後連貫的作文就有可能得到 4 分以上的分數。

　　指示詞是特指某一單字或事物的詞。指示詞有兩種：指示代名詞和指示形容詞，也叫「限定詞」。指示代名詞和指示形容詞都指代前面提到的事物，這就是它們有助於文章銜接自然的原因。

　　指示代名詞有四種：this、that、these 和 those。這些代名詞指代前面提到的名詞或代名詞，以避免重複。例如，上篇高分範文中的 these 用法。

Of course, there are some programs which exert a positive influence on children. Examples are *Sesame Street* and the science programs found on the Discovery Channel. From these, children can acquire practical skills, develop cognitive abilities and gain basic facts about nature, general science and culture.

在上述句子中，指示代名詞 these 指放映的優秀電視節目，例如《芝麻街》和科學節目。this 和 these 指在時間或空間上距離較近的事物；that 和 those 則指時間和空間上距離較遠的事物。

指示形容詞修飾名詞，如 this plan 和 those students。這些名詞片語的功能和指示代名詞的功能一樣，指代一個具體的人、物體或觀點，如：

Movies shown on television, like their counterparts on the big screen, contain violent behavior, including fist-fights, guns and rude language. Some children imitate this behavior, consciously and unconsciously.

在上述例子中，指示形容詞 this 修飾名詞 behavior 指代前面提到過的打架和說髒話等不良行為。

指示詞並不難掌握。考生只需注意單複數一致和名詞空間距離的遠近。

再看一個指示形容詞的例子，摘自本章的高分範文：

Yet young people need someone knowledgeable to confide in when they run into problems at school. To address this need, teachers and counselors should proactively set up appointments to meet with the new student.

在上述句子中，this need 指的是年輕人需要有可信任的人這件事。指示詞的運用使上下兩句的語義銜接緊密、句子的表達流暢。

在新托福寫作考試中，指示形容詞（名詞片語）可能比簡單的指示代名詞更有用，因為前者更具體。評分人看重作文的表達是否清晰，指示形容詞能夠做到這一點。

透過指示詞使作文銜接自然的策略

1. 使用指示代名詞和指示形容詞時，要考慮單複數一致和空間距離的遠近。
2. 指示代名詞代替名詞或名詞片語。
3. 指示形容詞表明人、物體或觀點是前面提到的具體的人、物體和觀點。
4. 定冠詞也可以讓作文銜接自然，所以可以交替使用定冠詞和指示詞。

建立自己的寫作句型庫

1. **Because these young people are still in their formative years, television watching is believed to have a great deal of influence on their x**
   因為這些青少年仍處於性格形成的階段，看電視會對他們的……產生很大的影響

   Because these young people are still in their formative years, television watching is believed to have a great deal of influence on their development.

   延伸說法 Because these young people are still in their formative years, television watching is believed to have a great deal of influence on their physical condition.

2. For example, there are adverse effects when children view programs containing x

例如，兒童收看含有……內容的電視節目會有負面影響

For example, there are adverse effects when children view programs containing violence and sexual content.

延伸說法 For example, there are adverse effects when children view programs containing adult content.

3. Another negative impact of television on children comes from x

電視對兒童的另一個負面影響源於……

Another negative impact of television on children comes from commercials.

延伸說法 Another negative impact of television on children comes from horror movies.

4. Perhaps the most regrettable influence is…

最令人惋惜的影響可能是……

Perhaps the most regrettable influence is the time wasted when children mindlessly sit in front of the screen.

延伸說法 Perhaps the most regrettable influence is the junk food that gets eaten and the lack of exercise.

5. Even programs that VERB can be beneficial to children if…

如果……，甚至有一些……的節目也有益兒童成長

Even programs that target broad audiences can be beneficial to children if parents discuss the content with children in an appropriate way.

延伸說法 Even programs that contain some fighting can be beneficial to children if they are presented in a historical context.

▶ Exercise 2

學完高分範文、萬用寫作範本、高分策略和寫作句型庫，運用所學的技能修改你的初稿，並認真看修改之處。然後用學到的新句型去練習下面五道預測題的寫作。

寫作預測題

1. How does x influence...

Many people think that weather influences people's moods and behavior. How does weather influence you in your daily life?
Use specific details to explain your answer.

189

寫作構思

> **Like warm weather**
> **Sunlight and longer days**
> **Cold and gray makes me want to hibernate**
> Light deprivation leads to depression
> England — rainy climate so British reserved?

高分範文 1　　Track 050

The area where I live has four distinct seasons: Spring, summer, autumn and winter. The weather is therefore very different throughout the year. Furthermore, in recent years weather patterns have become very strange and unpredictable, perhaps due to greenhouse gases. I have found that varying weather conditions affect me profoundly, both mentally and physically.

First, I should confess that I prefer warm weather. That means I am happiest in late spring and summer. I find I wake up earlier, probably because the days are longer. The sunlight comes shining into my window and somehow I am eager to hop out of bed, ready to start my day. Outside, the birds are singing and flowers are starting to grow. How can one not feel energetic? The sunshine makes me feel more alert all day long.

Not only do I like the bright light; I like the heat. Many people cannot handle hot weather and complain that extreme heat makes them get headaches and become fatigued. Personally, however, I vastly prefer hot temperatures to the alternative.

Cold weather makes me want to stay in bed. If I could, I would hibernate for the entire winter season. It's true that snow is beautiful, but after the first snowfall, I don't enjoy winter days very much. The sky is often gray, which is depressing, especially when it continues day after day. For some reason, the short days of winter make me feel trapped and somewhat claustrophobic.

I can't imagine living in a place where it is always dark, cold and rainy; for example, places such as England and northern Germany. Cold rain is worse than snow! I think I would become a miserable person if I had to live in that kind of climate. However, I know many people who feel the opposite from me. Some people love extremely cold weather. In fact, some people love rain, saying that rain washes the streets clean. Thus, it is clear that individuals vary tremendously in terms of how each person reacts to weather conditions.

托福總監評析

　　這道寫作題要求考生討論天氣對人們情緒的影響，和上一道「電視對兒童的影響」寫作題有相似之處。前一篇作文寫電視如何影響兒童，而這篇作文必須寫天氣如何影響人們的情緒。這表示考生需要描述天氣狀況及考生對此的感受。注意句子：I have found that varying weather conditions affect me profoundly, both mentally and physically. 這個句子提醒讀者下文討論天氣對人們心理和生理的影響，因此這個過渡句起到了增強本文銜接性和連貫性的作用。

　　在第一段，考生談了自己居住地的氣候，為接下來的四段做了一個鋪陳。第二段主要講述考生喜歡溫暖的氣候，描述了溫暖氣候的特徵和自己的感受。第三段在第二段的基礎上，進一步說明自己還喜歡炎熱的天氣。這使句型變得複雜，文章讀起來更有趣。第四段談寒冷的天氣，可以預見這種天氣考生並不喜歡。注意考生如何描述自己對這種天氣的感受。最後一段繼續討論寒冷天氣，但明確說自己不喜歡這種氣候。本文的結論只有一句：Thus, it is clear that individuals vary tremendously in terms of how each person reacts to weather conditions. 儘管結論很短，但之前的段落寫得非常詳盡，集中談論了自己喜歡的氣候以及氣候如何影響自己的情緒，因此一句話的總結足夠銜接整篇文章。

　　切記，在考試中如果時間不夠用，考生可以用一句話來總結全文。

....

2. How have people changed...

> **Many people have pets these days, including cats, dogs and other small animals. How have people's attitudes towards pets changed in recent times?**
> Use specific reasons and examples to explain your answer.

寫作構思

> **Small dogs are popular**
> **Dog and cats on farms**
> Don't discipline animals so they misbehave
> Socialization – People walk dogs together
> **Pets in cities**
> **Smaller families**

高分範文 2   *Track 051*

When I went home for my summer vacation, I noticed that practically everyone who lives in my parent's apartment building had a cat or a dog. Small dogs seemed to be especially popular. At dusk, after work, my neighbors could be seen walking their dogs within the apartment compound. Ten years ago, this scene would have been virtually impossible. That is because people nowadays seem to treat dogs and other pets as members of the family.

For example, owners these days often let their dogs and cats sleep with them at night in their bedrooms. In earlier times, animals would never have been allowed into a person's bedroom. In fact, in farming communities, animals were never allowed into the home; they had to stay outside. This is because in a rural society, cats and dogs are supposed to work outside. Cats kill rodents and dogs help herd cows and sheep, as well as guard the home against unwanted strangers. From this, we can see that previous generations considered cats and dogs to be dirty creatures that belonged outside, together with the other farm animals.

There are several reasons why people have allowed pets into their homes in recent times. For one thing, more people are living in cities now, and their economic standing has vastly improved. In cities, cats and dogs don't have any "farm work," such as catching mice or herding sheep. The animals' owners usually keep them inside to protect them from getting lost or hit by cars.

Another reason that owners are becoming closer to their pets is that people are having fewer children. A cat or dog is in some ways like another "child." A pet can provide companionship to people, regardless of their age. Pets also make life more lively and interesting. Pets do tricks and make us laugh. In turn, people buy their pets small toys and special treats.

Thus, we can see that our new preoccupation with pets reflects a transition from an agricultural to an urban society. It also reflects a move toward a relatively affluent society with smaller families, where people can afford to spoil their animals.

托福總監評析

　　考生會經常遇到這類獨立寫作題：How have attitudes towards x changed? 對於這類 How 題型，考生要比較過去和當前的狀況、過去和當前的態度，並說出變化的原因。如果考生能夠給出足夠的細節，就能取得高分。

　　在這篇範文中，為了讓第一段更有趣，考生講述父母公寓大樓的院子內有許多寵物，並給出了細節，如小型犬特別受歡迎。為了使該段銜接自然，考生是這麼寫的：Ten years ago, this scene would have been virtually impossible. That is because people nowadays seem to treat dogs and other pets as members of the family. 這兩句為下文的比較做了鋪陳（十年前和現在），並大致說明了變化原因。為了緊扣 how have attitudes changed，第二段描述了一種變化：允許寵物在臥室裡睡覺。第三段說明了寵物主人讓寵物進家門的原因：從農村生活方式到城市公寓的轉變。第四段列舉了當前社會寵物主人和寵物更親近的原因：他們的孩子少了。第四段實際的理由緊扣 How have attitudes changed，評分人會注意到這一點。總結段總結了人類和寵物關係更親密的原因。

3. How can x help...

Moving to a new school can be stressful for students. How can schools help students who have changed schools?

Use specific reasons and examples to explain your answer.

寫作構思

New set of friends

New teachers

Assign an old student to be a "sponsor" for semester

Have each new student join one club

Different curriculum

Safety net

高分範文 3 *Track 052*

Moving to a new school is often a traumatic experience for a student. Young people tend to rely on a circle of friends as they learn to master the skills of dealing with people. When students are abruptly plunged into a completely new environment, they often find it hard to adjust in the beginning. Whenever possible, the school should actively monitor and support the new student's transition.

Several problems present themselves in a student's adjustment to a new school. First, as it is difficult or unpractical to maintain close contact with old friends, the student has to quickly find compatible people. Making friends can be a long and trying process when you are the only unfamiliar face in a group of people. One thing the school can do is organize activities with the express purpose of introducing the newcomer to his or her classmates. This might very well encourage existing students to reach out to the new classmate, paving the way for the formation of new friendships.

The next challenge is the change in teachers and counselors. Young people work better with adults whom they trust; they tend to be shy when faced with unfamiliar adults. Yet young people need someone knowledgeable to confide in when they run into problems at school. To address this need, teachers and counselors should proactively set up appointments to meet with the new student. The meeting does not have to be long; the main purpose is to let new students know that the school is there for them, available for consultation whenever there is a need.

Additional hurdles that new students may face include adjusting to the new curriculum and worrying about being able to compete with other students. In these situations, as in the challenges discussed above, the school needs to reach out to the new student and offer help before help is needed. If that can be done, the student will realize that there is a safety net in place as he or she looks for ways to fit into the new environment.

托福總監評析

這道寫作題實質上是問學校如何幫助轉學生適應新環境：How can schools help students who have changed schools? 因此這篇作文必須包含詳細的步驟以及採取這些步驟的原因或依據。

第一段先說學生轉學是一種痛苦的經歷，然後描述可能會遇到的情況，到這裡讀者開始理解，轉學生需要得到哪些方面的幫助。Whenever possible, the school should actively monitor and support the new student's transition. 這一句使本文很自然地過渡到下一段內容，即步驟。第二段和第三段分別表述了新生可能會遇到的問題或困難，學校應如何幫助新生融入集體、適應新環境。總結段又提出了新生可能會遇到的兩種困境，緊接著指出，跟上文提到的所有問題的解決方法一樣，學校應聯繫新生，及時提供幫助。最後一句點明學校應這麼做的原因。

---

4. How does x differ from y...

Each generation of young people is different. How does your generation differ from your parents' generation?
Use specific reasons and examples to explain your answer.

寫作構思

New Generation
Technology, computers, Internet
Packaged food, junk food, microwave
Better economic situation
Doesn't understand or appreciate old art forms
Leisurely lifestyle

高分範文 4 *Track 053*

When we are teenagers, we think we know everything and that we are special. We think our entire generation is unique, and perhaps in some ways it is. It is likely, however, that our parents felt the same way when they were teenagers. This said, it is true that the world in which my parents grew up was very different from my world.

Perhaps the most profound difference between my generation and my parents' is the pervasiveness of technology. The wide impact of personal computers, mobile devices and the Internet have allowed young people today to be linked to each other and the world in ways never imagined. My father and mother had to rely on a landline telephone and occasionally a fax machine. For them, a "social network" meant a group of neighbors getting together for a barbecue. They did not have mobile phones. When they communicated with other people, it was usually in person.

Another significant difference between our generations is food — what we eat and how we prepare it. In my parents' time, there were no microwave ovens. People did not go out to restaurants very often. Rather, they ate simple home-cooked meals. The family meals my mother prepared were not fancy, but we sat down together every evening to eat. In contrast, my generation eats at irregular times. Sometimes we grab a sandwich or some other "junk food." It is no coincidence that my generation suffers more from obesity.

Finally, my father and mother had a more leisurely lifestyle, even though neither of them came from wealthy families. However, when my parents were young, they played after school with other children in nearby parks. In the summer, they went to my grandparents' home and relaxed. When I was a child, I felt a lot of pressure to study and often participated in structured activities like piano lessons and karate. My generation also had tutors to help us get higher scores on our exams. In contrast, my parents just studied on their own, without tutors.

As I have described, my parents' lives were quite different from my own. In many ways, they lived in simpler times. To be sure, there was less technology, but people seemed to have time to have a nice family meal and enjoy one another. To me, this pace of life seems vastly preferable to the rat race of the 21st century.

托福總監評析

　　這篇非常連貫的範文描述了兩代人之間的差異。第一段很有趣，因為該段描述了每個年代青少年的「自戀情結」。在說完了兩代人之間的相同點後，考生說實際上這兩代人差異較大，為接下來幾段的對比做了鋪陳。第二段至第四段分別描述了考生這一代和其父母這一代的差異。這些差異表現在：現代通訊科技使兩代人在社交方式上的差異較大；飲食習慣不同；業餘時間從事的活動也不同。總結段重申觀點，即這兩代人差異較大，然後總結了作文主體部分的分論點。同時，考生表明了自己的觀點：更喜歡上一代人的生活節奏。

5. How would you...

Imagine that you have received a large sum of money to give to the charity of your choice. How would you use this money?
Use specific details to explain your answer.

寫作構思

Help disaster victims
Save pandas and their habitats
Use money to set up educational foundation
Help poor children
Dorm and classroom building
Staff

高分範文 5 *Track 054*

As a college student, when I am not studying, I am often participating in university clubs. One of these activities is a volunteer group where students tutor children. These children come from poor families and don't have a proper school. Consequently, if I received a large sum of money, I would use it to create an educational foundation for the children's education.

I would begin by using a portion of the money awarded me to build a modern boarding school complex. I envision a student dormitory building with comfortable bedrooms and clean showers and bathrooms. The dormitory rooms would be wired for the Internet, and laptops would be provided for student use. The school building would have a large teachers' lounge where faculty could drink tea and relax. Classroom windows would be large, so that light could shine in. This state-of-the-art classroom building would be equipped with a computer lab, a library and a gymnasium.

With the remainder of the gift money, I would hire and train a full-time person to work for the foundation. The job would entail promoting the educational foundation and soliciting additional donations from people around the city. The ideal person for this job would be enthusiastic, socially minded and good with children and adults. If this employee could successfully bring in funds, that extra money could be spent on textbooks, school uniforms and lunch subsidies.

As soon as this infrastructure was in place, the elementary students could begin attending school there. Teachers could work with local education officials to make sure the curriculum was as good as possible and the school was up to standards. Student volunteers from my university could continue to do tutoring in the subjects that are difficult for them. For example, we could help them with English, mathematics and science. I believe that this way of allocating the financial gift would be an excellent investment, providing many children with an improved learning environment.

托福總監評析

　　這道寫作題是一道假設情形題。題目假設考生收到一大筆錢，問怎麼利用這些錢，因此這篇作文應該用虛擬語氣（I would spend the money on...）。

　　範文第一段中，考生先交代自己做家教義工的情況，自然過渡到中心觀點：Consequently, if I received a large sum of money, I would use it to create an educational foundation for the children's education. 文章接下來描述這些錢究竟怎麼花。第二段和第三段分別詳細描述了自己要建一所寄宿學校、這所學校的基礎設施建設和員工聘用等。最後一段繼續說明學校的運行，提到校友擔任家教義工，呼應第一段。最後一句重申論點，強調這筆錢應該用於創辦這麼一所學校。

建立自己的寫作句型庫

1. I have found that x affect me profoundly, both mentally and physically.

我發現……對我的心理與生理都有極大的影響。

I have found that varying weather conditions affect me profoundly, both mentally and physically.

延伸說法 I have found that eating healthy food at home affects me profoundly, both mentally and physically.

2. x makes me feel more alert all day long.

……使我一整天都保持敏銳的思維。

The sunshine makes me feel more alert all day long.

延伸說法 Jogging in the morning makes me feel more alert all day long.

3. For some reason, x make me feel ADJECTIVE and somewhat ADJECTIVE.

出於某種原因，……讓我覺得……，並且稍微有點……

For some reason, the short days of winter make me feel trapped and somewhat claustrophobic.

延伸說法 For some reason, studying independently makes me feel bored and alone.

4. Thus, it is clear that individuals vary tremendously in terms of how each person reacts to x

因此，每個人對……的反應差異性很大，這是顯而易見的

Thus, it is clear that individuals vary tremendously in terms of how each person reacts to weather conditions.

延伸說法 Thus, it is clear that individuals vary tremendously in terms of how each person reacts to living in a big city.

5. That is because people nowadays seem to VERB

那是因為現在人們似乎……

That is because people nowadays seem to treat dogs and other pets as members of the family.

延伸說法 That is because people nowadays seem to enjoy taking risks.

6. From this, we can see that previous generations considered x to be y

我們由此可知上一代人把……看作……

From this, we can see that previous generations considered cats and dogs to be dirty creatures that belonged outside, together with the other farm animals.

延伸說法 From this, we can see that previous generations considered eating at home to be an important thing.

7. There are several reasons why people have VERBed in recent times.

近來，人們之所以會……是有原因的。

There are several reasons why people have allowed pets into their homes in recent times.

延伸說法 There are several reasons why people have become less physically active in recent times.

8. Thus, we can see that x reflects a transition from an agricultural to an urban society.

因此，我們可以發現……反映了社會由農業型向都市型的轉型。

Thus, we can see that our new preoccupation with pets reflects a transition from an agricultural to an urban society.

延伸說法 Thus, we can see that modern architecture reflects a transition from an agricultural to an urban society.

9. Whenever possible, the school should VERB the new student's transition.

學校應盡可能隨時……新生的過渡。

Whenever possible, the school should actively monitor and support the new student's transition.

延伸說法 Whenever possible, the school should ease the new student's transition.

10. If that can be done, the student will realize that there is x as he or she looks for ways to fit into the new environment.

如果能夠做到這一點，當學生試圖融入新環境的過程中會發現有……

If that can be done, the student will realize that there is a safety net in place as he or she looks for ways to fit into the new environment.

延伸說法 If that can be done, the student will realize that there is help available as he or she looks for ways to fit into the new environment.

11. Perhaps the most profound difference between my generation and my parents' is…

也許，我們這代人跟上一代最大的不同在於……

Perhaps the most profound difference between my generation and my parents' is the pervasiveness of technology.

延伸說法 Perhaps the most profound difference between my generation and my parents' is the fast pace of life nowadays.

12. It is no coincidence that my generation suffers more from x

我這一代人之所以遭受更多……，絕非偶然

It is no coincidence that my generation suffers more from obesity.

延伸說法 It is no coincidence that my generation suffers more from stress.

13. Consequently, if I received a large sum of money, I would use it to VERB

所以，如果我得到一大筆錢，我將用它……

Consequently, if I received a large sum of money, I would use it to create an educational foundation for the children's education.

延伸說法 Consequently, if I received a large sum of money, I would use it to invest in the stock market.

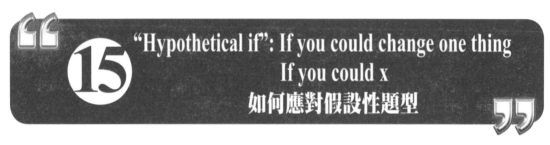

15 "Hypothetical if": If you could change one thing
If you could x
如何應對假設性題型

66 在本章，你將學到…… 99

★描述假設性情景的具體語言策略

解讀常考題

典型題型：If you could change one thing 和 If you could x。

獨立寫作題中，假設性題型是最有趣的一種題型。因為考生要想像一種情形，可以自由地寫自己喜歡的話題。但在文法上，假設性題型是對考生的一種挑戰。表達假設的文法並不簡單，要使用特定的動詞形式。本章會詳細說明這部分的重點。

假設性作文題通常有以下幾種形式：

1. **If** you **could** VERB, what **would** you do?
2. **If** you **were asked** to [choose a piece of art that best represents your country], what **would** you [choose]?
3. **If** you **were** a [university president], what kind of person **would** you hire to be a [professor]?

先來看一看假設性題型的例子。

▶模擬試題①

閱讀以下的短文並聆聽講座，完成以下這道作文題。

Directions:

Read the question below. You have 30 minutes to plan, write, and revise your essay. Typically, an effective response will contain a minimum of 300 words.

If you could create a new invention, what product would you make?
Use specific details to explain why this invention is necessary.

這道寫作題假設進行一項創造發明，問「你」最想創造什麼。從某個角度來說，這道寫作題也是一道 Why 題型寫作題，因為該題有一層隱含的意思：Why is this invention necessary? 一篇優秀的作文應該往能滿足現實需求的物品上想，還需要提供幾個例子說明某項創造發明對人類的意義。

▶ Exercise 1

根據上面例題的題目要求寫一篇作文。初稿完成後，繼續學習下部分的內容。仔細研讀高分範文、萬用寫作範本、賦能技能和寫作句型庫，運用所學的新知識完成 Exercise 2。

寫作構思

Machine that could accurately translate audio input
Use it to translate foreign languages
Spacecraft to travel in space
Speed of light
Resources
Emigration

高分範文　　*Track 055*

If I were able to create something new and revolutionary, it would be a spacecraft that travels at close to the speed of light. The availability of such a vehicle would serve many purposes, chief of which are outlined below.

First, this vehicle would give us the ability to explore far-flung places in the universe, so that we could look for things that we need back on Earth. As we all know, many of the natural resources we rely on are fast depleting. Examples are oil, coal and uranium. Even though scientists are trying hard to develop renewable energy sources, would it not be nice to have more of the traditional energy sources? Planets such as Mars, for example, may have concentrated mineral ores with great concentrations of precious metal ores.

Second, the invention would allow us to travel around the universe. People love to travel. Many of us have experiences visiting beautiful or exotic places, but why should we limit ourselves to places on Earth? Space tourism has always been something that businesses and potential tourists have wanted. I have no doubt that there are many weird and wonderful places beyond our solar system, just waiting for us to discover and enjoy.

Finally, my new vehicle might just be what we need to find the next home for humanity. Some people estimate that the Earth will continue to provide a livable habitat for oxygen-based animals, including humans, for another 500 million years. It seems inevitable that our descendants will have to emigrate to some other planet before that time comes. Without a fast intergalactic transport, it will be unlikely that humans can ever find a future home.

To recap, through my spacecraft, I would like to better the future of humanity. Both the commercial exploitation of distant resources and the development of space tourism would add value to our lives. Most importantly, my invention would enable us to find a compatible safe haven before the demise of planet Earth, allowing us to prepare for our eventual emigration to that planet.

萬用模板

If I were able to create something new and revolutionary, it would be a [一項發明] that _____. The availability of such a _____ would serve many purposes, chief of which are outlined below.

First, this _____ would give us the ability to _____, so that we could _____. As we all know, [用兩三個句子來描述第一個用處的必要性].

Second, the invention would allow us to _____. [用兩三個句子來描述第二個用處的必要性].

Finally, my new _____ might just be what we need to _____. [用兩三個句子來描述第三個用處的必要性].

To recap, through my _____, I would like to better the future of humanity. Both the [改述第一個用處] and the [改述第二個用處]. Most importantly, my invention would enable us to [改述第三個用處], allowing us to [進一步闡述第三個用處].

　　在這篇高分範文的第一段，考生說想創建一艘飛行速度接近光速的太空船。第二段至第四段分別描述了太空船的用處：開採外星球上的能源、太空旅行以及為地球不適宜人類居住時做準備。總結段先籠統地說了說發明太空船的原因（... I would like to better the future of humanity.），然後總結了上文提到的三個用處。注意考生把最重要的用處放在最後來說明。

描述假設性情形

　　新托福考試獨立寫作題常要求考生討論假設性情形，例如：If you could create a new holiday, what would it be? 但就像前面所說的，假設性作文的語言規範比較不好掌握。很多考生可能都知道條件句的文法規則，但真正運用的時候，有些考生就不知道如何正確使用虛擬條件句了。

　　在假設性題型中，考生幾乎都要用到虛擬條件句（問偏愛的 What would you do? 題型也同樣）。用陳述語氣 I will... 來回答假設性題型是不正確的。這一點要切記，因為許多考生都會犯個錯誤。

1. 描述假設性情形需要掌握三個方面的知識

1）如何用獨立子句和非獨立子句寫出複雜的句型。
2）如何寫出虛擬條件句。
3）作文中如何靈活運用虛擬條件句和陳述句兩種句型。

2. 假設性題型的典型錯誤表達

寫作題	正確說法	錯誤說法
If you **could** create a new holiday, what **would** it be?	I **would** create a day for health.	I hope people have a day for health.
	I **would like** to create a day for health.	I will create a day for health.
	A Health Day **could** be created.	A Health Day can be created.
	A day celebrating good health **might** be created.	A Health Day may be created.

　　從上述例子可以看出，如果題目是假設性作文題，文中的時態也就應用相同的時態，即虛擬條件句的時態。作文中的所有例子和原因也用相同的時態。

　　注意上面這個表格，「錯誤說法」欄裡的句子如果單獨出現都是正確的。但在一篇假設性情境的作文裡，這些動詞形式則是錯誤的。

3. 假設性題型作文裡的情態動詞

　　需要運用虛擬條件句的寫作題，考生要用情態動詞 would、could、should 和 might。would 用來表達喜好與意願；could 用來表達可能性。

　　would 在獨立寫作中可以有兩種文法形式：Subject + would + VERB 和 Subject + would + VERB + infinitive VERB，如：

If I could create an invention...
I **would** invent a robot.

If I could create an invention...
I **would** choose to invent a robot.
I **would** love to invent a robot.

　　在獨立寫作的假設性題型作文中，考生應該避免使用 can 和 may，而應該使用 can 的過去式 could 或 may 的過去式 might。這些情態動詞表明某人假設做某事。

　　在假設的情境裡，could 和 might 的用法是：Subject + could + VERB 和 Subject + might + VERB，如：

The holiday **could** educate people about good health practices.
The invention **might** help senior citizens move around town.

此處情態動詞 could 和 might 解釋在假設情境裡某種情況會呈現什麼狀況，這會在段落中起到非常好的論證效果。

改變一下上述用法，可以增加副詞 maybe 和 possibly，如：

The money **could possibly** be used for orphans.
If I had time, **maybe** I **would** travel to Australia.

總之，在虛擬條件句中，考生要正確使用情態動詞，尤其是描述要做的事情時。但討論事實情況時，考生要用陳述語氣。下面來看一段從以上高分範文中摘取的內容：

First, this vehicle **would** give us the ability to explore far-flung places in the universe, so that we **could** look for things that we need back on Earth. As we all know, many of the natural resources we rely on are fast depleting. Examples are oil, coal and uranium. Even though scientists are trying hard to develop renewable energy sources, **would** it not be nice to have more of the traditional energy sources? Planets such as Mars, for example, may have concentrated mineral ores with great concentrations of precious metal ores.

加粗的動詞形式是虛擬條件句裡的情態動詞。考生透過這些情態動詞告訴讀者自己想要什麼或者認為可能的情況。加框的動詞形式是陳述語氣形式，表明事實情況，例如：many of the natural resources we rely are fast depleting 是一個客觀事實。最後一句用了 may have，因為考生認為這個陳述是對現實的推測。

假設性題型的策略

1. 掌握獨立子句和非獨立子句的複雜句型。
2. 要會寫虛擬條件句。
3. 學會用來表達偏愛或意願的情態動詞 would 的基本用法，並多加練習，如：If I were given a sum of money, I would buy my parents a house.
4. 學會用來表達可能性的情態動詞 could 和 might 的基本用法，並多加練習，如：The holiday could teach people about the space program.
5. 考試時仔細看清楚題目意思，確定題目是假設性題型還是要用虛擬語氣的其他題目類型。
6. 看題目時，注意題目中是否有 would，如：Would you like to travel somewhere you have never been before? 這是作文裡需要用情態動詞 would 的提示。
7. 可以在 could 和 might 句子中加上副詞 maybe 和 possibly，使句型多樣化。
8. 虛擬條件句要用情態動詞，而事實性句子則用陳述語氣的動詞形式。

建立自己的寫作句型庫

1. If I were able to create something new and revolutionary, it would be a(n) x that VERB
如果我能創造出突破性的新事物，那將會是……

If I were able to create something new and revolutionary, it would be a spacecraft that travels at close to the speed of light.

延伸說法 If I were able to create something new and revolutionary, it would be a drug that could cure cancer.

2. To recap, through my x, I would like to better the future of humanity.

總而言之，透過我的……，我希望讓人類的明天更美好。

To recap, through my spacecraft, I would like to better the future of humanity.

延伸說法 To recap, through my new drug, I would like to better the future of humanity.

▶ Exercise 2

學完高分範文、萬用寫作範本、高分策略和寫作句型庫，運用所學的技能修改你的初稿，並認真看修改之處。然後用學到的新句型去練習下面五道預測題的寫作。

模擬試題

1. If you could create...

Many holidays call attention to important issues. If you could create a new holiday, what cause would you celebrate? What would people do on that holiday?
Use specific reasons and details to support your answer.

寫作構思

Senior Citizen Day
Good Neighbor Day
Reach out to lonely people
Make a good community
Home Day
Mother Nature
Abundance
Fragile

高分範文 1 *Track 056*

If I had an opportunity to create a new holiday, I would use it to heighten people's awareness of the fragility of the Earth's environment. My holiday would honor Mother Nature, who endowed us with the rich but fragile environment in which we live. I would name my holiday "Home Day" to emphasize that the Earth is our common home.

Aside from the Sun, we obtain everything we need to survive from the Earth. From the rich fauna and flora which provide us with food, to the minerals and energy sources which allow us to build our modern society, the Earth's natural resources sustain us. I cannot imagine living without the material abundance of the Earth. Moreover, the physical environment of this planet is both dramatic and soothing. When I travel into the mountains, I am often struck by the sheer beauty of the natural landscape.

However, in spite of its beauty, the Earth is extremely fragile. I see everywhere the destruction humans have brought to the environment: Smoggy air filled with pollutants, rivers churning with dirt and silt because of deforestation and entire hillsides littered with manmade garbage. Less obvious, but perhaps more dangerous to living creatures are our waters, which are slowly being poisoned by chemicals and the greenhouse effect. These destructive forces need to be reversed.

If I could, I would make Home Day a national holiday so people could have a day off to enjoy nature or attend educational events. Companies could sponsor events throughout the country and promote their own environmentally friendly products.

There is a saying that "Ignorance brings destruction, whereas education brings protection." Through the enactment of Home Day, we could educate ourselves. Our citizens would learn to be good stewards of the land we inhabit so future generations can enjoy the abundant resources and beauty the Earth has to offer.

托福總監評析

　　這道假設性寫作題要求考生假設可以創立一個新節日。高分作文應包含三個方面的內容：提出一個有意義的節日、給出充分的理由並描述節日當天要開展的活動。

　　在這篇高分範文中，第一段先說明創立節日的目的（to heighten people's awareness of the fragility of the Earth's environment），然後告訴讀者要創立什麼樣的節日。第二段描述了地球豐富的自然資源和美景。第三段描述污染和其他人類活動對地球的毀滅性破壞。在第四段，考生針對題目中 What would people do on that holiday 做了陳述。總結段非常有力度。先是引用名言，接下來強調進行保護地球生態系統教育的必要性。

2. If you could change...

> If you could change one thing about your living accommodations, what would you change?
> Use reasons and specific examples to support your answer.

寫作構思

> **Parents' apartment**
> **Street noise**
> **Pollution**
> Add a shower to the bathroom
> Just a bathtub now, want a hot shower

高分範文 2　 *Track 057*

I am generally satisfied with my living accommodations, for I have a fairly large space in my parents' downtown apartment. My room is nicely decorated, according to my wishes, and the apartment has all the modern amenities one could hope for. There is just one thing that bothers me: the location. If it were possible, I would pack up all my things and move to a different place.

The first problem solved by the move would be noise. There is a terrible racket coming from the street below my room. Not far from our building is a street market where vendors gather before daybreak. They are a noisy bunch, calling out to advertise their low prices. There is also the honking of passing cars; the drivers are angry at the traffic jams. Even though the vendors are supposed to use the sidewalk, they put their carts in the narrow street, which blocks the flow of cars. The uncivilized drivers honk their horns persistently just to vent their anger. It is enough to drive anyone crazy.

The second problem that would go away is pollution. Our city is an old industrial town. Steel mills and coal mines line the outskirts of the city, making the air gray and heavy. Consequently, I can never leave my room windows open. If I do, even for half an hour, I end up cleaning for hours. My furniture, bedding and audio equipment are covered with a layer of soot and dust. I would not have this problem if I could move to the small mountain town where one of my classmates lives. Although the town is not as prosperous as my city, they leave their windows open throughout the day. Sitting in their apartments, one can enjoy the fresh breezes blowing into the window.

I love my city because I have grown up here. I have gotten used to its rhythms and customs. Nevertheless, I would be happy to give everything here up for a quieter and cleaner environment. I am sure that once I settled down in the new town, I would be very comfortable there.

托福總監評析

　　這道假設題同時也是一道 What 題型，因為該題要求考生說一說自己住所的問題以及改善措施。高分作文一般都會舉例說明改善措施，可能還會對比改善前後的情景。對比中可以對不同特點作正面或負面評價。

在這篇高分範文中，考生詳細描述了目前居住的公寓。提到了公寓的幾個優點和讓人難以忍受的缺陷，即地理位置。第二段和第三段分別描述了缺陷：周邊的吵鬧和空氣污染。在第三段，考生特別提到了一個地方：一個同學居住的山區小鎮。在最後一段，考生說自己很喜歡目前居住的城市，但仍下定決心找一個安靜、環境乾淨的地方居住。

---

3. If you could ask someone...

> If you could ask a celebrity one question, what would you ask? Give detailed reasons to support your choice.

寫作構思

> **Genetically modified food**
> **Public debate**
> **Scientific facts**
> Ask Johnny Depp what his proudest moment was
> Understand his value system

高分範文 3 *Track 058*

If I had a chance to ask a celebrity a question, I would ask about genetically modified foods (also known as GM foods). Specifically, I would pose this question: "Do you think GM foods are all right? Why or why not?"

Quite frankly, I would be curious about how the celebrity would respond to this kind of question. I would not be surprised if the celebrity had strong feelings on the matter but could not provide any legitimate reasons to support those feelings. My experience is that people in general don't have knowledge of the facts on this important topic. For example, most of them are not aware that when a certain gene is inserted into a crop such as cotton, farmers can grow this crop using very little pesticide. It would be interesting to see if the celebrity is as uninformed as ordinary folks.

Because of the importance of food economics, I would try to use this opportunity to publicize the issue. No matter what the celebrity's response was, it would be good to debate the issue. If the celebrity was not knowledgeable, it would demonstrate to the public that we really need education in this area. On the other hand, if the celebrity knew a lot about the issue, his or her response would serve as valuable input to people following the news.

During our conversation, I would also try to get the celebrity to react to a claim made in a major newspaper, that crop modification by molecular methods is not any more dangerous than crop modification by traditional methods. I would ask him, why do you think we are suddenly so concerned with this efficient new technique of cross breeding? After all, humans have experimented with cross breeding for centuries and never worried whether it would create adverse effects. Hopefully, the media would report on all of these points.

In fact, my rationale for asking this question is that famous people create controversies, which then get covered in the media. What better thing than to use my questions to create some buzz about genetically modified foods? If public discussions are generated because of this query, we might be able to dispel many misunderstandings about the science of GM foods.

托福總監評析

這道假設題可以有很多種寫法。例如，考生可以問名人一個有趣的問題：If you were a flower, what would you be? 或者問嚴肅的問題：What do you think the key to a successful career is? 或 What can people do to fight global warming?

注意兩個方面：第一，提出問題之前要考慮好你向名人提出這個問題是出於什麼原因。第二，作文裡可以提到名人的名字，也可以泛泛地說 a celebrity 或 a movie star。

儘管這篇高分範文中的第一段很短，但把考生感興趣的話題（基因改造食品）和考生要提問的具體問題都交代清楚了。第二段的風趣之處在於考生說儘管自己提問了，但他懷疑名人是否答得出自己的問題，因為世界上大多數人對基因改造食品的瞭解並不多。第三段沿著這個思路繼續論述，說不論名人是否博學，基因改造食品的對話有利於提高公眾對此話題的認識。很顯然，透過名人的影響力使該話題出現在媒體上，這是考生向名人提問基因改造食品的原因。第四段順著這個問題陳述了考生想問名人的其他幾個問題。提問的目的都是想透過媒體的報導，提高公眾對「雜交育種」的意識。最後一段總結了考生提問的原因，強調媒體的爭議和公眾的討論有助於破除基因改造食品的謠言。

---

4. If you were asked to...

If you were asked to write a book about your hometown, what would you write about? Why?
Use specific details and examples to support your answer.

寫作構思

Cuisine
Imperial homes
Traffic and pollution
Future
History of universities in my town
Long tradition of university students coming here
How it affects the town

高分範文 4　 *Track 059*

My hometown, Beijing, is not only the capital city, it is also one of the most interesting places in China. If I were to write a book about it, I would focus on three aspects: Its food, its imperial past and its future as a cosmopolitan city.

All Chinese pay a lot of attention to food. Beijing is especially blessed because it is a city of immigrants, who have brought their home cuisines to their new adopted home. A trip to a neighborhood restaurant can turn out to be a culinary adventure. Every corner of Beijing has restaurants operated by people from all over the country. Oftentimes the wait staff comes from the owner's hometown and speaks the local language; for example, the Cantonese and Sichuanese dialects, or Mongolian, Uyghur and Dai. Writing about the friendly staff in these small restaurants and the diversity of dishes would be a pleasure.

The second aspect of Beijing I would write about is the imperial homes and gardens which were once inhabited by emperors and their households. For example, I would talk about the Forbidden City and the Summer Palace. After describing the landscaping, architecture, and furnishings, I would devote a few pages to the historical conditions that led to one single family living in splendor while the masses lived in poverty.

At the end of the book, I would speculate about the future of my hometown. Beijing today is literally a lab and playground for international architecture. Everywhere one looks, there are landmark office buildings and even residential communities designed by foreign firms. In contrast to the standard traditional Chinese buildings found in the hutong, the new designs lend the city a cosmopolitan air. Of course, congested traffic and pollution have come along with the new prosperity.

Throughout, I would try to strike a balance by describing the things I enjoy as well as the city's problems. Moreover, I would certainly write about the ways in which my hometown could work toward a brighter future.

托福總監評析

　　這道寫作題要求考生假設寫一本以家鄉為主題的書。一篇優秀的作文應該包含兩項內容：選取家鄉最有特色的幾個點、選取這幾個點的原因。

　　第一段很簡潔，談到自己的家鄉是北京，北京是中國的首都，然後列出下文要講的三個方面：美食、古都的歷史和國際化都市的未來。第二段至第四段分別從這三個方面來描述。總結段說北京好的一面「我」會寫，存在的問題也會寫，還會對其未來的發展提出建議。

5. If you could go back in time...

> **Time travel is not yet possible. However, if you could go back in time, when and where would you go?**
> Use specific reasons and details to explain your answer.

寫作構思

Travel to Paris around 1900
See Picasso and other artists and writers in coffee houses
Time warp
Peking Man
Bering land bridge
Fact-finding trip

高分範文 5　 *Track 060*

Most of what we know about the prehistoric world is based on speculations by paleontologists and archaeologists. By traveling in time, I could see for myself what happened in prehistory. Consequently, if I could go through a time warp, I would choose to go to two prehistoric times and places.

First, I would travel to a location southwest of modern day Beijing, an area where the remains of Peking Man were found. I would want to see if Peking Man (a Homo erectus species) was still there when Homo sapiens arrived. If both Homo erectus and Homo sapiens were in the area, I would observe whether there was any mingling between the tribes. This might shed light on the Chinese gene pool.

After that, I would set the time travel machine for a point in time 12,000 years ago and travel to Siberia. I would hike across the Bering land bridge, thinking about the great forces of nature that made it possible for humans in Asia to travel to North America. I would marvel how climate change could eventually melt so much ice that the entire land bridge would become part of the ocean floor. In addition, I would muse about how nature closed off the Americas. When this happened, native Americans lost contact with other continents and had to develop their cultures all by themselves.

From Alaska, I would continue to walk south along the coastline until I reached the area that is now Washington State. I would chat with the local tribes and observe how they lived. As I trekked southwards, I would keep my eyes open for giant mammals such as saber-toothed cats and ground sloths. I would explore whether they became extinct because humans killed them off or whether they were driven to extinction by climate change.

Essentially, I would turn this opportunity into two fact-finding trips. I would put modern theories to the test. This would certainly put to bed some controversies and allow future science to be built on a more solid foundation.

托福總監評析

　　這道寫作題的假設屬於幻想類的，讓考生想像時光之旅。作文應該包含年代、目的地以及選擇此目的地的原因。注意，原因是評分中最重要的因素。

　　在這篇高分範文的第一段，考生開門見山談自己時光之旅的原因：人們都是透過古生物學家和考古學家的推測來瞭解史前世界的，「我」想親自去體驗。「我」想去兩個歷史時期：第二段描述了第一個目的地，訪問北京猿人的遺址。第三段和第四段描述了第二個目的地。考生詳細描寫了旅行路線（從西伯利亞穿過白令海峽，到達今天的華盛頓州），同時還提到了想去這些地方的原因。這些目的地是和科學探索聯繫在一起的，如：I would explore whether they became extinct because humans killed them off or whether they were driven to extinction by climate change. 這些內容使作文前後更連貫。總結段非常簡潔，重申了這次旅行的原因：科學探索和發現事實。

建立自己的寫作句型庫

1. If I had an opportunity to create a new holiday, I would use it to heighten people's awareness of x
如果我有機會設立一個新節日，我將利用這個節日來增強人們對於……的意識

If I had an opportunity to create a new holiday, I would use it to heighten people's awareness of the fragility of the Earth's environment.

延伸說法 If I had an opportunity to create a new holiday, I would use it to heighten people's awareness of water conservation.

2. I would name my holiday "x" to emphasize that…
我將我的節日命名為……，藉此強調……

I would name my holiday "Home Day" to emphasize that the Earth is our common home.

延伸說法 I would name my holiday "Water Day" to emphasize that clean water is a treasure to be protected.

3. Through the enactment of [HOLIDAY NAME], we could VERB
透過設立……節，我們能……

Through the enactment of Home Day, we could educate ourselves.

延伸說法 Through the enactment of Family Day, we could take time to appreciate the people in our families.

4. There is just one thing that bothers me: the x
唯一讓我煩惱的事情是……

There is just one thing that bothers me: the location.

延伸說法 There is just one thing that bothers me: the cost.

5. If it were possible, I would VERB and VERB
如果可能的話，我會……並……

If it were possible, I would pack up all my things and move to a different place.

延伸說法 If it were possible, I would tear down the existing bathroom and build a new one.

6. If I had a chance to ask a celebrity a question, I would ask about x
我若有機會向名人提問，我將問關於……的事

If I had a chance to ask a celebrity a question, I would ask about genetically modified foods (also known as GM foods).

延伸說法 If I had a chance to ask a celebrity a question, I would ask him what the secret of his success was.

7. In fact, my rationale for asking this question is that…
事實上，我問這個問題的理由是……

In fact, my rationale for asking this question is that famous people create controversies, which then get covered in the media.

延伸說法 In fact, my rationale for asking this question is that celebrities can help get funding for a good cause.

8. If I were to write a book about it, I would focus on three aspects: Its x, its y and its z
如果我要寫一本這方面的書，我將側重以下三個方面……

If I were to write a book about it, I would focus on three aspects: its food, its imperial past and its future as a cosmopolitan city.

延伸說法 If I were to write a book about it, I would focus on three aspects: Its history, its people and its economy.

9. Writing about the x and y would be a pleasure.
寫一些關於……和……的內容將會是一種樂趣。

Writing about the friendly staff in these small restaurants and the diversity of dishes would be a pleasure.

延伸說法 Writing about the fishing industry and seafood restaurants would be a pleasure.

10. The second aspect of [HOMETOWN NAME] I would write about is the x and y which…
我要寫……的第二個方面是……和……

The second aspect of Beijing I would write about is the imperial homes and gardens which were once inhabited by emperors and their households.

延伸說法 The second aspect of New York I would write about is the development of the Broadway shows which became popular in the 19th century.

11. At the end of the book, I would speculate about x
我會在書的結尾推測……

At the end of the book, I would speculate about the future of my hometown.

延伸說法 At the end of the book, I would speculate about ways that mass transportation could be improved.

12. By traveling in time, I could see for myself what happened in x
透過時光旅行，我能親眼看到……發生了什麼事

By traveling in time, I could see for myself what happened in prehistory.

延伸說法 By traveling in time, I could see for myself what happened in medieval Japan.

13. After that, I would set the time travel machine for a point in time x years ago and travel to y
之後，我會將時光機設定到……年前的某個點，去……旅行

After that, I would set the time travel machine for a point in time 12,000 years ago and travel to Siberia.

延伸說法 After that, I would set the time travel machine for a point in time 100 years ago and travel to my great-grandfather's home.

16 Open-ended describe and discuss: Discuss the causes Describe a custom

如何應對開放型題型

❝ 在本章，你將學到…… ❞

★如何描述、討論或解釋一種相對抽象的現象
★如何建立邏輯連貫性

解讀常考題

本章討論的「開放型題型」是指要求考生進行「描述」和「討論」某事件或某一現象的寫作題。很多情況下是要求考生討論原因、描述某一習俗等。

開放型寫作題是獨立寫作題中最難的題型之一，因為考生需要以一種相對抽象的邏輯方式討論或解釋問題。例如，寫作題經常會問影響因素或隱含的根本原因；有的開放型作文題會問影響某一趨勢的因素；有的要求考生描述本國文化中，哪些文化較為重要；而有的要求考生闡述影響他們的某一事件。

儘管寫作題庫裡的開放型題型並沒有「二選一」題型多，但考生還是需要認真準備。

開放題型的寫作題通常有以下幾種形式：

1. **Describe** an animal that is important to your country's national identity. **Explain** how it contributes to your country's culture.
2. Some events seem to occur randomly. **Describe** a significant event in your life that you did not expect. **Explain** how it affected your life.
3. Access to clean water is becoming increasingly important. **Discuss** the **factors** contributing to this trend.
4. One reason that people attend university is to find a job. What are **other reasons** why people attend university? **Discuss** one or more of these reasons.
5. In the 21st century, more and more people are choosing to work for themselves. **Discuss** the **causes** of this trend.
6. The birth rate in many developed countries is declining. Many reasons for this trend have been put forward; for example, the lack of money. Discuss how having children can influence a young couple's lives.

現在看一則例子：

▶ 模擬試題①

閱讀以下的短文並聆聽講座，完成以下這道作文題目。

Directions:

Read the question below. You have 30 minutes to plan, write, and revise your essay. Typically, an effective response will contain a minimum of 300 words.

> **Describe a food that is important to your country's sense of identity. Explain how this food contributes to your country's "food culture."**
> Use specific examples and details to support your answer.

就深度和廣度而言，這道寫作題是典型的開放型寫作題。本題要求考生描寫一種能夠代表本國形象特徵的食物。換句話說，國民會把這種食物看作本國飲食文化的一部分。如果這不足以構成挑戰的話，本題還進一步要求考生解釋這種食物是怎麼促成該國一種文化的形成。

考生可以採用多種方法來寫這篇作文。一種方法是選擇一種該國人民最常吃的食物。例如：日本人以米為主食。另一種方法是選擇一種有特殊象徵意義的食物，要嘛對本國人民有特殊意義，要嘛對外國人有特殊意義。例如，在美國，由於有許多像麥當勞一樣的全球連鎖快餐企業，起士漢堡就有其象徵意義。不論考生採用哪一種方法，都應該從文化的角度看待食物，就像人類學家看待問題的方式一樣。考生舉的例子應該能夠全面解釋為什麼這種食物會成為該國的一種文化。

▶ Exercise 1

根據上面例題的題目要求寫一篇作文。初稿完成後，繼續學習下部分的內容。仔細研讀高分範文、萬用寫作範本、高分策略和寫作句型庫，運用所學的新知識完成 Exercise 2。

寫作構思

Rice
Soy sauce
Pigs / pork
Ease of raising them
Cuisine
Meat, skin and blood

高分範文　 *Track 061*

Pork is extremely important in many ways to China's sense of identity. In fact, when we say the word for "meat" ("rou") in Chinese, we are referring to pork. Among the Han people of China, pork is by far the preferred source of protein.

For one thing, pigs are the most widely bred livestock in China. They are easy to breed, so pork is relatively affordable to the majority of the population. This is because pigs can live in a variety of climates. In fact, they can even live in where there are concentrations of people. Secondly, pigs are quite tenacious and do not contract disease easily. As a result, one does not need much expertise to raise them. In fact, many rural families raise pigs for their own consumption. Pigs eat almost everything, "recycling" kitchen leftovers people would otherwise throw away. No wonder pigs are so ubiquitous.

Pork is a favorite in Chinese cuisine. In the South, my native region, pork is particularly beloved. My mother prepares at least one pork dish a day. I have been exposed to dozens of dishes that make use of the meat, skin and even the blood. Sometimes we even have several pork dishes at the same meal. Although our family rarely makes pig blood soup, there are many little shops that sell it. For a snack, Western children might grab a chocolate bar or some chips, but we would usually buy some cooked food. I still remember when I was little, on our way home from school, we would stop by little stands and choose from a variety of foods, such as fish ball soup and fried sweet potatoes. For me and many of my classmates, however, the snack of choice was pig blood soup.

Some foreigners may think that rice is the food with the most significance to Chinese, but in fact not everyone in China likes to eat rice. Northerners often prefer noodles or other flour-based staples. Pork, on the other hand, is well-loved across the country, at least among the Han people. It has become an integral part of our culture. Unless we all turn into vegetarians, I cannot imagine us living without pigs.

萬用模板

[食物名稱] is extremely important in many ways to _____ sense of identity. In fact, [用一兩個句子說明某種重要食物].

For one thing, [食物名稱] are the most _____ in [China]. [用兩三個句子說明這種食物的來源、產地等資訊].

[食物名稱] is a favorite in [Chinese] cuisine. [用三四個句子說明這種食物怎麼受國人的喜愛，怎麼烹飪、食用。如果能加上自己生活中的例子更好].

Some foreigners may think that [第二種食物的名稱] is the food with the most significance to [Chinese], but in fact not everyone in [China] likes to eat [第二種食物的名稱]. [舉例說明哪些人不喜歡吃這種食物]. [第一種食物名稱], on the other hand, is well-loved across the country, at least among the Han people. It has become an integral part of our culture. Unless we all turn into vegetarians, I cannot imagine us living without [第一種食物名稱].

範文第一段，考生直入主題，說豬肉對中國人意義重大，人們常說的「肉」就是指「豬肉」。第二段解釋中國人普遍食用豬肉的原因，即豬具有容易飼養、不易得病等特點。第三段描述了豬肉在中國飲食中的重要性。考生用講故事的形式給出了具體的例子和細節，提到自己家的飲食習慣和放學後吃小吃的故事。總結段緊扣主題，說明食物如何和民族文化相關。最後一句很簡短，強調了豬肉在中國人飲食中的重要性。

邏輯上做到前後連貫

在前面的篇章裡，我們學習了如何透過有技巧地重複關鍵字來增強文章的連貫性，而本章也將繼續討論連貫性，說明如何透過內容的選擇、文章結構的組建來建立上下文的邏輯關係。內容的選擇主要是指選擇例子和論據等，文章結構的組建主要指內容的邏輯順序，這些都是決定考生作文分數的因素。

增強連貫性的三個簡單步驟

1）寫作前，考生先選一個自己能夠「勝任」的話題。不僅熟悉該情境的詞彙，還要能夠想出和提綱相符的兩到三個例子或分論點。

2）想一想以什麼邏輯順序排列論點和例子。如果準備講故事，可以按時間順序排列論點；如果是解釋某個現象的原因，可以按原因的重要性進行排列，最重要的原因放在後面。

3）考慮好文章的內容和結構後，開始動筆。寫作文的過程中銘記要讓讀者理解所有論點的邏輯結構和各論點之間的聯繫。

許多考生因為不知道如何為一篇作文設計結構，所以很苦惱。以下面這道寫作題為例，我們來看一看如何設定一篇作文的結構。

Life is full of events that change our lives. Some events occur because of a decision we make. Others are due to circumstances outside our control. Describe a significant event in your past and explain how it affected your life.

面對這道題目，考生需要做三件事：第一，選擇一件改變了你生活的事件；第二，描述該事件；第三，說明該事件怎麼影響你的生活。

構思時，考生可以列出每一個論點以保證每一段都有足夠的內容可寫。因為題目問該事件如何影響了考生的生活，所以至少要講述兩到三個方面的影響。

	事件（主題）	影響
第一段	What happened on that **[Shanghai] trip would change the course of my life.** [It **changed** in several ways.]	
第二段		Because my aunt had an **accident** and I went to Shanghai to see her, I realized that **I wanted to be in that city**.
第三段		My aunt asked me to stay and **live with her in Shanghai**.
第四段（如果需要，而且有時間的話）		With my **aunt's financial support**, I went to school in Shanghai up **through high school**.
總結段（轉述）	It was in this way that **the trip I took** to visit my injured aunt **changed my whole life**.	My aunt will **pay for my college studies** in the US. I will definitely work hard to take care of her because **I am grateful**.

　　考生的上海之旅改變了其生活。第二段至第四段分別講述了故事情節的發展。從某種程度上說，每一個故事情節的發展都是這次旅行的結果。

　　因為題目要求陳述過去的某個事件，所以每一段都是故事某個環節的陳述。但是每個環節裡都必須說明這件重要的事（這次旅行）是如何影響考生生活的。例如，第四段：My family could never have afforded to send me to schools in Shanghai, let alone America. 這說明這件事的「影響」之一是考生能夠上更好的學校。這個例子證明了緊扣題目的作文是如何建立邏輯連貫性的。透過這個例子大家可以知道，帶著明確的寫作目的寫好每一個段落，這有助於把每一個分論點有機地和論點聯繫在一起。

　　因為考生只有 30 分鐘的寫作時間，直接在第一段陳述論點會好一些。然後，接下來的每一段都根據這一論點進行論述。

　　建立連貫性的另一個策略是在段落第一句陳述本段的論點。這種策略不適用於講故事性質的作文；但題目若是要求考生分析原因，這種策略非常有用。

　　考生可以自由地闡明論點，但要記住，構思過程中就要確定接下來要講什麼。如果所有的段落都能構成一個整體，即使文中出現幾個不嚴重的文法錯誤也是沒關係的，因為評分人看重的是「統一性、漸進性和連貫性」。

要使文章富有邏輯連貫性，可運用以下策略

1. 文章結構層次清晰、有序。例如，如果需要用兩三個原因來解釋現代人們的結婚年齡比以前大這一趨勢，就一定不能毫無次序地列舉原因，要按從不重要到最重要的邏輯順序排列原因。

2. 每一個符合邏輯的論點都要用一個段落來闡述。這可以讓評分人一眼就能看出文章的結構層次。

3. 把每一個段落都當做一篇「小文章」來對待。也就是說，段落的展開也要做到富有邏輯連貫性。

4. 段與段之間的銜接要符合邏輯，承接自然。可以透過分論點和例子的排列順序實現文章的流暢性，也可以像 Another factor is... 句型一樣透過信號詞 another 來實現文章的流暢性。

5. 運用連接詞（consequently 等）和指示詞（This food）等來銜接上下文。

6. 除了總結段需要重複論點或論據之外，其他地方不要重複論點或論據。

7. 在總結段，總結句要呼應上文的論點。

建立自己的寫作句型庫

1. For one thing, x are the most ADVERB x in [COUNTRY]
首先，……在（某國家）是最……

For one thing, pigs are the most widely bred livestock in China.

延伸說法 For one thing, bread is the most commonly eaten food in Russia.

2. x is a favorite in [COUNTRY ADJECTIVE] cuisine.
在（某個國家的）菜餚裡，……是最受歡迎的食物。

Pork is a favorite in Chinese cuisine.

延伸說法 Curry is a favorite in Thai cuisine.

3. Some foreigners may think that x is the food with the most significance to [COUNTRY PEOPLE], but in fact not everyone in [COUNTRY] likes to eat x
一些外國人可能認為……是（某國人民）最重要的食材，但事實上，並非所有的……人都喜歡食用……

Some foreigners may think that rice is the food with the most significance to Chinese, but in fact not everyone in China likes to eat rice.

延伸說法 Some foreigners may think that pizza is the food with the most significance to Italians, but in fact not everyone in Italy likes to eat pizza.

▶ Exercise 2

學完高分範文、萬用寫作範本、高分策略和寫作句型庫，運用所學的技能修改你的初稿，並認真看修改之處。然後用學到的新句型去練習下面五道預測題的寫作。

寫作預測題

1. Describe a significant event and explain how it affected...

Life is full of events that change our lives. Some events occur because of a decision we make. Others are due to circumstances outside our control. Describe a significant event in your past and explain how it affected your life.

寫作構思

Had to take the college entrance exam a second time
Taught me to stand up after a setback
Trip to Shanghai
Aunt had an accident
Went to school
Learned Shanghai dialect

高分範文 1 *Track 062*

I would not be sitting here taking the TOEFL test had it not been for a trip I took in the summer ten years ago. My aunt was in a Shanghai hospital due to a bad fall, so I was going there with my mother. What happened on that trip would change the course of my life.

My first impression of Shanghai is hard to describe. Even though I had already seen pictures on television, the enormity of the city did not hit me until I was there. As we walked into the gated compound where my aunt lived, I was amazed at the immaculate landscaping that greeted us. It included a huge fountain and an elaborate garden. I said to myself then, this is where I want to live in the future.

We dropped off our luggage at the apartment and rushed to the hospital. Fortunately, she was doing much better, and she came home three days later. We ended up staying at her apartment for over a month, taking care of her and keeping her company. My aunt's affection for me grew as she regained her health. Towards the end of our stay, she asked my mother if she could keep me in Shanghai indefinitely. My mother said it was up to me to decide. Needless to say, I accepted my aunt's invitation.

I subsequently transferred to an elementary school in Shanghai and went on to high school there as well. My aunt treated me like her own daughter. She financed my education and biannual trips to visit my parents. Now, she also plans to finance my education in America. My family could never have afforded to send me to schools in Shanghai, let alone America.

It was in this way that the trip I took to visit my injured aunt changed my whole life. Now I have another set of "parents" in my life. I shall work hard to repay my debt to them and take care of them when they are old.

托福總監評析

    實際上這道寫作題要求考生講述一個「因果」故事。這種寫作題給考生一個講述個人故事的機會，但要連貫地說明是故事中的什麼因素引發命運的轉折。

    在這篇高分範文中，考生以一句戲劇性的開場白說現在自己坐在考場上參加托福考試，這是十年前的上海之行帶來的後果。然後敘述了整個事件：阿姨發生了一場意外以及「我」和母親的上海之行。第二段描述了自己對這座城市的第一印象：I said to myself then, this is where I want to live in the future. 第三段繼續敘述事件的發展：阿姨康復之後請考生留下來和自己一起生活。第四段敘述了從小學到高中的學習費用全部由阿姨支付，她還打算送「我」去美國留學。總結段重申了第一段的論點，即這件事改變了自己的人生。考生在最後一句表達了自己的感激之情和報答親人的心願。

....

2. Discuss the factors contributing to this trend...

The ability to read and write is more important than ever. Discuss the factors contributing to this trend.

Use specific reasons and examples to support your answer.

寫作構思

> **Speech and human evolution**
> **Written texts**
> **Printing press**
> **Internet**
> Complexity of work
> College education is needed for jobs, so need literacy
> Global businesses, e-mail more important

高分範文 2 *Track 063*

In the 21st century, the ability to read and write is vital, and the importance of these skills will only continue to grow. There are many reasons why this is true. For one thing, we live in a time when most the information we need for our lives and jobs is not coded in our biological genes. Rather, it is found in written form, stored in printed books and digitally, on computers. Because the amount of written information is increasing all the time, it is vital that we find efficient ways to absorb it.

Of course, it was not always the case that written texts were essential. One reason for this is that our earliest communication was accomplished through hand gestures and speech. During the long history of human evolution, we slowly developed the capacity for language. Because we could communicate with one another, we were able to compete and survive, adapting to hostile environments. A written form of language started to appear, as our hunting and foraging lifestyle gave way to an agricultural lifestyle.

Another important factor influencing the increasing importance of reading and writing is the emergence of the printing press. The earliest written texts were chronicles of historical events and religious teachings. These were handwritten and then passed down from generation to generation. However, when the printing press was invented, philosophical ideas and scientific theories blossomed and were quickly disseminated. As a result, people naturally began reading and writing more than before.

The recent birth of the Internet and the digitalization of information has further speeded the publishing of information, leading to what some people call an "information explosion," also requiring us to read and write.

All of these events have shaped a world whose speed and complexity could not have been foreseen by our forefathers. From the little things in life such as reading manuals and learning to use a cell phone to accessing materials in the workplace, written information flows from one individual to the next at an unprecedented pace.

托福總監評析

　　寫好這篇作文，考生要交代人類歷史上對讀寫產生深遠影響的幾個階段，藉此說明現在讀寫能力為什麼越來越重要。

　　在第一段，考生先陳述當今社會的大部分資訊都儲存在人腦以外的地方，這表示如果人們想使用資訊，必須能找到資訊並對其進行處理。第二段描述了在人類歷史早期階段，人們只能透過手勢和言語進行交流，直到後來出現了文字。第三段描述了印刷的出現（以及當時哲學思想和科學理論的發展）如何影響對讀寫的需求。第四段提出網際網路是致使「資訊爆炸」的一個因素。總結段換句話說了作文主體部分提到的幾個因素，認為現代的資訊以前所未有的速度傳播著。

3. Discuss one or more of these reasons...

One reason that people work is to obtain money. What are other reasons why people work? Discuss one or more of these reasons.
Use specific examples and details to support your answer.

寫作構思

Boring
Health
Friendship
Fulfill potential
Lets people be creative
Allows people to experience new things
Other people need my skills

高分範文 3 *Track 064*

People seem to enjoy play more than work. But all play and no work makes for a boring life. Work not only provides us with the necessities we need to stay alive, it also satisfies the needs for health, friendship and self-actualization.

First, work keeps us in good health. In order to stay both mentally and physically healthy, we need to be active. Studies have shown the more we exercise our brains and our bodies, the better shape we will be in. For example, there are many instances of people's health quickly deteriorating as soon as they retire. Doctors have suggested that this is caused by the lifestyle change which deprives retirees of activity. Personally, I hope to continue to work until the day I die, simply to stay clear-headed and strong.

Second, work brings us friendship. When we are young, most of our friends tend to be our schoolmates. However, after college most of us have to leave our school friends and move to wherever our jobs take us. That means we must either find new friends in our new surroundings or be alone. Imagine a young man who comes from a wealthy family and decides not to work. When his college friends all go off to their new jobs, he will feel very much alone.

Third, work allows us to fulfill our potential. We are all endowed with special talents. It is important to prove to ourselves that we can do certain things well. For example, I believe I have a knack for organizing people in order to complete a certain task. At my company, we generally work in a team setting for whatever assignment we have been given. I am usually the person who gets everybody to contribute ideas. I derive a sense of accomplishment from using my interpersonal skills, especially when I see that my efforts help our team do a better job.

I have listed but three reasons for working; there are doubtless many more. Almost everyone craves the energy produced during work and is searching for meaning beyond money.

托福總監評析

　　這道寫作題要求考生討論人們賺錢以外的其他工作原因。這並不難寫，因為人們工作有很多原因。考生可以選擇一個或幾個原因來寫。注意，這道寫作題還有暗含的一層意思，即要求考生比較工作和賺錢的不同動機。

　　高分範文第一段，考生開門見山地提出中心論點，還有列舉了人們工作的三個原因：健康、友誼和自我價值的實現。第二段至第四段分別陳述這三個原因。總結段簡短但很有力度。在全文的最後一句，考生陳述了自己的信念，即除了賺錢外，每個人都渴望工作帶來的活力，都在尋找生命的意義。

4. Discuss the causes of this trend...

> **On average, people live longer these days. Discuss the causes of this trend.**
> Use reasons and specific examples to support your answer.

寫作構思

"Average" life span
Humans getting stronger
Nutrition
Sanitation, Bacteria
People read about health on the Internet
Modern medicine

高分範文 4　　 *Track 065*

From ancient times, people have always tried to find ways to live longer. In many societies, attempts were made to invent some wonder drug that would make a person live forever. They have all failed. However, it is an undisputed fact that the "average" life span — a statistical number — has increased dramatically over the last few centuries. The three causes most often cited for this increased longevity are nutrition, sanitation and medicine.

First, we all know malnourished infants tend to get sick more easily. Without adequate nutrition, many children never reach adulthood. Moreover, in agricultural societies, famine and the lack of water can lead to deaths in adults. The Industrial Revolution brought us new agricultural technologies which increased food production, providing more nourishment for children and adults. This contributed significantly to the lengthening of the average human life.

Second, unclean conditions lead to diseases and early death. Bacteria, quite harmful to humans, thrive in environments with discarded garbage and raw sewage. To thwart bacteria, modern societies now use flush toilets to help dispose of waste. In addition, communities set up sanitation departments to make sure garbage and sewage is safely removed and processed. Better sanitation leads to fewer pathogens, which obviously helps lengthen human life.

Finally, modern medicine has helped treat and even prevent many diseases. For example, penicillin and other antibiotics have helped stem infections. Modern societies have harnessed new drugs and techniques, as well as building clean hospitals to provide efficient care to sick people. Every life saved this way increases the average life span of a society.

There may be other factors that cause increased life expectancy, but I think the above three are the chief ones. One day, if scientists can figure out how to slow the aging process using genetic or other technologies, I am sure the average life span will get another huge boost.

托福總監評析

　　這道寫作題要求考生討論目前人們越來越長壽的原因。談原因的文章至少要談到兩點。
　　在第一段，考生透過描述兩個事實引出話題：過去，人們總在尋求長生不老的仙丹；幾個世紀以來，人們的平均壽命延長了很多。在這一段的結尾，考生提出自己的觀點：現代人長壽的原因有三點：營養、衛生條件和現代醫藥。第二段至第四段分別講述了這三點原因。和上一篇作文用到的寫作方法相同，考生在結尾段先說現代人長壽可能還有其他原因，然後展望了基因技術讓人們更長壽的可能性。

----

5. Discuss how x has taken place...

> **Some things are learned outside the classroom. For example, one can learn from a parttime job or from other people. Discuss how this type of learning has taken place in your life. Explain in detail what you have learned.**

寫作構思

Language
Social behavior and values
Meaning of friendship
On-the-job training
Problem-solving in the real world

高分範文 5　　 *Track 066*

Before public schools were common, especially in rural areas, many people gained practical and important survival skills in informal settings at home or out in the wild. Formal schooling is a relatively new phenomenon and has certainly not replaced the need for learning outside the classroom.

One of the first things that all of us learn is language. I doubt that anyone learns to speak his or her native tongue in the classroom. The minute we are born, our mother, father and other family members start to speak to us and we begin to learn our language. At school we continue to learn our own language, such as learning to write. Moreover, we may choose to learn foreign languages. The amount of language learning that takes place before we start school is mind-boggling.

Another vital lesson we learn outside the classroom is social behavior. From our parents, we learn how to act properly. Some people learn important moral values from the church. Our behavior is also shaped by interaction with other children or by observation of adults. Before we step into a school building, we have already absorbed many basic values.

Lastly, I would like to mention on-the-job training. School introduces us to necessary knowledge. However, there is no way that standardized education in group settings can foresee every knowledge or skill that an individual will need in the future. When I first started to work a few months ago, I was shocked to hear my colleagues speaking a professional jargon that was like a foreign language to me. It was only after a few months of learning about our trade that I gradually began to grasp the basic terminology and concepts that industry people use.

To be sure, I think schools provide an efficient and necessary means of educating a large population in modern societies. But we cannot rely on them for everything we need to learn. My education began at home and continues now in the company where I work. With an inquisitive mind, one can always keep learning.

托福總監評析

　　這道寫作題要求考生談談自己對課堂內習得與課堂外習得的觀點，構思時不要忘了個人生活中的故事和例子。這道題目困難的地方主要是能否迅速想到課堂外可以學到的東西，並能夠拿來討論。

　　在這篇範文中，考生先從歷史的角度來談學習：人類在課堂之外已經學習了很多個世紀。第二段介紹了在課堂外學習的第一個例子：母語學習。第三段講述了社會行為的學習，即孩子如何受家人和周圍環境的影響從而形成自己的價值觀。第四段講工作中的學習。注意作文中的觀點呈線性發展，從人類歷史早期到兒童時期，最後到職場。這是作文富有連貫性的典型例子。總結段談到，課堂學習有價值，但許多重要技能都是在課堂外學會的。

建立自己的寫作句型庫

1. I would not be VERBing had it not been for a x I VERBed… [TIME PHRASE IN THE PAST]
如果我沒有……，我現在就不會……

I would not be sitting here taking the TOEFL test had it not been for a trip I took in the summer ten years ago.

延伸說法 I would not be working in this bank had it not been for an internship I had during my senior summer.

2. What happened on that x would change the course of my life.

……發生的事改變了我的人生。

What happened on that trip would change the course of my life.

延伸說法 What happened on that day would change the course of my life.

3. I said to myself then, this is… in the future.

然後我告訴自己，這就是將來……

I said to myself then, this is where I want to live in the future.

延伸說法 I said to myself then, this is the man I want to marry.

4. I subsequently VERBed in [PLACE] and VERBED there as well.

我隨後……，還在那裡……

I subsequently transferred to an elementary school in Shanghai and went on to high school there as well.

延伸說法 I subsequently volunteered in Africa and learned some medical techniques there as well.

5. It was in this way that the x changed my whole life.

……以這個方式改變了我的整個人生。

It was in this way that the trip I took to visit my injured aunt changed my whole life.

延伸說法 It was in this way that the job interview changed my whole life.

6. In the 21st century, the ability to VERB is vital, and the importance of these skills will only continue to grow.

在 21 世紀，……的能力至關重要，而且這些技能只會越來越重要。

In the 21st century, the ability to read and write is vital, and the importance of these skills will only continue to grow.

延伸說法 In the 21st century, the ability to speak multiple languages is vital, and the importance of these skills will only continue to grow.

7. Of course, it was not always the case that…

當然，……也並非總是如此。

Of course, it was not always the case that written texts were essential.

延伸說法 Of course, it was not always the case that mobile phones were so common.

8. All of these events have shaped a world whose x could not have been foreseen by our forefathers.

這些所有的事件決定了一個……的世界，這是我們祖先無法預見的。

All of these events have shaped a world whose speed and complexity could not have been foreseen by our forefathers.

延伸說法 All of these events have shaped a world whose connectivity could not have been foreseen by our forefathers.

9. Work not only provides us with x, it also satisfies the needs for y

工作不僅提供給我們……，還能滿足我們對……的需求

Work not only provides us with the necessities we need to stay alive, it also satisfies the needs for health, friendship and self-actualization.

延伸說法 Work not only provides us with money to support us, it also satisfies the needs for social interaction.

10. The three causes most often cited for x are a, b and c.

……的三個提到最多的原因是……

The three causes most often cited for this increased longevity are nutrition, sanitation and medicine.

延伸說法 The three causes most often cited for global warming are fossil fuels, methane emissions and deforestation.

11. This contributed significantly to the x

這對促成……具有極大的作用

This contributed significantly to the lengthening of the average human life.

延伸說法 This contributed significantly to the popularity of movies.

12. There may be other factors that cause x, but I think the above three are the chief ones.

也許……還有其他因素，但我認為以上的三點是最主要的因素。

There may be other factors that cause increased life expectancy, but I think the above three are the chief ones.

延伸說法 There may be other factors that cause students to plagiarize, but I think the above three are the chief ones.

13. x is a relatively new phenomenon and has certainly not replaced the need for y...

是一個相對較新的現象，肯定不能取代……的需求

Formal schooling is a relatively new phenomenon and has certainly not replaced the need for learning outside the classroom.

延伸說法 Distance learning is a relatively new phenomenon and has certainly not replaced the need for traditional classroom education.

14. It was only after [TIME PHRASE] that I gradually began to grasp the basic terminology and concepts that x use.

……之後我才逐漸掌握了……的基本學科術語和概念。

It was only after a few months of learning about our trade that I gradually began to grasp the basic terminology and concepts that industry people use.

延伸說法 It was only after a year of practice that I gradually began to grasp the basic terminology and concepts that musicians use.

Appendices

特別收録

Appendix ▶ The Scoring of the TOEFL® iBT
特別收錄 新托福考試的評分

★新托福考試成績概述

新托福考試為決策機構提供了兩套分數：總分和各部分得分。各部分的分數由「標準分」組成，標準分由原始分根據一個通用比例轉換而來。標準分很重要，因為它可讓決策者對學生進行更為公平的比較。

新托福考試成績的滿分如下：

閱讀： 30

聽力： 30

口語： 30

寫作： 30

───────────

總分： 120

考生會收到被稱為「成績回饋」的資訊。該資訊旨在告訴考生該如何瞭解自己的整體表現。例如在閱讀和聽力部分，考生得分情況有 Low（0～13）、Intermediate（14～21）或 High（22～30）。口語部分，考生得分情況有 Weak（0～9）、Limited（10～17）、Fair（18～25）或 Good（26～30）。寫作部分，考生得分情況有 Limited（1～16）、Fair（17～23）或 Good（24～30）。

但是請注意，提交給大學的成績單中不會有該成績回饋資訊。只有考生個人會收到此資訊。

★新托福寫作部分的分數

1. 評分人

一般情況下，會有四個評分人為同一份作文評分。這表示新托福寫作的評分比較客觀，不是基於個人的主觀看法。而且，ETS 還會用自動評分系統評分，作為人工評分的補充。

2. 如何評分？

新托福考試結束之後，考生作文的數位檔會被發送到 ETS，然後透過評分網路系統將兩篇作文分配給評分人。

評分人根據新托福寫作評分準則給考生的作文打分數。有兩套獨立的評分準則：一套適用於綜合寫作，另一套適用於獨立寫作。這兩道作文題目都考查考生的整體語言能力。兩道題目的分數為 0～5，但是一般不會打 0 分。

綜合寫作題的評分準則有嚴格的要求：文章必須包含講座中的重要資訊。如果考生遺漏了講座中的一些資訊，評分人會扣分。

評分準則中所說的「重要資訊」是指教授在講座中提到的三個分論點。得 5 分的綜合作文必須連貫而準確地描述講座中的三個分論點；對於試圖描述三個分論點卻因為詞不達意而沒有將論點之間的關係表達清楚的作文，得 4 分；如果考生只正確描述了兩個分論點，能得 3 分；如果只正確描述了一個分論點，只能得 2 分；1 分的作文是那種遺漏講座的重要資訊，只抓住細枝末節資訊的作文；如果作文的語言難以理解，也只能得 1 分。0 分作文往往是因為考生交空白卷、完全離題，或者考生照抄題目或閱讀短文的內容。

對於獨立作文，結構嚴謹、邏輯連貫、話題充分展開，這樣的作文才能得 5 分。4 分的作文可能只是邏輯連貫，但是話題沒有展開。3 分的文章可能邏輯不太連貫，文章意思有時難以理解，文中有文法和拼寫錯誤。2 分和 1 分的作文有一些更加嚴重的問題，例如結構不清晰、語言運用能力差等。如果考生幾乎沒寫出什麼實質性的內容、離題，或者內容完全抄襲題目，那就只能得 0 分。因為獨立寫作題完全靠考生自己去構思，所以這道題對主題的展開和連貫性的要求比綜合寫作題高。

評分人給每篇作文判分之後，取平均分數並轉換成 0～30 的標準分，這個分數就是官方成績單上的分數。

透過下面的轉換表格，考生可以大致瞭解原始分和標準分之間的轉換機制：

原始分	標準分
5.00	30
4.75	29
4.50	28
4.25	27
4.00	25
3.75	24
3.50	22
3.25	21
3.00	20
2.75	18

2.50	17
2.25	15
2.00	14
1.75	12
1.50	11
1.25	10
1.00	8
	7
	5
	4
	0

　　一般情況下評分人會給整數，例如 2 分，不會出現給 2.5 的情況。把原始分數轉換成標準分需要計算，上面的表格只是一個數學推定法，幫考生大致瞭解轉換過程。

3. 成績單

　　在兩週之內，官方的寫作分數（0 ～ 30 之間）與閱讀、聽力和口語分數會一起寄給考生和考生申請的所有大學。除此以外，考生還會收到每篇作文的分數，形式如下：

Writing based on Reading and Listening (Task 1)

Writing based on Knowledge and Experience (Task 2)

　　考生會看到兩篇作文 0 ～ 5 分的原始分數。在成績單的回饋分析部分，這個分數會被分成三個等級：Limited (1.0 ～ 2.0)、Fair (2.5 ～ 3.5) 和 Good (4 ～ 5)。這個回饋不會寄往考生申請的大學，而只是作為一個參考，供考生提高自己的能力。

★其他重要資訊

1. 成績單

　　考生可在完成考試兩週後線上查看成績單，郵寄成績單的耗時則會更長一些（一週到一個月）。每位考生都會收到成績單，同時考試機構會將最多四份成績單的正本寄往考生所選定的教育機構。成績單上只顯示一次考試的成績，如果你以前參加過新托福考試，以前的成績將不會出現在最新的成績單上。新托福成績的有效期是參加考試後的兩年之內。

2. 所需的最低總分

許多考生問：「需要在新托福考試中得多少分才能被大學錄取？」答案是：「視大學而定；視級別（大學或研究生）而定；有時還會視大學裡的某個系而定」。目前，很多公認較有名的教育機構要求新托福總分最低為 80 分。頂尖學院，如哈佛大學、麻省理工學院和芝加哥大學，總分可能至少需要 100 分，尤其當該考生申請的是商業、法律或傳播學這類科系時更需要高分。相反地，理工科的學生可能只需要 80 分，甚至更低。也有院校總分只需 69 分便可入學。

3. 各部分所需的最低分數

有些大學對新托福考試各部分的最低分沒有要求，但有些大學會要求，也會規定最低總分。還有些大學雖然對各部分的最低分有要求，但沒有單獨列出最低總分。舉例來說，你可能會發現你要申請的學校要求你閱讀最低 21 分、聽力最低 18 分、口語最低 23 分、寫作最低 22 分。如果考生滿足上述最低要求，則考生的總分至少為 84 分。

4. 如何查詢你的目標大學對新托福成績的要求

如果你正在申請出國留學或獎學金，想瞭解你想去的學校對英文能力的要求，必須到目標大學的網站上查看是否規定了最低托福分數。查找此類資訊的最好方法是：先點擊 Admissions（招生），再點擊 International（國際），然後查找 English language proficiency（英語語言能力）或類似這樣的標題。

原來如此 系列 *E109*

托福命題總監教你征服新托福寫作

托福總監親自出馬！真的不是權威不出書！

作　　　者	秦蘇珊
顧　　　問	曾文旭
總 編 輯	王毓芳
編輯統籌	耿文國、黃璽宇
主　　編	吳靜宜
執行主編	姜怡安
執行編輯	李念茨、林妍珺
美術編輯	王桂芳、張嘉容
封面設計	阿作
特約編輯	費長琳
法律顧問	北辰著作權事務所　蕭雄淋律師、幸秋妙律師

初　　版	2014年12月初版一刷 2019年再版六刷
出　　版	捷徑文化出版事業有限公司
電　　話	（02）2752-5618
傳　　真	（02）2752-5619
地　　址	106 台北市大安區忠孝東路四段250號11樓之1

定　　價	新台幣320元／港幣107元
產品內容	1書

總 經 銷	采舍國際有限公司
地　　址	235 新北市中和區中山路二段366巷10號3樓
電　　話	（02）8245-8786
傳　　真	（02）8245-8718

港澳地區總經銷	和平圖書有限公司
地　　址	香港柴灣嘉業街12號百樂門大廈17樓
電　　話	（852）2804-6687
傳　　真	（852）2804-6409

本書由外語教學與研究出版社有限責任公司以書名《托福命題總監教你征服新托福寫作》首次出版。此中文繁體字版由外語教學與研究出版社有限責任公司授權捷徑文化出版事業有限公司在台灣、香港和澳門地區獨家出版發行。僅供上述地區銷售。

捷徑 Book站

現在就上臉書（FACEBOOK）「**捷徑BOOK站**」並按讚加入粉絲團，
就可享每月不定期新書資訊和粉絲專享小禮物喔！
http://www.facebook.com/royalroadbooks
讀者來函：**royalroadbooks@gmail.com**

國家圖書館出版品預行編目資料

托福命題總監教你征服新托福寫作 / 秦蘇珊著.
-- 初版. -- 臺北市：捷徑文化, 2014.12
　　面；　公分（原來如此：E109）
ISBN 978-986-5698-29-4(平裝)

1. 托福考試　2. 作文　3. 考試指南

805.1894　　　　　　　　　　103021302

TOEFL
iBT WRITING

不是權威不出書！練托福，
當然就讓最專業的托福總監帶你練！

捷徑文化
Royal Road Publishing Group